Farr into the Future

The Third Book in the Farr Family Saga

ANITA D. BOSEMAN

ISBN: 979-8-88945-004-7
eISBN: 979-8-88945-005-4

Brilliant Books Literary
137 Forest Park Lane Thomasville
North Carolina 27360 USA

Printed in the United States of America

Acknowledgements

This book is dedicated to my late husband Vann for putting up with my prolonged bursts of writing and to my sister, Carolyn, who is my primary editor and greatest fan.

This is also a work of fiction. None of the characters, events, etc. are real, it's all just a figment of my very active imagination!

Contents

Prologue
[1885]

The letter had arrived by an early morning delivery and was brought to Richard Farr's office by one of the clerks. Richard didn't open it, but let it lay on the desk. He knew who it was from. Richard recognized the neat, measured handwriting of his mother and if it hadn't been for what the rest of the unopened envelope indicated, he would have smiled.

The return address was Farr Cottage, a place where his mother hadn't lived since the death of his father in a hunting accident at Aldwin House, the ancestral home of Lord and Lady Oswin. When Richard's oldest brother and the first son assumed the title of Viscount of Gibbons, his mother moved into the Dower house. It was a smaller establishment where she could have her own household and would not be burdened in her widowhood by the rigors of entertaining.

If the change of address wasn't enough, the envelope was banded in black, a sign that the person who wrote the letter and the house where they lived, was in mourning. Richard was relieved the letter was from his mother because, since she had written it, she was not the one who was being mourned. However, the fact she had written to him from Farr Cottage and the envelope indicated a death in the family, it would mean the one who had died was important.

Children and wives died quite often. It was still the 1800s and many children, even in the most affluent of families, did not live beyond five. Childbirth was also quite hard on women and although there had been advances, losing a wife to childbed fever or because of hemorrhage after delivery was not uncommon. Because of these facts of life, a child or wife's passing, although tragic, was not usually a public affair. The family would mourn within the extended family.

No, the envelope which sat on Richard's desk contained bad news and until his day was finished at the bank, he would keep the letter to read at home. Miss Lucy, Richard's new bride, was with child but she would still help him deal with whatever was in his mother's note. Until the evening, he would put it from his mind.

The New Year
[Present day]

"Pinky … Pinky!" Melody called with an ever more strident note to her voice, "where are you?"

LT Chadwick, the object of the colorful call, winced. Melody Fitzhugh Farr was his goddaughter and the daughter of his best friend, her late father, Charles Andrew Farr. The nickname no longer applied, his mane of light strawberry-blond hair had long since turned to white, but he was still known as 'Pinky' to the older brother who had given him the name and to Melody.

LT had been named Lionel Tyrone by his mother, in honor of her two favorite movie stars, Lionel Barrymore and Tyrone Power, but his father had insisted he be called LT and the appellation had stuck. LT was the Chairman and CEO of Chadwick Holdings, Inc., a privately owned conglomerate that consisted of energy, ranching, land, medical, and real estate interests. The Harris, Higgins, Lopez, and Chadwick families all owned a piece of the company and benefited from LT's running of the firm.

"Melody, I'm right here," LT said as he sauntered into the study at Farr House. "I just needed to have a word with Bellamy before we went out to look at the progress on the pool and lanai. Patience girl!"

"Alright, but did they finish? Is it all gone?" she asked plaintively. "I love Christmas but it seems like this one lasted forever!"

LT laughed, "The last light, strand of tinsel, and nutcracker has been safely stashed until next year. Bellamy and the girls did a wonderful job of putting the house back to the way it was. So now can we see the pool?"

Bellamy was Melody's butler and the 'girls' LT referred to were the maids, Glenda and Pauline. They were sisters and preferred being called Glen and Paul. They were part of the staff LT had sent to Melody from his house after his wife left him and he put the home on the market. Mrs. Bellamy, the wife of Bellamy, was the cook and rounded out the full-time employees at Farr House.

As if on cue, Bellamy appeared and asked his employer if she needed anything. "I don't think so Bellamy, but thank you for getting all the holiday decorations taken down. I thought we would never see the last of them." Looking over at LT and realizing it was after five, somewhere, she changed her mind. "Hmm, I guess you should bring LT a whiskey before we go out to check the progress of the pool and when you do, bring me a drink, also."

Bellamy nodded his assent and silently left the room. When LT first recommended having a staff, Melody wasn't quite sure she would need all of the extra help. She and her mother had gotten by with a girl that came to clean a couple of times a week, but since the arrival of Bellamy and the rest of the staff, her home had run much smoother.

The original Farr House was built in the late 1800s by Melody's great great-grandfather, Richard Farr. He had emigrated from England and established a bank, first in partnership with Samuel Newhouse, and later, after buying out his partner, simply as Farr's Bank. In the 1980s, when Texas passed the law that allowed branch banking, Melody's father, Charles Farr, sold Farr's Bank to one of the bigger banks and assumed a seat on the new bank's board and a position on staff.

The study where Melody and LT were sitting was the only room of the original house that was left after the Great Storm of 1915. The hurricane took the house, except for this one room, the stables, and only left the old round barn standing. When the replacement house was built by Melody's great-grandfather Avery Farr, it was modeled after an Italian Palazzo where Avery and his bride Constance had stayed on their honeymoon.

Melody's grandmother, Mary Catherine, added the conservatory. Melody's father, Charles, originally commissioned the pool, patio, and outdoor kitchen, all under a lanai. Now it was Melody's turn to add her stamp on the home.

Evangeline (Evie) Farr, Melody's mother, had done very little up-keep on the home after her husband, Charles, had passed away. LT, as her father's best friend and trustee of her father's estate, insisted that the needed repairs be done to the house and grounds. Although Melody was the only child and inheritor of her father's estate, the will had an age clause in it that kept her from having full possession of his legacy until she turned thirty or was married to "a gentleman acceptable to the trustee(s)."

The same attorney who had done the will for Melody's father had written the one that Evie Farr had left when she died. The estate passed to Melody, but because she was not yet thirty years old, she had to have, as her guardian, the closest male Farr relative who was over the age of majority. A search was made and the male relative was Sir Arthur Roland Farr, Viscount of Gibbons. Sir Arthur was the sole heir to the Farr family's titles and the ancestral home in England, Farr Cottage.

Following the death of her mother, Melody had gone to England to stay with her guardian and there she was able to work on the Farr family history. Melody had a master's in history and the subject fascinated her. Her cousin, Sir Arthur, was also a historian and during the time Melody stayed with him, they had worked well together.

Melody met another man in England, a kind of neighbor to the Farrs, Sir Alfred Oswin. His estate, Aldwin House was not far from Farr Cottage, but the town houses the Oswin and Farr families owned in London were within a few yards of each other. Both the Oswin and Farr families were from Anglo/Saxon stock and proud of their long heritages.

Alfred and Melody had become quite close, much to the chagrin of Lord Arthur. Also, Alfred was always hinting the two men might even be related, a charge Lord Arthur disputed but would not allow to be tested. It was because of the worrisome possibilities of Melody and Alfred becoming a couple and the realization, by Arthur, that he also had feelings for Melody, he allowed and encouraged her to return to her native Houston, Texas for the Thanksgiving and Christmas holidays.

Melody returned to her home in Houston and it was then that LT had sent her the staff, directed the repairs and improvements that were being done to the house, and begun to tell Melody about all to which she was heir. An old map her father kept in his study and was later moved into the library by her mother was the first lesson. The old, yellowed map was of Houston before 1900. The red shaded areas were parcels of land her great great-grandfather, Richard Farr, had acquired and subsequent pieces his son, Avery, added to the family's estate. Melody's father, Charles, also bought property which was a part of what Melody would inherit when she turned thirty in a little over a year.

LT was still revealing various parts of the estate and although he was the trustee, some items were unknown even to him. The study was one such secret. A large envelope with wax seals was a part of what he didn't know. The study, the only room left from the original house Richard had built, was full of secrets and the envelope was the key to them.

As a banker, Richard often brought cash or valuables home and kept them in a safe in his study. The interior dimensions of the room were smaller than the outside ones which would indicate and it was all because of the hidden compartments built into the study. When he had had the original house built, Richard designed and directed that the door to the niche where the safe was located be hidden in the paneling. A bar was another item concealed in the room and was currently used quite often. However, there were other panels that masked a niche where he had kept other items.

With their drinks in hand, LT and Melody walked to the new lanai area which was in the middling phase of construction. The old pool had been removed and the form for the new one was in place. The various water features, the rock grotto, waterfall, water slide, and diving platform were either marked out or had been roughed in by the company doing the work.

Jose` Lopez, LT's project manager, had finished the refurbishment of the cabana as far as they could. Some of the features for the pool had to go in before the work could be completed, but the updates and upgrades which had been done were impressive. The building had two large bathroom/dressing rooms, two bedrooms for guests, a lounge area, and a kitchenette. The new equipment for the pool would be placed in a hidden room and it was this equipment that was keeping Jose` crew from finishing the building.

The item LT was most interested in was the bar/grill area. He as a grill master and at least once a week since his own house had gone on the market; he had used the one at Melody's house. Looking over the changes which had been made, LT commented, "my penthouse on top of the Chadwick Building is nice, but I do miss my own barbeque grill, I'm just happy you let me use yours. It looks like the fridge, drinks cooler, and items in the bar area have been installed." Turning to the new smoker unit on the barbeque pit, "I'll have to come and cure this little baby one day!" LT said as he lovingly moved his hand over the flat-black component.

Melody laughed, "I'm surprised you haven't had Jose` over at your place trying to figure out how to turn one of those five bedrooms into a patio/grill deck."

"Don't laugh girl; the place is too big, but the building just wasn't engineered for that type of thing; besides, the insurance company kind of frowns on people having open fires on the roof of a multimillion dollar building."Taking Melody's arm, he steered her back toward the study. "Any way, I can always use your setup. Come with me, I have a few things I want to discuss."

Melody frowned. When LT wanted to 'discuss' something it was usually quite important and she had just finished several weeks of 'important'. Right now she just wanted to enjoy the absence of Christmas decorations, guests, and the round of parties she had just endured. She liked a good dinner party, Christmas or New Year's Eve party as much as the next girl, but the list of invitations she had received since the charity ball the first Saturday of December was astounding and a bit overwhelming.

xxxxx

Their Lordships, Arthur and Albert, decided the Holidays in England would not be the same without her and so she invited them, (or did they invite themselves?), to visit her in Houston. The first social event they all attended was the charity ball for St. Luke's Anglican Hospital, an institution built by the original Dr. John Harris, and it had been a social success for her and her guests. Another young man, Jeremy Higgins, was a marine officer on leave from his unit and stayed with LT over the Holidays. Melody had a feeling LT was hosting the young man as a counter-weight to the two Englishmen.

After the ball, the invitations to teas, dinner, and cocktail parties poured in. If Melody and her guests had accepted all of the invitations, they would never have eaten lunch, dinner, or even had a drink at Farr House. The interest was in her but also extended to their Lordships and in a couple of instances; she had encouraged them to accept the invites.

On one of the days when she sent Lord Arthur and Lord Alfred to a dinner party without her, she had gone to dinner, alone, with Jeremy. Unlike their Lordships, he was laidback, casual, and his favorite mode of transportation was a Harley. This wasn't to say he was a slouch, far from it. Even out of his marine officer's uniform, the military bearing was unmistakable.

Jeremy was the great, great-grandnephew of the best friend and mentor of Melody's great, great-grandfather, Richard Farr. When Melody had returned to Houston, she found Jeremy wandering around the graveyard at St. John's looking for the final resting place of his namesake. LT was having a farewell barbeque at his house and after showing Jeremy where he could find the original Jeremy Farr, she took him to meet LT and several of his distant cousins.

LT and Jeremy really hit it off. LT insisted Jeremy stay with him at the apartment on top of the Chadwick Building and he talked the young man into spending several weeks of unused leave time in Houston. Melody knew it was probably so she could get to know Jeremy; LT was on a search for a suitable husband for her and in LT's eyes, Jeremy fit the bill.

Melody enjoyed the dinner with Jeremy. He had called with the invitation just after the limo left with their Lordships. "Put your jeans, boots, and a leather jacket on, like the one you were wearing the day we met and I'll be by to pick you up in about fifteen minutes. We're going out tonight!"

When she thought about it, he really hadn't 'asked' her if she wanted to have dinner with him, it was more of a 'get dressed, we're going' kind of non-invitation invitation. She was dressed and ready when he pulled up on a rented Harley. He handed her a helmet and they sped up the drive to the main road.

Bellamy had done the initial background/security checks on Jeremy and knew his military record. As a former special operations officer, Bellamy knew how to read the kind of things the young man was into and he found Jeremy to be quite impressive. Part of the duties Bellamy had in Miss Melody's household was her security and trusting her to Jeremy was not a problem. Bellamy wasn't too enthusiastic about the motorcycle, in a safety sense, but he knew Jeremy would and could protect her.

As Jeremy stopped the cycle to wait for the traffic passing the gate to Farr House, he half turned and asked his date where the best 'Tex-Mex' restaurant was. Melody gave him directions and when there was a break in the flow of cars, Jeremy expertly pulled the bike onto the street. Several minutes later, they parked in front of the café.

La Cosina was not a chain restaurant. The same family had owned and operated it for more than fifty years. The food was flavorful, plentiful, and the staff was friendly. The original owner, Memo, had died several years ago, but his sons and daughters took what he had started and moved it into the future. Now there was another generation of the family working in their grandpa's café.

The woman who seated them recognized Melody with a big hug and asked her why she hadn't been in for so long. Melody told her she had been in England and would be going back there for a few months, but she had wanted some of the Padilla family's excellent food before she left. She introduced Jeremy and then the couple sat down.

The conversation over dinner was casual and fun. Melody and Jeremy talked about experiences they'd had in college and, in Jeremy's case, in the field. He told her there were some things he couldn't tell her, but she patted his hand and said it was OK, "I don't think you need to explain, secret should mean secret."

More than two hours later, they finally left the table. Jeremy and Melody had passed a couple of clubs on the way to *La Cosina* and he asked her if she wanted to stop and get a beer or something. Melody had never been able to drink beer, but she agreed to a glass of wine.

The parking lot was a mix of cars, pickups, and motorcycles. Music could be heard every time the door opened. Jeremy took Melody's hand as they entered. The place wasn't very big on the inside. Two pool tables took up quite a bit of floor space in an alcove off the main bar area and there was also a small dance floor. The bar itself was a square with stools all around and off to each side there were small tables. Most of the seats at the bar and many of the small tables were full.

There was no live band but they did have a DJ who took requests. Jeremy went up to the bar to get a beer for himself and a white wine for Melody. After putting them on their table he went to ask the DJ to play a couple of requests. Melody saw Jeremy pull a folded bill out of his jacket pocket and hand it to the man who smiled and nodded enthusiastically.

It was much too loud in the club to hear anyone talking without shouting so Melody and Jeremy simply sat and sipped their drinks, listened to the music, and watched a couple of men playing pool. One or two men looked over to the table, but Jeremy kept his eyes on that kind of thing and a look from him let the others know, this was his date, and they should stay away.

Three songs played before the one Jeremy had requested came on, but then, without even asking her, he led her to the dance floor. It was a slow tune and only one other couple joined them. Melody was happy to dance with Jeremy. He was a take-charge kind of guy and where other men might have asked her if she wanted to dance, he just assumed she did and behaved accordingly.

When the song finished, they sat down to finish their drinks. A man from the bar who had not seen the 'Jeremy look' came up to the table, leaned over Melody, and started to put his hand on her. In a flash, Jeremy was out of his seat and wedged himself in between Melody and the man.

Melody didn't hear what Jeremy had shouted in the man's ear, but he backed off and took up his seat at the bar. A scowl on the intruder's face made the female bartender look over to where Jeremy and Melody were sitting. Jeremy gave her a big grin and raised his bottle of beer. She smiled back and understood that the man had made an unwelcome advance. She was just happy nothing was broken, no fights had started, and no bottles of beer had been hurled; it was still too early in the evening for that.

The last song Jeremy had requested came up and he again led Melody onto the miniature dance floor. This time they were alone. Melody felt safe in Jeremy's arms and when the song finished, she wished it had gone on longer. It was, however, time to go.

Jeremy took Melody to the door when he got her home, but didn't go inside. For the first time he felt like he could kiss her and was sure she wanted him to. He hadn't, however, figured on Bellamy. Just as Jeremy leaned down, the door opened, and the butler greeted them.

Bellamy very calmly asked, "Good evening Miss, will you and Mr. Jeremy be wanting coffee or brandy this evening?" The mood broken, Melody shook her head no and Jeremy gave her a peck on the cheek as he said goodnight.

xxxxx

Melody and LT sat in the study for more than forty-five minutes going over the things LT wanted to talk to her about. There were still a few things in the house which needed fixing or replacing and he wanted Jose` to come and get those either done or started before Melody left for England.

While they talked, Bellamy quietly gave them refills on their drinks before calling them into dinner. They ate at the small dining table in the breakfast room. Mrs. Bellamy made a lite but filling meal that both Melody and LT appreciated after the many dinners and lunches they had attended over the last month.

LT put his fork down and turned to Melody, "there is one last thing I wanted to tell you. I want to get some insurance on you before you return to England. The agent and a nurse will be here tomorrow around ten to get the necessary information and it will take about a week for the policy to be issued. Having you in a foreign country and I'm sure you want to travel to the Continent while you are there, well, I would just feel better if we had this for you."

Melody frowned. "What kind of insurance are we talking about? I have medical and a life policy my parents bought me when I was little. Why would I need more?"

"Melody, this is a kind of terrorism insurance. We can watch over you here, but in England or anywhere else you might go, it would be difficult. I just want to make sure we would have the facility to pay a ransom if you were kidnapped. Many people have this; I've had it for several years."

Melody looked worried. "OK, uh, but why the nurse?"

Bellamy had just come quietly in to take the empty plates when he stopped to hear the answer. He knew what Mr. LT was talking about; they had discussed the subject when Bellamy had first started working for Miss Melody.

"For the policy, they need a sample of your blood, fingerprints, we will get your dental x-rays, and a DNA swab. It's really very routine. These are just things that would help with identification." LT had seen the look on Bellamy's face when he mentioned DNA. The cock of the butler's eyebrow almost made LT stutter. "It will all be perfectly safe and no one will use any of the information unless it is necessary."

Melody nodded. She knew, after what LT had told her about the Farr estate, she could be a target, but had never wanted to acknowledge the possibilities. "If you think it's necessary. Fine." Looking over at Bellamy, "I think we can take coffee and brandy in the study."

xxxxx

The insurance agent and nurse were exactly on time. The whole procedure, from the questions the agent needed answered to the items the nurse collected, took a mere forty-five minutes. When the procedure was finished the agent asked Melody when she was planning to travel and was pleased the planned date of departure was more than a week away. "It will give us time to get the policy in place. I hope you have a wonderful trip!"

Bellamy showed the people out and Melody sat back in her father's chair in the study. A box of her great great-grandfather's papers lay in front of her and she pulled the first few things out to have a look. In the bottom of the box lay a journal and packet of letters. The journal was in Richard Farr's handwriting and the letters showed the familiar, practiced hand of Richard's mother.

Melody still had a few minutes before Bellamy would come in with the morning sherry and cake. She decided it wouldn't hurt to take a quick look. Before she left for England at the end of the next week, she wanted to spend some time on the part of the family history represented in the journals, letters, documents, and diaries of her American ancestors. This would give her an idea with what she had to work.

xxxxx – [1885]

Richard and Miss Lucy finished a lite supper before retiring to the lounge. The evenings were still cool and the open windows helped to cut the heat which had built up during the day. The windows had light net summer curtains over them and a spring breeze made them flutter ever so slightly.

Miss Lucy was only six months into her pregnancy, but she was already having the difficulties of a woman close to her lying-in time. Doc John Harris, the young doctor Jeremy had brought with him to the Chadwick ranch when Richard had hurt himself in a fall, was their physician and he had ordered Miss Lucy to keep her feet up when she was sitting down. Doc Harris suspected that Miss Lucy was with twins, but he wouldn't know before at least another month and maybe not until the time of delivery.

The letter from his mother was in his coat pocket and Richard decided to open it before he got his brandy.

xxxxx

Farr Cottage March 11, 1885

My Dear Richard,

It is with a very heavy heart I must write to inform you that your brother, Harold Charles Farr 16th Viscount of Gibbons has died. Your brother, Major Roland Arthur Farr, will be named to the title.

Your brother Harold and his two young daughters, Virginia and Harriett, became ill just after Twelfth night with fever and cough. The two girls lived through three weeks of constant torment. Lord Harold seemed to be recovering, but when the girls died one within a day of the other, he took a bad turn.

The local doctor consulted with a colleague in Harley Street, but nothing was found to aid him. Time was the only thing that might have helped him. He had started to recover, but his constitution had been sorely compromised. A late winter chill was too much for him. He expired a fortnight ago.

I have been in contact with Lord Boxten about hastening the return of your brother from India, but he is with his regiment in the Northwest Territories. The fighting has been sporadic in Waziristan and the group your older brother is with has been in constant contact with the insurgents. I expect Roland's return at any time.

Your last letter was a bright spot in this difficult time. Your marriage and the anticipated arrival of your first child have made me very happy. Please stay well.

Lady Annis L. Farr, Dowager

xxxxx

Richard folded the fine linen paper and put it back into the black-banded envelope. Unlike many families of his time and station of life, he and his brothers had all been very close. Their father and mother had employed nannies and tutors for the four boys as they grew up, but when it came time, they had all gone off to public school. With so many boys to be educated, however, it made more sense to have Dons from the university come and live for a couple of years to extend the education at home as long as possible. Then, when they needed more than the homeschool could provide, each of the boys went on to public school.

For Harold, as the oldest and the one who would inherit the title and estates, four years at public school and two years at university were sufficient. The second boy, Roland was destined for the military and following two years in public school was sent to a military school to assume his place in a regiment that had known

Farrs for many generations. As the third son, Edgar was fated for the clergy and a vicarage at the local church, St. Alban's.

Arthur Charles Farr, Richard's father, had been very fortunate to have four sons. In the Farr family it was tradition for the first to inherit, the second was meant for the regiment, the third for the church, and the fourth, well, a fourth was expected to make his way in the world and not sully the name of Farr. Richard was the fourth son and much to the delight of his tutors and father was very intelligent, especially in math. When Edgar was sent to public school prior to entering Oxford to study theology, Richard went with him.

At Oxford, the young Edgar Farr pursued his path to the ministry and Richard studied math. It was during his time in Oxford that young Richard was approached by a group of gentlemen who persuaded him to take a position in a banking house in London. Upon completion of his course of study, Richard accepted the offer.

The Farrs were a very old, established Anglo/Saxon family. Their roots went back to before the Conquest and the Norman Invasion. They had always served their king or, in rare cases, queen when called upon. They were, however, considered to be rather dull when it came to things such as scandal, riotous living, or anything other than sober rectitude. They were not spendthrifts and husbanded their lands, estates, and fortune for the future generations of the family.

Richard was a typical example of the male Farr. He was tall, well over six feet, slender but strongly built, had light brown hair, and deep blue eyes. Although he did drink, it was never to excess, and thought gambling was for people of a lower class. Richard knew he had to take care of himself, financially, and the work in the bank was something at which he was good and he saw a future for himself there.

The same group of men who had recommended Richard take the position kept close watch on his progress. Each of them had investments in the United States, mainly in cattle ranches and they were grooming Richard to become their representative in America. Having a man who could look after their interests first hand and who was a gentleman would make each investor feel easier. Richard was asked to go to America.

Richard consulted with his father when the offer was made. Few decisions of this magnitude were taken in the Farr family without discussing the matter within the family. Both men knew that if Richard took the position he might never see England or his family again. They also knew that as the fourth son, Richard had no hope of inheriting the title and all that went with it even if he were to stay in England. However, in America, the possibilities for building a future were endless. Lord Arthur gave his son his blessings and wished him well.

Richard fared very well in Texas and the young city of Houston. He worked as the agent for the investors in London for a few years and in that time met people who would forever be close to the American branch of the Farr family.

Jeremy Higgins was his mentor and best friend. Jeremy was an older man who had a large family that managed his various ranches. When Richard's father suddenly died in a hunting accident and left a sum of money for him to use to build an independent future, it was Jeremy who counseled him to go into the local banking business. He also became something of a surrogate father to Richard.

'Big Red' Chadwick and his sister Elbeth were friends who would be a part of the Farr family's extended network of close friends on into the future. Samuel Newhouse, the man Richard went into partnership with at a bank stayed close even after Samuel moved back to New York to be with family. Doc John Harris set up a clinic in Houston after his marriage to Elbeth Chadwick and became everyone's family doctor.

Miss Lucy, though, was the most important of anyone he had ever met or was likely to meet. The first time he saw her she was just seventeen and was helping her aunt Abbey cope with an illness. Richard had gone to Jeremy's 'little' ranch to discuss the death of Richard's father and the bequest he had made. Jeremy introduced Richard to his wife's niece. While Richard was attracted to Miss Lucy, he also knew he was in no financial condition to take on a wife and children.

Richard worked hard to make the partnership with Samuel Newhouse flourish. The Newhouse and Farr bank was a success and Richard was looking forward to the day when he could buy out his partner and make the bank simply Farr's Bank. The subject had been discussed, but both Samuel and Richard knew it was not quite time for the buyout. Richard wanted a few more years of Samuel's involvement before going it alone.

Samuel Newhouse was also looking forward to the day when he could take his new family back to New York. When he had originally taken Richard as a partner, he did it because he wanted to take his granddaughter Ruth back to New York to be married within her faith. The Newhouses were Jewish and Samuel worried for her future. While he was in New York, he also married and then brought his bride, Sarah to Houston with him.

As Richard looked at his wife, Miss Lucy, his mind's-eye saw her as she had been that first day they met. She would always be "Miss Lucy" to him, the seventeen year-old girl with the long gold tresses and cornflower blue eyes. Now, however, in her pregnancy, she had taken on a glow which seemed almost magical to Richard. He never thought she could be more beautiful than on the day they met, but when they married, she surprised him with her added beauty as she walked down the aisle of the newly built St. John's church and became his bride. However, the longer she was pregnant, the more radiant she became and Richard marveled at the girl who was now his wife.

Miss Lucy sat quietly reading while Richard read the note from his mother. She knew it was important because her husband had waited to open the envelope rather than simply reading it at the office. The fact he waited until after dinner made the letter even more momentous. Miss Lucy could tell by the look in her husband's eyes that it was more than just the news his mother sent that was going through his mind and she decided to wait until he was ready to talk about it before she would interrupt his reverie.

Richard laid the envelope on the side table and picked up his brandy. His brother was dead. Harold was much older than he was, but like his other brothers, the years they spent growing up had been happy and now that was all over. His father's death had been difficult for Richard, they had also been close, but now with a brother gone, mortality became ever more real.

Richard looked at his wife and her growing belly. His son or daughter was nestled within her and that child, along with the others that would surely come, would be his future. He smiled at Miss Lucy and was again struck by his love for her.

Miss Lucy laid her reading down and rested her hands on the baby she was carrying. A slight shudder passed through her as the little one gave her a hefty kick. Richard saw the change in expression and was immediately at her side.

"Oh Richard dear, it's nothing. Just the baby kicking. He's been very active these last few days, but John, (Doc Harris), says that is good. An active baby is a sign of a healthy baby." Miss Lucy shifted in her chair. She took her husband's hand and placed it on her belly. "Here, see? Oh! That was a big one!"

Richard liked feeling his little one. It reminded him of how far he had come in his life. The property where his house sat, the church he helped to found, the bank, and now his growing family, it was his 'little piece of heaven' but he was also aware of how easily things could slip away. His brother Harold had probably thought he could look ahead to a house full of children, a bevy of grandchildren, and dying at a ripe old age. Nothing could be taken for granted and Richard vowed that nothing would.

Normally, he wrote to his mother once a week. He always started a letter to her on a Monday morning and as the week progressed, he would add a few lines or thoughts, and would then finish and post it by Friday. In the morning, he would write a special letter to her expressing his love and concern for her and for Harold's widow. A page or two would also be included for his brother Roland.

Miss Lucy could almost hear her husband's thoughts and wanted to comfort him, but he needed to start the conversation. After several minutes, Richard removed his hand from her belly and brushed her neck with a kiss. "Thank you my dear, no one can put the world into perspective like you can. What do you say we take our little one and go to bed? I've had a long day."

Miss Lucy nodded as he led her up the stairs. Later, as she nestled in his arms, they talked about the letter, Harold, and the future. She knew he had nothing more to worry about when she heard his soft snore and it was then she could find her own sleep.

xxxxx

LT was coming to dinner. While this was true many times during the week, this evening was special. In the morning, Melody was again leaving Houston and going to her guardian's house in England.

For the last week, she had been preparing the things she would want and most of the items had been boxed and sent via FedEx. Melody hated dragging mounds of luggage through airports and by shipping the bulk of her items; she would only have a small carryon and a wheeled suitcase for a few day's stay in London.

LT had taken her to dinner a couple of times, but his habit was to at least pass by for a drink if not dinner itself on most evenings. Tonight, though, he wanted to spend some time going over a few things and so the request and invitation were more formal. He would be there at five thirty and dinner would be at six thirty.

Melody was in the study when LT arrived. Bellamy took his coat and showed him into a room with which LT was already quite familiar. Without asking, Bellamy set a whiskey down beside his former employer and a scotch for Miss Melody. LT was carrying an old leather satchel, which he put on the top of the highly polished desk.

After a few moments of light banter and a couple sips of his drink, LT began. "I brought you this," motioning to the bag on the desk. "It was your father's and before him, well, maybe your grandfather's or great grandfather's. All I know is your dad put instructions in his will that I was to have this bag until it was given to you, either on your thirtieth birthday or marriage. I just thought, uhm, since you're leaving again tomorrow, it might be better just to give it to you now."

"I don't know exactly what all is in there." LT continued, "I do know it has that envelope I've told you about, the one about this room." LT motioned with his hand to encompass the room, "but what else is in there, well, that is up to you now, isn't it?"

Melody didn't make a move toward the bag. Instead she sipped her drink, put it down, and chuckled. "If I wasn't supposed to have it yet, then why are you giving it to me now, am I supposed to keep it and not open it until my birthday?"

LT squirmed, "I don't know how long you'll be in England, and by the time you get back, things may be different. I want you to have as much information as possible before you leave or make any long-term decisions. I would ask, however, that you don't open it or look through the contents until after I leave this evening. Whatever is in there your daddy wanted it to be just for you. Will you do that?"

Melody nodded. "I can do that, but right now, what about another drink before we go in for dinner? Mrs. Bellamy has made your favorite dishes and I'm sure she is anxious for you to have time to enjoy them."

zzzzz

Melody stood at the front door and waved goodbye to LT one last time. He would not be seeing her off in the morning so it would be several months before they would see each other again. Turning, she asked Bellamy to bring her some tea into the study. She wanted to have a look at the leather bag LT had brought and she might be in there for some time, depending upon what she found in the satchel.

Several minutes later Bellamy brought her the tea and inquired if there was anything else, she might need. "No, Bellamy, I'm just going to have a look at what's in here and then go up to bed.

"Yes, Miss." Bellamy turned and left the room. He would wait, as always, to retire for the night until his employer was safely in her room. By the looks of bag on the desk, she might be an hour or so.

The first thing Melody pulled out was the brown envelope LT had mentioned. When she turned it over, she found a heavy wax seal and the signature of her father over the flap to show it had not been opened. As interesting as it looked, she laid that aside and looked at the rest of the contents. A half hour later, the various papers and items had been sorted into two piles; important and 'not so much'.

In the 'not so much' pile were a couple of invoices for things bought by his grandmother years before and were no longer relevant. A pair of symphony tickets with an autograph, and a dinner receipt. Two or three dozen small check-stubs for a club that was no longer open and the picture of a young boy and his dog were also included. The picture had no date on it and no inscription. It didn't look anything like her father and Melody didn't know who it was, thus it's designation of 'not so much' pile.

The important pile had a couple items which were interesting but not really very relevant. Melody looked at the receipt for her grandmother's limousine, the one for which Tommy Hernandez had found a good home. The cost, new, was a fraction of what a small, inexpensive car would cost in today's market. Melody chuckled and put it away with a sticky-note to remind her to give it to Tommy one day.

The second thing was a repair bill for the electric gate. When the new gate was installed, sometime after the Second World War, the dragon, which had been on the original one, was not added. It was made of wrought iron and the man who made the gate said it was too heavy for the motor on the gate to handle the weight. According to the receipt, the dragon had been affixed and a very heavy-duty motor bought to accommodate the ornament. It looked like an expensive thing to have done, but it had lasted all these years with little problem. Melody made a note to see if it needed replacing or how long it might last into the future.

A stack of pictures was also included in the important pile. Melody had seen many of the people in them, but these were either copies or different poses taken on the same day and place as the ones she had seen. There were, however, a couple of pictures of Annis and Chet Lowell that Melody had not seen and she wondered why they were in this bag. She shook her head and put all of the pictures on the side. There was also the stray letter or two that seemed to be of no importance.

The only item left was the brown envelope with the seals. This was a part of her inheritance but it was also something she wasn't supposed to have access to until her thirtieth birthday or she married. Why did LT want her to have it now? Hmm, she turned it in her hands. Should she open it or wait? Would it be safe here in her father's big desk? It was supposed to tell the secrets of the study, this room, the only room left intact from the original house Richard Farr had had built in the 1880's. Could she not open it?

The sterling letter opener with the imprint of Farr's Bank on it which usually lies in the top drawer of her dad's desk slit through the brown envelope very cleanly. Melody was ready to see what all the mystery was. She tipped the envelope so its contents slid onto the desk.

A small notebook, a diagram, schematic, and an old skeleton key were the sum total of the contents. She recognized the diagram immediately as the room where she was sitting and she had seen her great great-grandfather Richard's neat handwriting enough to know he was the one who had written in the legend and directions. Melody set it aside while she examined the rest of the items.

The notebook had an advertisement for Pomeroy's Hay and Feed embossed in the cover. It had probably been a promotional item given away to steady customers. Inside; each page was headed with a name, address, and loan amounts. Then below was the tally of loans and payments made with most showing a zero balance. A few, however, still showed balances. In the inside of the back cover was a notation that these were personal and not bank loans but with a further direction to "collect these if possible but do not force payment if it would cause undo hardship." Melody looked back over some of the pages and recognized her great grandfather's hand; he must have done as his father directed.

The schematic was the next thing Melody examined. At first it was hard to determine what the thing was until she realized it was a wire-frame drawing of the partner's desk where she was sitting. When Richard Farr and Samuel Newhouse had been in the banking business together, they had each sat at this desk, one side for Richard and the other for Samuel. When Richard bought out the partnership he moved this massive desk from the bank to his study and put a smaller desk in his office at Farr's Bank. Melody's father had put the smaller desk in the library when Farr's Bank was sold in the 1980's.

Melody laid the drawing down to examine it. She had played around this desk as a child, done homework on it through her master's degree, and recently, held lengthy discussions with LT at this desk. What was the reason for the drawing, was it simply a rendering an artisan would use to build such a piece?

Finally, she turned the diagram around on the desk so that it matched 'drawing-to-desk'. She referenced the drawers on each side, the fittings, and the shelves but couldn't find any differences. It was when she looked at the side view of the desk that she found why this paper was in the brown envelope, a hidden compartment. The partner's desk was a puzzle box! Melody pulled the chairs out, crawled under the desk, and going by the diagram, found a piece of trim that turned easily at her touch. She had to open the drawers in a particular way and turn one of the legs, but then she heard a soft click. Where the two sides of the desks were joined, a compartment was revealed.

Melody pulled gently on the panel and the compartment slide out to reveal a pocket large enough to hold something, but was currently only hiding a single sheet of parchment. She took the paper, pulled the chair back up to the desk, and sat down to read.

It was a letter from her great, great-grandfather Richard Farr.

xxxxx

If you have found this, it has only been by following the instructions which are to be passed from one generation to the next. I know my son, Avery, will sign his name and add his thoughts, but will my grandson Charles also do so? That is for the future to decide, but it is my hope that my grandson, his son, and may it be so ordained, more generations shall also add their names.

In my time, this compartment held gold, a few sensitive documents, and a pistol for protection. Be so kind to those who will inherit after and tells us, pray, what did you find worth hiding?

Signed – Richard Arthur Farr – 1922

The letter continued with the addition of Avery's note.

I regret my one and only son, Charles Arthur Farr was unable to carry on the tradition. He was killed two days after landing at Omaha Beach, Normandy on D-Day, June 6, 1944. During my time, this compartment held gold coins to keep them out of the hands of that traitor to his class, FDR! Well, and a few other things were hidden here also, buy only a few deeds and things I didn't want the staff to find.

Signed – Avery Richard Farr – 1965

A small notation was found on the back of the paper:

I've just learned of this from grandfather. How odd this desk has been here all this time and I never knew. It is my hope the line of Farrs can reach into the future the way great grandfather would have wanted. I know I will do my part! So far, do not know of anything I would want to put in here, but I may in the future.

Signed – Charles Andrew Farr - 1984

xxxxx

Melody caressed the parchment. The line of Farrs; yes, she would do her part, but with whom? Unlike some of the friends she knew, she had more than one suitor. Where they had none, she had three, but how to choose, what if she chose unwisely. She laid the letter from Richard Farr back in the compartment and snapped it shut. She just didn't want to think about this right now.

The last items to examine, the diagram of the room and the skeleton key were next. Melody stood and oriented herself with the drawing in the room. The bar was evident, it was used daily, the two safes, which were secreted behind the oiled oak paneling on the walls, were also known, but had not been used since her father had passed away. What else was there? Slowly turning with the illustration in her hand, she scanned the walls and the document.

One of the built-in bookcases caught her attention. While some of the shelves in the room were open, the two that flanked the fireplace were covered with glass doors. In the days before the house was air-conditioned, the Houston humidity and the need to have windows open made it imperative to keep some things dust free and undamaged from moisture. Melody couldn't remember there ever being anything more than figurines or, as her mother called them 'dust-abeles' on the shelves.

The key didn't fit into the lock on the doors, but then they had never been locked. She opened the one on the left, compared it to the diagram, but found nothing odd about it. The doors on the right swung open to her touch. A heavy Chinese urn stood on the center shelf while lesser pieces of china occupied the other four shelves.

Something just didn't look right. Melody laid the drawing down on the lower shelf and compared it with the actual shelves. Then she saw it, a slight variation in the width of the center shelf. The size of the urn drew the eye to its intricate design and masked the size of the compartment. On the right side of the shelf, the trim hid the deviation.

Carefully, so she didn't disturb the urn, Melody felt around on the side wall of the compartment that was different from the others. It seemed solid; there were no pressure points that would have given way under the force of her fingers. The trim didn't seem loose or moveable either. It didn't make sense, why would Richard Farr have included this in the diagram of the study?

Melody took a step back and looked at the bookcase on the other side of the fireplace. Was it the fact there was a flaw in the workmanship which made the differences memorable? The whole study had been so carefully constructed, it just seemed off. She closed the left side doors again and then went back to the right side. Well, it was getting late and she had the trip in the morning; better just to go to bed and worry out the problem another time.

As she felt around one last time before closing the glass doors, she accidently bumped the urn. It didn't move. That was odd. She had been careful, but the brush with her arm was enough it should have shifted, but it didn't. Was it that heavy? Melody pulled the little library steps over to the front of the case, stood on the lower step to give herself the added advantage, and reached in to lift the urn. It still didn't budge.

Hmm, now what? She had tried lifting it by the base, but it seemed to be stuck fast to the wooden shelf. The urn had two stubby little handles up near the top and she tried those. Nothing, except, when she took her hands away, it seemed to turn ever so slightly. Maybe that was it; turn the vase. Putting equal pressure on both sides, she tried rotating the urn by using the handles.

The urn moved and when it had gone almost a quarter turn, Melody heard a soft click. The oak panel next to the bookcase opened like a door, but ever so slightly. Stepping down from the library steps, Melody used her fingers to open the panel further. Inside the cavity, it was dark, dusty, and cobwebs adorned the corners and rear of the little cubbyhole. A chair and small table with a lantern on it, sat inside. On the door, a handle would allow the panel to be opened from the inside.

A piece of paper was tucked under the corner of the lantern. Melody picked it up to read what it said. She again recognized Richard's handwriting. It was only a few lines and it made her laugh. "Where else would you hide someone you didn't want any-one to know was in your study?" was all he said, but in her great grandfather Avery's hand, "right father, but it is better for hiding the whiskey from the Temperance League!"

Melody put the paper back where she had found it, looked to make sure she hadn't missed anything, and stepped back into the study. She turned the Chinese urn back into its original position and then closed the door. At the desk, she took all of the items she had found in the satchel and put them back. There was one item left; the skeleton key. Now what did it go to? Well, she was getting tired and it was time to go to bed.

Melody opened the paneling that hid the larger of the two safes and put the bag inside. She knew the combinations to both of them, but she liked this one because the combo was so easy. She twirled the handle and closed the panels that hid it from sight. Everything would be safe until she returned from England.

Taking her tea things, Melody put the items in the kitchen before going up to bed. When he heard her leave the room, Bellamy left his wife sleeping in bed and washed the teapot and cup, checked the security system and armed it, then went to bed. As always, he was the last one in the house to go to sleep.

Blood Will Tell

Melody stepped out of the international arrivals hall at Heathrow Airport. She had shipped her luggage before leaving Houston and didn't have to wait for anything to be unloaded from the plane. Dragging her wheeled case with an attached carryon behind her, she headed for the taxi rank. However, before going two steps she saw a welcoming party waiting for her.

Lord Alfred Oswin was accompanied by Lord Arthur Farr who was her cousin and guardian by decree of her father's will. Melody was pleased to see them and they seemed to be getting along in each other's company without the abrasive demeanor they had shown when she first became acquainted with them. Alfred stepped forward and hugged and kissed her only to relinquish Melody to the arms of Arthur. His hug and kiss was the most amorous she had ever received from him.

Almost like twins, the two men said in unison, "Did you miss us?" They looked at each other and broke into smiles, another sign the coldness toward each other had melted considerably.

Alfred took her carryon while telling her, "I'll take this," and the three walked through the doors to get a taxi to town.

Settling in the back seat, Melody sat between the two men who had so recently been her guests for the Christmas and New Year's holidays in her Houston home. Each man took one of her hands. The trip into London to the quiet street where each gentleman had a townhouse took almost an hour. The traffic was always heavy, but today it seemed heavier than usual.

Alfred was doing most of the talking, leaving Arthur to savor the closeness of his ward. At first, Arthur had been oblivious to Melody's beauty, grace, charm, and intelligence. They had worked side by side in the library at Farr Cottage for months when Melody had originally come to England to fulfill the terms of her father's strange will. Since Arthur was her closest male relative on the Farr side of the family, well, actually he was her only relative on the Farr side of the family, as a very distant cousin he accepted the duty of taking Melody in until she would become thirty years old and could inherit her father's estate.

Alfred had befriended Melody from the initial day she arrived in England all those months ago. Arthur had a very important obligation he had to fulfill at the time of her arrival and had been unable to meet her until she had been in the Cottage for almost a week. Nedda, Arthur's housekeeper had installed his ward in the servant's quarters and this angered him and most especially when Alfred brought it to his attention. He and Alfred had never gotten along very well although they were both country and city neighbors, of a sort, and both of their families could trace their lineage to Anglo/Saxon England before the Conquest.

A few days in London before going down to the Cottage would be nice. Alfred was busy telling them of the changes he was making in his townhouse and how Arthur had been kind enough to invite him to stay in his while Alfred's was being renovated. Mrs. Jones, the old cook from Arthur's London house, had been asked to take care of the meals and her niece, Angie, to do the cleaning.

Arthur described the activity in his townhouse. "I know we don't have the staff you have in Houston, but we've been able to muddle through. The cleaners have been in to do a top to bottom polish of the old place and it is looking better. There are just so many things that could be done," Arthur sighed, "but there hasn't been time to do it. Your room is all freshly aired and I even had a new featherbed set put in to keep you warm."

Melody simply smiled as the two men talked. She *had* missed them and was looking forward to the next few months. Her birthday was only two months away and then she would be twenty-nine. When the will was read after her mother passed away, she was shocked and surprised at the special nature of the estate. Her father's will had decreed she would not inherit until she was thirty or married and until that time, she was to be the ward of her closest male Farr relative who was over the age of thirty. A search was made and that male relative was Lord Arthur Roland Farr, Viscount of Gibbons. As it turned out, he was the only male relative, unless what Alfred has been saying since she met him was true, that there was a blending of the two lines at some point in the past and Alfred and Arthur were, in fact, distant cousins.

She thought about LT, or as she had known him since a small child, 'Pinky' and how he saw this process. While at first she had chaffed under the terms of her father's will, she now saw it as a learning experience. From the time of her great great-grandfather, Richard Farr, the American estate had been preserved for the Farrs of the generation (s) to come. Her mother didn't inherit anything except for a fully paid living and could have had anything she wanted from the estate. But since she was not a Farr, she was not eligible to call any of it hers. She had carefully watched what she spent and made sure it would be secure when Melody came of age.

The trip home to Houston had been the real revelation. LT, as her father's best friend, her godfather, and Trustee of the Estate; he had been the one to begin to educate Melody in what her family had left to her. A yellowed, framed map which had always hung in the study but had been moved to the library by her mother was the first part of the elucidation.

The original American Farr, at least the Texas part of the family, Richard, had been the fourth son of the Viscount of Gibbons, Lord Arthur Charles Farr. Knowing he would never inherit the family titles or estates, Richard accepted a position with a group of London investors as their agent. In the mid-to late 1800's, investors in London were heavily engaged in the American cattle and ranching business. Richard had shown he had a head for numbers when he was up at Oxford with his next oldest brother, Edgar. After a few years of training in one of the City's banks, Richard was offered the post in Texas.

The map, LT explained to Melody, showed several of the properties the Farr estate owned. Ricard Farr had started the acquisitions, but his son Avery, and Melody's father, Charles, had all added to the family's fortune. There was also the bank, Farr's Bank, which had been started during her great great-grandfather's time when he bought out his partner, Samuel Newhouse. In the 1980's, when Texas had changed the banking laws to allow branch banking, Melody's father had sold the bank and assumed a position with the purchasing bank as well as serving on its board.

Yes, Melody was not the penniless, plain girl her British cousin had believed would be coming to stay in his home. When Arthur and Alfred had descended upon her home for the Christmas Holidays, they found her to be the chatelaine of a mansion called Farr House, boss of a staff of four, and still with the humility and demeanor of a naïve young woman. Both men were smitten before the visit and the time with Melody in her Houston home only made each of them more committed to winning her affections.

Melody began to recognize various streets and building so she knew they must be near the townhouse. Both men still held her hands and Alfred continued talking about the renovations on his townhouse. "Granted, it's not the big double that Arthur has, but it does have several quite stylish and historically significant elements."

The mention of the big double townhouse Arthur owned brought up a question Melody had been waiting to ask. Turning to Arthur she said, "Cousin, in the last few days before I left home, I happened to find a packet of letters from Richard's mother, Lady Annis Louise Farr, which were written to my great, great-grand-father, Richard. She was informing him of the death of her oldest son, Richard's oldest brother, and Viscount of Gibbons, Harold Charles Farr. She had sent to India to have the second son, Roland Arthur Farr returned from his regiment. Is this the Farr connected to the merger of the original townhome with the one next to it through marriage you spoke of before I left London last time?"

The two men looked at each other. Melody was only in a position where she could see the look on Arthur's face and she couldn't read the strange expression he had. Alfred had fallen silent waiting for Arthur to answer the question.

Clearing his throat, Arthur stammered, "Well, let's see, hmm, I suppose I might have mentioned it, but it's not important. Roland Farr, uh, Major Roland Farr was the second son who came back to assume the title when Lord Harold died. And, yes, Roland did marry the daughter of the people who had the adjoining town-home. But it was the kind of thing that happened once in a while, the second son having to step into the place left by a first son."

Arthur was now showing a bit more strength in what he was saying, "in fact, I was hoping you would look into the Farrs who were shown in the painting I showed you from around the time of the English Civil War. That has a lot more interesting people."

Alfred stirred and Melody could feel his grasp of her hand stiffen. "Why Arthur, if she wants to look into Major Roland, then she should. I know I would like to see it studied."

Arthur shot him a stern look back, "Humph, I'm sure you would!" Focusing again on Melody, "I will leave it up to you, but really, there is nothing to see with Major Roland."

The taxi slowed outside of the townhouse and Alfred took her carryon inside while Arthur paid the hack. "I'll give you all the information my family has on Major Roland if you think it might be useful. Just let me know when you'll want to start."

xxxxx – [1885]

Major Roland Farr sat back in the hackney carriage and watched the scenery he passed by on his way to the London house. He hadn't been in England since the year his father died and his regiment had been sent to India. While he could have returned on home-leave a few times down through the years, he had decided the horrors of sea travel were more than he wanted to endure.

Roland was convinced the Farr men were attracted to the army because they would never have made it as sailors. He did recall there had been two or three naval officers on one of the distant branches of the family tree, but the majority of military service provided to the crown was via the army. Roland followed the tradition in his family which was the first born inherited; the second went to the regiment, the third to the church. His fourth brother would have to make his way in a profession.

The clip-clop of the horse pulling the cab echoed in the streets. It was very early in the morning and few people were awake. Most of the residents would still be in their beds, but their servants would be up preparing their employers' homes for breakfast and since today was a Sunday, for church.

London at this time was the major power in the world militarily, socially, and financially. Queen Victoria sat on the throne and it was her extensive brood of children and grandchildren who were marrying into most of the royal houses of Europe. This offered a certain stability to everyday life. The Empire was at its most magnificent and it could be seen in the life of the capital city; London.

Turning down the street where the family's townhouse was located, he noticed a young woman dressed in the maid's uniform of his mother's household. While most maids wore a black dress, white cap, and white apron his mother fancied a grey dress with a black and white striped material for the cap and apron. As soon as the girl noticed the carriage, she scurried to the stairs that would take her to the kitchen area of the house.

Roland was sure the news of his arrival was being spread throughout the house as the cab was pulling up to the front door. The horse had no sooner come to a stop when the door of the house opened and a butler and footman descended the stairs. A second footman joined the first in removing the luggage from the back of the coach while the butler opened the door. "Your Lordship, welcome home Sir. Your mother is having her breakfast in the morning room; if you would please follow me I'll show you the way."

Roland looked up and down the street then at the butler. "No need, I think I can find it."

"Very good sir, your bags will be in your room if you would like to freshen up before going in to eat." The butler then turned his attention to the cabby. The cabby had removed his hat as he waited to be paid. The butler pulled a small leather coin purse from his jacket and gave the man the price of Sir Roland's cab from Victoria Station to the townhouse.

By the time the butler finished his business with the cabby, Roland had disappeared into the house. He stood in the foyer for a few moments while a maid took his hat, gloves, and overcoat. Roland looked up the stairs but decided to bypass going up to his room before seeing his mother. With purposeful steps he made his way to the morning room to join his mother for breakfast.

Lady Annise Louise Farr sat at the small table near the garden windows with a plate of eggs, bacon, sausage, and a half-full toast rack. A coffee cup was held in her dainty hands as Roland entered.

Roland went to his mother and kissed her on the cheek. "Mother, I am so sorry about Harold and the children. I came as soon as I could, but as you know transport from the Northwest Territories is not very modern in any way imaginable." Lady Annise raised her face to receive the kiss, put her cup down, and motioned for him to sit. A small silver bell sat near her left hand and she rang it to summon the servants.

The butler, Milton, entered and Roland told him what he would like for his breakfast. The traveler hadn't eaten since leaving Portsmouth. The ship Roland had been on from Alexandria, Egypt had docked only the night before and there were no trains to London until the very early one he had used. "I'm famished. Eggs, bacon, sausages, oh, and if you've got kippers, that with toast should make a good start."

Annis sat watching her son as he ordered his food. It had been several years since he had gone out to India and she was beyond pleased to have him back. Many times, she had wished he had taken advantage of the home-visits opportunity, but knowing his aversion to sea travel, she understood why he hadn't. She loved all of her sons and having one of her two absent boys back home was a treat.

However, now she looked at her second son with a critical eye. Roland was the Viscount of Gibbons and inheritor of the lands, estates, titles, and everything which went with it. He was also unmarried, closer to fifty than to forty, and was expected to fulfill his duties as the male head of the family. He needed a suitable wife, children, and to establish himself as the Viscount.

Lady Annis was aware Roland had never expected to inherit nor be anything more than an army officer. Now, he had to readjust his whole way of thinking. He needed to be transformed from a Major in Her Majesty's Army of Bengal into a titled member of the English Aristocracy. The first step in that transformation would be a visit from the tailor and bootmaker.

"Rolly," it had been years since he had heard his mother's nickname for him, "oh, sorry, Roland." His mother corrected herself and she reminded herself not to use the appellation again. Now was not the time to take her son back to the days of his youth, but forward to the future of the family. "After we finish our breakfast, you and I need to have a long conversation about your future."

"Mr. Oats, your father's old tailor, will be here in the morning. We also have an appointment with the bootmaker in Knightsbridge." Lady Annise saw the look on her son's face. "I understand this is not something you enjoy, but it must be done. This is March, well, actually, the end of March and the Season has already begun. I want you ready to accept invitations to dinners, parties, or balls as soon as possible."

Roland started to interrupt, but Lady Annise did not let him. She raised her hand to silence him, "Let me finish before you express discomfort with this. I am also very uncomfortable with the need to socialize right now. You lost a brother, but I lost a son. My grief is great, but the needs of the family and the future far outweigh my sorrow and should do the same for yours. We can't wait the customary year to mourn Harold. You must have a suitable wife. You must have children from this wife as soon as possible. This imperative takes precedence over any grief either you or I have."

Roland sat back in his chair. He knew his mother was looking out for his, well, actually, everyone's best interests and there was nothing about it that could be done. The Farr line was long, but there had been times when death, either by war or disease, had tried to interrupt or stop the flow of lands and titles from proceeding along the Farr family line. He did know his duty, but it didn't mean he liked having to do it.

Being the second son was a position Roland had liked. He had been acquainted with other second and third sons who chaffed at having lost the birth-order lottery, but not him. The life he had laid out for himself was the one he wanted. In his mind, he pictured a long stay with the Regiment in India, maybe even a transfer from the Bengal to the Madras armies after a few years, then retirement to home.

On the Farr Cottage estate stood a sizeable stone cottage which he had been dreaming of occupying since he left for the sub-continent. The place was quiet, had a small garden where he could putter if he wanted, and was close enough to a stream for fishing. His pension would keep him quite comfortable. Nowhere in those dreams were provisions made for a wife. Perhaps a maid to clean once or twice a week, but that was the extent of his need for a female. He was especially leery of children. He didn't like them and was sure they would not like him. No, now he wondered if it was too late to renounce his claim to the estates and titles in favor of his next younger brother, The Reverend Edgar Charles Farr.

However, as nice as that might sound, renouncing in favor of his younger brother went against his very being. He was the second son and it was his duty to step into the void created by the death of his older brother. No, Farrs didn't quit, they slogged through the problem until it was solved. Besides, Edgar might be a Vicar and all, but his wife had only been able to produce one daughter and she didn't strike him as a woman who would undertake another pregnancy to try for a son.

Lady Annise watched as her boy processed what she had said to him. She knew he would come to the proper solution, but it might take some time for him to be comfortable with it.

Roland had never shown any interest in girls even as a boy. She had insisted her brood of boys must have cotillion classes. A woman called 'Madam Louisa' held them in her home every week and the local gentry sent their young ones there. The lessons in manners, deportment, dance, and various social graces were adequate but it helped the boys most of all. Lady Annis' boys were all very good dancers and each one had been more than comfortable at any London party to which she had ever taken them. However, Roland was the only boy that had bonded more to his regiment than to civilian life. She knew he had it in him to do his duty, but would he balk at the idea of marriage?

She reached out to touch his hand. "Roland, I know you are not fond of girls, but do you think you could at least try?"

The contact with his mother's hand lifted him out of his reverie. "Hmm, yes, well, um, about that. I want you to know, up front, it's not that I prefer men to women, well not like that, um, what I mean to say is I prefer the *company* of men to women. At least with the men of my acquaintance in the regiment and those beyond that, you know where you stood. Chaps respected each other's boundaries and possessions. Oh sure, you would get a bad apple in the bunch once in a while that would try cheating at cards or not take his responsibilities with his men seriously, but they didn't last long in the Territories. It was a comradery, discipline, and order that kept things moving along as it should. You just don't get that with a woman."

Lady Annis was sure she saw a slight blush on his cheeks as he continued. "With women, you never know where you stand. I've seen too many chaps get waylaid by some girl who had come out to India for no other purpose than to find a husband. They would take a position as a nanny, governess, or companion to a family traveling out from England then charm some mid-level officer into marriage. No sooner would the nuptials be over than she would be crying to return to England. Phift!" Roland snapped his fingers" and we would lose another officer from our ranks."

"I must admit, I have danced with a couple of these women. Even dinned with one in the officer's mess, but their interests lay more in what prospects a man had back home than his ambitions in the regiment. I suppose," Roland looked down and picked an invisible dust particle from his trousers before continuing, "when I told them I would be staying on in India until the time when I could either pension out or was sent on to another posting overseas, they lost interest. She couldn't waste time on an officer who would not want to leave and besides, unless you are somebody like Sir William Lockhart, the Lieutenant General of the Bengal army district, having a wife out there is just silly."

Lady Annis nodded. She was relieved to hear her son was not totally opposed to women, he might just need the correct female and circumstances. It would be her job to put him in the right place with the right person. However, finding this girl might be tricky. It wasn't even half-way through the London season and many of the debutants who had been presented at Court were already either spoken for or arrangements were being discussed.

Besides, Roland was not a young man anymore. He needed a wife who might be a little older, but not so old as to preclude children. She had a couple of friends looking through their acquaintances for someone suitable, but finding a girl might take some time. However, no time could be wasted preparing her son for the life ahead. The tailor and bootmaker would take care of the outer appearance, but she also needed to bring Roland into the inner workings of the estate and titles which he had inherited.

"Very well, on Monday afternoon the family solicitor, Mr. Niels-Smyth, will be here for the official reading of the will and the transfer of the various instruments of the title and estate. You'll have some papers to sign and such, but with that, you'll officially be the Viscount of Gibbons."

Roland watched his mother as she spoke. He had been at Farr Cottage on the day when the solicitor had traveled down from London to effect the transfer to his older brother Harold. Roland's father, her husband, had just been killed in the hunting accident at Aldwin House. His mother had been through a great deal of sadness and he gave a silent prayer she would not have to see any more. He squared his shoulders and resolved to do what had to be done to secure the future for the Farr family.

xxxxx – Present day

Melody was impressed with some of the changes in the London house. True, the striped wallpaper was still faded, but the whole place had been dusted, flowers put in the vases, floors polished, and light streamed through clean windows. The drab house she had left in November was much cheerier in January.

Angie, the niece of the cook, Mrs. Jones; took Melody's things up to her room and Alfred and Melody followed Arthur into the lounge. The curtains were still open but the sun was setting fast and with it, the temperatures would drop. However nice these old houses looked, they were still the products of eighteenth and nineteenth century construction with all the drafts, lack of insulation, and vintage fixtures in need of repair and replacement.

"While we are all together in London you must come and see the house I am redoing about two streets over. Like this one and mine, we're not allowed to change the outside, historically it's embargoed, but I have spent the last few months changing the whole of the interior. I think you'll like what I've done with it and it might," Alfred turned and directed his comments specifically to Arthur, "show you what can be done. I know my house is going to be totally updated when I finish but I'm also keeping the wonderful design elements."

Melody nodded, "I would like to see it. I understand the idea of not changing the historical character of the buildings, but it must be difficult doing the insides and bringing it up to modernity. Have you been lucky enough to find any treasures, surprises, or secrets in the places upon which you have worked?"

Alfred threw his head back and laughed. "It depends on what you consider a treasure or secret. Dead rat skeletons are surprises when we find them, but most of the old places have been cleared out quite thoroughly by the time I get to them. The lofts on the old docks turn up an odd coin here or there, but nothing of real value. No, the only thing that any of these places could yield might be the odd ghost, but since I don't believe in them, they don't even register."

Melody smiled, "I don't believe in ghosts either so there's no problem with that. I was just wondering if, during your refurbishments, you have uncovered any carvings, scrollwork, or fancy design items. I know how one generation can decide that what gran had was not to their liking and they would have it painted over, covered up, or removed to the attic. Anything like that?"

Alfred thought for a moment. "Hmm, we did run across that very thing in my house. The man who originally built the house must have been quite impressed by the Baroque style. He did a couple of the large bedrooms, probably his suite and the one his wife occupied, in a kind of Baroque revival thing. We found some of the more highly carved wall sconces in the attic and after peeling several layers of wallpaper off those particular walls, the outlines of the items could be seen."

"Will you be putting them back, restoring the house to its former glory?" Melody queried.

Alfred shook his head, "No, I'm keeping a lot of the other elements, but some of the wall sconces border on the "gargoyle" and it's not for me."

Arthur jumped in, "look, I hate to interrupt your talk of houses, ghosts, and sconces, but Melody," he directly addressed his ward, "you've just had a long flight. I'm sure you want to go to your room, maybe have a lie-down, and perhaps a long hot bath before you need to dress for dinner. Remember, we meet in the lounge at 5:30, sharp, for drinks."

Melody nodded, "I am a bit tired, and a hot bath sounds wonderful. I'll see you both for drinks."

xxxxx

During the next few days the old routines fell into place and Melody felt like she had never been away. The three enjoyed each other's company and had long talks over dinner and drinks each evening. During the day, Alfred left to work on his projects and Arthur spent most of his time in either the library or the British Museum doing research. Melody spent her time puttering around the big London house and exploring all of its rooms, hallways, and attics.

On the third day back in England Melody finally took a long afternoon nap that cured her of the jetlag to which she seemed to be sensitive. After that nap, she was back on GMT and able to stay up in the evenings and, without much trouble, rise as early if not earlier than her host.

Two days before they were scheduled to return to the country and Farr Cottage, Alfred took Melody to the house he was almost finished refurbishing. It was quite close to Upper Brook Street where they were currently staying.

Walking up to the house it looked like any other on the lane. The white façade had been repaired to its historical elegance and freshly painted. The interior was something else entirely. From the front foyer to the servant's quarters on the fourth floor, the house had been gutted and everything made new.

The ground floor had most of the public rooms, but the kitchen had been moved from "below stairs" to the back of the house. The former area it had occupied had been turned into a wine cellar, storage for pantry items, and, to what in America would be called a "man cave" that was simply the gent's game room. It had comfy, overstuffed chairs, a big sectional sofa, and it all faced a huge flat-screen telly. At the back of the room were two games tables, a foosball table, darts board, and a substantial oak bar. If you're going to have a man's playroom, it would have to look something like the one Alfred had built.

On the ground floor[1], the kitchen, butler's pantry, and dining room were all on one side with the dining room looking out over a small but very well landscaped back garden. The lounge also shared the same views of the garden and the study covered the remainder of the floor. The morning room on the first floor also had the garden view, but next to it was the library with high windows that were for light but didn't let in the sun's rays to damage the books or fade the furniture or carpets.

What had been the typical ballroom space had been divided into a media room and a lovely master with walk-in closets and a large bathroom. The sitting area of the bedroom area looked over the garden and had a view over the wall to the mews. An elevator had been installed so the entire house could be reached by anyone in any physical condition.

The second floor had the rest of the bedrooms, bathrooms, and a sewing room. There was also a nursery for young families. The third floor still held the attics and servant's quarters, but the servant's quarters in this house were nothing like the ones Alfred had originally found. These were small studio apartments with kitchenettes, sitting areas, private baths, and ample closet space. It would be rare to get a servant who would agree to work in a house if the quarters were like the ones he had ripped out, but there would be several takers for the new ones.

Alfred looked around the servant's lodgings and chuckled. "You know, in 1900 there were over a million people "in service" in Britain, but now …" He shook his head, "now it will be difficult to find enough people to fill these spaces. Nobody wants to be a maid, housekeeper, or butler. The idea of being a servant is beneath

---

1   In the U.S.A., the ground floor would be the first floor, the first the second, etc.

most of the young people. They would rather go on the dole (government assistance) than be a maid or work in a house like this."

Melody looked around. Her house was grander than this house, hers was not just bigger, but with her staff, would be well taken care of while she was gone. Thankfully, LT Chadwick had been so insistent on having her take the people who had worked so faithfully in his house. London was nice, but it was time to go back to the country where there was room to walk. She didn't like views from windows which were only streets, brick walls, or tiny gardens, and it was time to see forests or large, well-kept gardens.

Alfred took her hand, "ready to leave?"

Melody nodded, "hmm, yes. I'm ready to go back to the country. It's a nice house, but London just feels so crowded. It's almost hard to breath."

Alfred laughed, "You are not the only person who has ever felt that way about the city, but after having seen your house, I can understand. So, let's go. Lunch first?"

xxxxx

Two days after the tour, with Alfred, of the refurbished house in London, Arthur was ready to leave London for Farr Cottage. The short days of winter meant it was dark when they arrived at Farr Cottage from the station. John, Nedda's husband, was at the station waiting with the old car, which Arthur kept for use in the country.

The fire had been lit in the lounge, dining room, and when Melody entered her room the warmth of the fire was inviting. A quick change into her dinner clothes and Melody was back in the lounge for the traditional before dinner drinks.

Melody had no problems staying awake. In Houston it was still early in the afternoon, but Arthur stretched to stay for a second after dinner brandy and coffee. He had some things he wanted to discuss with Melody by decided they would best be left for the morning.

xxxxx

Sunlight slipped through the slender gap between the curtains in Melody's bedroom, traveled across the oriental carpet on the floor, and traversed the featherbed on the large four-poster. Slowly, Melody awoke to the light shining on her eyelids. For the first few seconds she found herself surprised by the different surroundings. Her mind sorted out the confusion and she lay there, thinking about Farr Cottage.

Alfred had stayed on in London, but would be down to Aldwin House by the end of the week. He had invited her to Sunday services. She and Arthur would probably attend with him. Until then, she would be working on the Farr family story and Arthur on whatever it was that he had to do at the moment.

Stretching and kicking off the covers, Melody knew it was past time to start the day, but it was, after all, Arthur's fault; the featherbed was just so warm and toasty, it made her want to stay in bed. Nedda did not like to keep breakfast for anyone and Melody understood that Cousin Arthur would be waiting to start the workday.

Hmm, Cousin Arthur, is that really what he was now? Sir Arthur, Lord Arthur, Cousin Arthur, even Viscount Gibbons, he had declared his love and affection for Melody and asked her to be his wife. So, now, what was he? And, to make matters more confusing, under the dictates of her father's will, Arthur was her guardian and she was his ward until Melody was thirty. She would have to think about this.

Arthur was in the foyer when Melody came down the stairs. Inwardly, he was smiling at the sight of her. Dressed in a warm wool jumper (sweater) and skirt, woolen tights on her shapely legs, and the heels she always wore he had missed her so very, very much. Her chestnut brown hair and beautiful eyes, which were always so inquisitive, still mesmerized him. She belonged in this house and he needed to do whatever was necessary to get her to stay and marry him. It couldn't be any other way; he needed her in his life.

Arthur took his ward's arm, "I hope this is not going to become a habit! You do know we start our day here much earlier than this, but I suppose your first day back, well, I'll make an exception. Come, Nedda has some breakfast for you and I'll have a cup of tea while you eat."

The breakfast was filling and the coffee, well, it was easy to tell the difference between the coffee Mrs. Bellamy made Melody in Houston and the morning beverage Nedda made. Of course the cold toast was different, but it was not as important as the coffee. She would have to see about getting a really good coffee pot and some strong roasted, freshly ground beans to go in it.

After breakfast, in the library, Melody and Arthur began their work. She showed her cousin the narrative on Annis Farr; daughter of Richard Farr, which Melody had worked on while she was in Houston. There were also several photos, letters, journal pages, etc. she had brought which would be important additions to the things she had written about Richard and the Houston Farrs before she had returned to Texas for the holidays.

"Before you start on the next part of the family story," Arthur said, looking at the treasures she had brought, "I'd like to see you put as many of these items in the proper places in the accounts you've already written as possible. The letters from Lady Annis to her son Richard when he immigrated to Texas are so beautifully written and these photos, they will really bring the history of this family alive."

"If the scanner you ordered for the computer system has arrived, it will take no time to add these to the writings. I think, even if we don't use everything, they should still be preserved onto disk for the future. We might think about having as many of the paper, photographic, and miscellany as we have from any period, secured on disk. Too many of the items you have here are fragile and wouldn't it be nice if future generations could enjoy them?"

Arthur nodded, "let's do these now and we'll look after the others when you finish." He hadn't thought about it much in the past, but she had just given him the perfect excuse to keep her busy scanning in bits and pieces and away from the story of Major Lord Roland Farr. Then he shook the notion out of his head. No, with Alfred so keen on her working on Roland, it would be difficult to keep her doing more than the items for the work she had already done. He just needed to resign himself to her working on Roland and Rand Oswin.

Melody was intent on what she was doing and did not notice the turmoil Arthur was enduring. A little too gruffly, he said, "well, if you've nothing else to discuss, let's get to work."

It was then Melody looked up to see her cousin begin reading her work. Bowing her head over her task, she got back to work. Sometimes she just didn't understand him. Had she done something to make him angry or was it a disappointment in her work. Whatever it was, she knew he would tell her if it was something she had done wrong, he always did!

For the next two days, Melody spent her work time sorting and scanning the items into the narrative. That done, she then set about scanning the other items she had brought so they would be readily accessible in a database.

The routine of the house still included the sherry and cake at eleven in the morning and dressing for dinner with drinks in the lounge at five thirty. Since she had been back at the Cottage there had been no guests, but on Friday evening, The Reverend Charles Paxton, vicar at St. Alban's Church, and his wife Livia joined them for supper.

On Saturday morning, Alfred arrived and before going to his own home, Aldwin House, he was having sherry and cake with Arthur and Melody.

"You missed a wonderful dinner party at Maude Harbison's. Beryl Somersby has gotten herself engaged to a Scotsman, Ian MacDougal. Big guy, close to six and a half feet tall and has to weigh close to two hundred and fifty pounds.[2] Beryl is so thin and wispy, but, she seems to be happy. Maude looked a little dejected. I think they had a thing going about who would marry first, but it doesn't look like Maude can win this one."

For the rest of the evening, Alfred told them funny stories of various members of his social circle. Melody had the feeling Beryl or Maude would have been more than happy to make Alfred a good wife, but perhaps they've given up and decided to look elsewhere. Most of his circle now knew of his interest in Melody and that would have dampened any girl's hopes.

The next day was Sunday and Alfred was going to church with Arthur and Melody. Lunch afterwards was being served at the Cottage and the ease and comfort Arthur showed in inviting Alfred still surprised her. The trip to Houston the men made together must have made a difference.

xxxxx

With the weekend over, scanning completed in the work Melody had done before leaving England, and the additional work she accomplished in Houston over the Thanksgiving and Christmas Holidays, it was time to start the story of Major Lord Roland Arthur Farr. Almost immediately, Melody found a phrase which puzzled her and found it would be necessary to research it before diving into the story, after all, "Napoleon's Niece"? She'd never seen or heard of that one …

---

[2]   Weights and heights are in pounds and inches for the American readers.

Napoleon's Niece 1796

Simon du St.-Dinard sat on his horse while his general spoke about the coming battle. As a colonel of the Chasseur a` Cheval of the Consular Guard, the light cavalry of the personal guard of Napoleon, he was 'at rest.' He had spent so many years in the saddle as a cavalry officer no one could tell he was not listening intently to what the new First Consul was saying; he had heard it before.

In the days before the Battle of Montenotte in 1796, he first saw the man who was the youngest general in the new army of the French Republic. Napoleon had risen fast and brought victories to the struggling new democracy. The Old Regime` was no more. The heads of many in the aristocracy were lost to 'Madam Guillotine'.

Simon was very fortunate he and his family's heads were not among those whom the Citizens wanted to see separated from their bodies. His grandfather had been the Duke du St.-Dinard, but a falling out with Louis XV had led to his being stricken from the rolls of France's elites. Simon's father had been mortified he would not inherit the lands and title from his father. However, shortly after Simon's grandfather died, the Revolution began and being an Aristocrat was not the path to a long life in France.

The family put the white cockade of Revolution on their hats and caps, addressed everyone as 'Citizen', and tried to keep out of the rabble's eye as much as possible. Simon's father had been an officer in the cavalry when he was younger and his older brother Jean-Marie was destined to inherit the title. Jean-Marie had started the scandal, which ended in the falling out with the king, and even Jean-Marie's death was not enough to assuage the royal ire. "Tampering" with the king's wife was treason, but with the king's favorite mistress it was personal.

Simon's father, Charles, would have been in line to assume the title of Duke. After the storming of the Bastille, the Revolution and the division between the Royalists who fought for the king and the Citizens who clamored for a France without a royal family, the du St.-Dinard men knew they were better off as loyal to France and not her king.

Like his father before him, Simon attended the military academy in Paris. Simon graduated mere months before the Bastille fell. He and his father both pledged themselves to the revolution and waited to see what the future would hold.

Simon's mother, Greer, had been Scots and there was serious talk about taking the family and going to the relatives across the channel. However, the Royalist forces enlisted the aid of the English, Austrian, and Spanish fleets and armies to try to regain the throne for a Bourbon King. France needed every military officer and enlistee they could safely use and the break with the former King's father served the family well.

Living in a modest house in the town once a part of their "lands and titles;" Simon's widowed father watched over Simon's wife, Marie-Juliann, and the two young children, Marcel and Marguerite. The idea of having to slip away to England for safety had receded into the background, but like many people in France, Simon and his father always knew the possibility was forever present.

As his General/First Consul continued his talk to his officers, Simon remembered the many battles, large and small, into which he had followed Napoleon. From the Battle of Montenotte in 1796, when most of the world saw the army of France as a joke to be overrun in days, to the one upon which they were about to begin the Battle of Marengo, Simon had led his group of cavalry bravely. He had been promoted on the battlefield for his heroism and loyalty to France and Napoleon. The only major campaign he was unable to participate in was the Egyptian and looking back on the outcome, it was good he didn't go with Napoleon.

It was funny, really, and he caught himself starting to smile, but knew it would give him away. Mustn't anger the First Consul! No, at the time, Simon was furious to be left behind, but each of the men to accompany Napoleon on the trip had to be in top physical condition and Simon wasn't. For a cavalry officer, the ability to sit a horse for long hours or to ride at top speeds, maneuver, and fight from the saddle was imperative. However, a boil in an, uhmm, uncomfortable, uh, place, could make that difficult and the chances of the site becoming infected was even worse. So, as the ships that carried the Army of Egypt sailed toward the Nile, he was at home, on his stomach, recovering from having the offending boil removed.

There were some of the generals who thought, after the outcome of the Egyptian campaign, Napoleon had lost his magic, but speculation like that could embolden an enemy. They had all poured over the maps, listened to the strategy, and assessed the enemy. The trek across the Alps, a feat which would be the subject of more than one famous painting of the First Consul in the future, was compared to Hannibal's bringing his war elephants to the siege of Rome.

Suddenly, Simon noticed a departure from the standard pre-battle speech. It was time to listen more intently.

Tomorrow, Austrian General von Melas will send us his best troops. Tomorrow, the battle will be fierce. This is a fight for the safety of France and the life of all French Citizens. Give everything you have and when I ask you for more dig deep and find it for me. Do not worry about your wife or children, they will be cared for like my own. No, tomorrow France is our child and its safety is in our hands. Do not disappoint! If you give your life for France, I will personally care for your children as if they were my own nieces and nephews.

xxxxx

The First Consul had been right. The fighting was fierce. In the early hours of the day the Austrians pushed and pushed on the French lines and moved them backwards. When Napoleon realized the intent of von Melas was different than first expected, a change of tactics on Napoleon's part began the path to a French victory.

When the smoke and clash of battle had settled that night, the Austrians had been pushed out of Italy at a terrible cost to their army. On the French side, the casualties had been much less. However, as the triumphant French army celebrated and the church bells of Paris announced the great victory, a young serving girl in St.-Dinard was sent to the local newspaper to get the casualty lists.

The du St.-Dinard household was steeped in mourning. Black-crepe was hung over the portrait of Simon in his uniform, a wreath of black-crepe was fashioned for the front door, and Madam Simon du St.-Dinard entered a mourning she would never abandon. Marcel and Marguerite became a nephew and niece of Napoleon. Each year, they received a small stipend for as long as Napoleon was in power. Marcel received an appointment to the

École Militaire in Paris, the same school as his father and grandfather, and Marguerite could petition for a dowry when she married.

As fate would have it, Napoleon did not last for as many years as he had envisioned and long before the first exile on Elba, Simon's father took his daughter-in-law and granddaughter to his late wife's family in Scotland.

Smugglers Cove

England and France have always wrestled with the problem of smugglers. However, France was so close and the merchants of London were always eager to get the contraband. French wines, brandy, and spices from the Orient filled the smuggling caves located in coves and inlets along the English Coast. Fine English wool and products from the Empire traveled to France. And, as always, people were a steady cargo. The temptation was too great and the profits were worth the risk.

Charles du St.-Dinard started moving his widowed daughter-in-law and granddaughter to his late wife's family by way of these smugglers onto English soil. The crossing of the Channel in a small boat was the first hardship, but it paled to the weeks they had to spend in the damp cave below the English cliffs.

Customs agents scoured the coast looking for any contraband and while they were not focusing on people smuggling, if found, the du St.-Dinard refugees would have been sent back to France and put to death. In high tide, the floor of the cave was covered with water, and although it was only a few inches, nothing was dry. Marguerite's mother was unable to survive the ordeal. Before the third week of their concealment had finished, she slipped away to join her husband Simon in death.

Charles du St.-Dinard was a harder man to kill. Rather than allow the circumstances to beat him, he used his military training to find a way out. It was easier for a man alone but his granddaughter, Marguerite, was all he had left. Unlike the girl's mother, he spoke excellent English and so did she. For anyone who asked, they were from the American city of New Orleans.

xxxxx

Angus MacLardie lived on the coast of Scotland near a town called Montrose. He was Charles du St.-Dinard's father-in-law and a man who forgave only grudgingly. Angus was a Laird, a Lord to the English, and much to most Englishman's dislike, a Catholic.

When they had married, Greer Marie and her family were promised she would be allowed to visit as often as practical and the children would be raised in the Catholic faith. One visit in thirty years did not suit the old man and the desecration of the French churches by the revolutionary rabble angered him even further. The meeting with Angus and Charles was short and acrimonious.

It was the child, Marguerite, who softened the old man. She joined her great grandfather Maclardie in the chapel each morning and could say her catechism of the virtues, but it was her blue eyes that turned his heart towards her. The same blue eyes of his daughter Greer and his wife Adele. Marguerite was allowed to stay in the house with Angus, but grandfather du St.-Dinard was housed in a crofter's cottage on the estate.

Sent to the best school, doted on by her Scottish great grandfather, Marguerite was a Highland catch. Her French grandfather, however, was ever watchful and the arrangement between the two old men diminished the list of possible suitors. Young men from

Catholic families were not plentiful, at least at the social level and class of Marguerite.

As Marguerite began to approach early spinsterhood, her prospects for marriage were reduced to nothing. Charles du St.-Dinard died and Angus Maclardie became feeble. Marguerite resigned herself to living out her days in the cold, drafty house of her great grandfather. When old Angus MacLardie died, his heir invited Marguerite to stay on, but the small inheritance she received gave her the income to move to London.

xxxxx

The industrial revolution was a boon to middle class men with vision and a strong work ethic. Men who were willing to put their ideas to the task of building something that would drive England and the Empire to the forefront of primacy in the world of innovation and wealth. Joseph Bannister was just such a middle-class man.

Jo Bannister was the son of a farmer. Working long hours doing heavy labor was nothing to him, it was simply how he had grown up, but he also liked to know how things worked. Not long after Jo turned nineteen, his father sat him down and explained the farm would be going to his two older brother and their families.

Outwardly, Jo let his father know how sad he was to not be able to stay on the farm but in his mind, he was relieved to know it would not be expected of him to stay. He was offered the opportunity to stay of course, his family wasn't putting him out with nothing. It's just that the farm wasn't big enough to support all of the people who were living on it. If Jo wanted to help buy extra land adjoining the family farm, he could stay on and farm it, but none was for sale nor likely to be anytime in the future.

Jo took his meager belongings and joined the other young men looking for work in the cities. A small machine shop employed him and Jo's life was forever changed. Fifteen years later, Jo owned the original shop and nine more just like it. The Industrial Revolution ran on machines and *Bannister's Machine Works* was known for the most innovative, strongly built, and best engineered machines. Also, 'any repairs needed' were done quickly. The shops were close to the factories where the equipment was located and this gave the various owners and managers' confidence that the builders of their equipment would be able to watch over these major expenses.

Jo still spent long hours in the shops. He had managers who worked for him and saw to the day-to-day work, but Jo made it his business to get to each place regularly. Sales of equipment to new or existing customers were also something Jo insisted upon doing himself.

It was during one of his trips to London that he met Marguerite. Jo had never taken the time to think about marriage, but one of his biggest clients had married into a family of solicitors in London. His wife was a school friend of Marguerite. At a small dinner party given for Marguerite, Jo was seated next to her.

Marguerite's blue eyes and chestnut-red hair intrigued Jo. And, although Jo had only a rudimentary education, he had schooled himself in what it took to be a successful businessman. The courtship was short, mainly just long enough for Jo to buy a house for his bride.

Located next to an old Anglo-Saxon family named Farr, the house in Mayfair came furnished and had a staff to help care for the newlyweds. Although Marguerite attended mass daily while she lived in the home of Angus MacLardie the influence of her French grandfather and his revolutionary teachings prevailed for the rest of her life.

The marriage only produced one daughter, Juliet. Jo Bannister spent most of his time doing the same as he had before he married. As the number of shops grew to keep pace with the exploding industrial economy of the Empire, there was less time to spend either making or attending to a family. Before he knew it, his little girl had finished boarding school, finishing school, and was being readied by her mother for her "season."

Juliet inherited the chestnut-red hair and blue eyes of her mother. With her creamy complexion, excellent figure, and impeccable manners she was popular as a dance partner in the round of parties that followed her coming-out. Her mother, as an 'Honorable,' gave her the place in society, but it was her father's money that helped make her as appealing as a possible marriage candidate with the eligible young men.

The Honorable George Fitzwilliam came from an old family with old debts and a crumbling house in the country. Before his father, Lord Charles Fitzwilliam, took to his bed with advanced syphilis, he had already spent his inherited money on women and gambling. His long-suffering wife, Clarice, saw Juliet as the savior of her son and his future.

Clarice Fitzwilliam and Marguerite Bannister didn't so much approve of the marriage of their children but negotiated an agreement for the two young people to marry. Jo Bannister immediately paid the debts of the Fitzwilliam family, refurbished the country house, and settled an income on Juliet until such time as she or her children could inherit. The only item Jo insisted upon was no money would go for the care of Lord Charles.

The wedding was small but tasteful and performed at the small church near the Bannister's London home. A wedding breakfast was eaten at the house before the young couple left for an extended honeymoon in Italy. The repairs to the country home were expected to be finished by the time they returned.

While the young couple was away, Lord Charles finally did the best thing he could have for his newly married son and died. Clarice Fitzwilliam informed her son of his father's passing and told him not to shorten his honeymoon because of the man's death. Lord George Fitzwilliam and his now pregnant bride Juliet arrived home two months after his mother had written him the news.

xxxxx

Lord George and Lady Juliet Fitzwilliam watched as their stunning daughter Charlotte was presented at court. She was dressed in a white silk court gown with the short train deemed appropriate by Queen Victoria. The white plume she wore in her hair was contrasted by the chestnut-red color. The same blue eyes of her mother were raised briefly to the Queen as she had her few seconds in the royal eye before the next girl was presented.

Before her grandfather Bannister died, the house in the country was sold and the widowed Lady Clarice Fitzwilliam was moved into the home in Mayfair. Both grandmothers helped Juliet raise Charlotte and lived to see her married to an impoverished young Lord, Andrew Percy of Northumbria.

The young couple was soon estranged. Lady Charlotte became pregnant with a girl the March after her June wedding and Lord Andrew left for the Continent with his lover, Robert Scott, soon after. Lady Charlotte's mother Juliet and father George were on hand to help her raise the new little girl. Within two years, Lady Charlotte was informed by the police in Genoa that her husband's 'friend', Robert Scott, had killed her husband, Lord Andrew Percy, and promptly committed suicide.

Lord George Fitzwilliam made the trip to Genoa to close that chapter of his daughter's life. The sordid details were kept from his little girl and they would go to the grave with him. He paid any debts the man had left and retrieved the few pieces of Percy family jewelry which had not been sold.

Jillian was a lovely girl with dark blue eyes and the same brown hair as her father. She barely squeaked through formal lessons, but did do better in finishing school. However, she didn't have the same seriousness her mother and grandmother had always exhibited. She was beautiful but rather shallow, preferred parties and dancing to reading, and despite her generous allowance, she never seemed to have enough money to pay her bills at the dressmakers, cobblers, or milliners.

At twenty-three, several suitors had inquired about her, but none seemed a good fit. A friend of Lady Charlotte's invited Jillian and her to their country house for a weekend. Although Jillian preferred the life in town, her mother insisted she go.

Aldwin House

Rand Oswin and his bride Laura were just returning from their morning ride when a coach arrived with more visitors. Rand's mother, Lady Grace Oswin, had invited several of her friends for the weekend and it would probably prove to be an older crowd that would be boring for the young couple. His mother, however, had insisted they come down from London to join the party.

Rand and Laura were in time to greet the newest guests as they stepped down from the carriage. It was an older woman, Lady Charlotte Percy, a friend of his mother's and her daughter Jillian. It was the younger lady that caught Rand's eye. Clothed in an emerald green traveling suit, he couldn't help but notice the tiny waist, flashing blue eyes, and coquettish demeanor. Maybe the weekend wouldn't be too bad after all!

Also in attendance were Grace Oswin's old friend Lady Annis Farr and Major Lord Roland Farr. The new Viscount had only recently returned from his regiment in India following the death of his older brother, Viscount Harold Farr. Lady Annis was in mourning black, but the son was sporting a country tweed with a black armband out of respect for his late brother.

Lady Oswin had promised to help Lady Annis try to find a wife for her son. He needed a girl who was still young enough for children but old enough to be a good wife. The Major was a handsome man, but his best marriageable years were behind him. Not many young ladies wanted to be tied to an older husband, regardless of their station, but the Farrs, like the Oswins, were not 'exciting' families with which to begin.

The Oswins and Farrs were Anglo/Saxons who could trace their linages to before the Norman Conquest. Two half-brothers, Harold and Henry d'Auffay, were part of the army which came from Normandy with the bastard William. Henry d'Auffay murdered the father-in-law and husband of Mercia Farr within feet of Farr Cottage. Henry claimed the lands and estate of Farr Cottage as well as Mercia for his wife. Unbeknownst to him, however, was the fact Mercia was pregnant with her late husband's child. In a matter of weeks following the forced marriage, while continuing to ride with William's army, Henry was killed. The priest at St. Alban's Church knowing the true parentage of the child listed him with the name of his blood father.

The Oswin conqueror, Harold, was the younger of the two half-brothers. He had been injured in the initial fight and was unable to ride with the army and his half-brother. Harold forced himself on the Lady Iseult as the body of her murdered father-in-law, Arielle, was being drug from the old keep. Lady Iseult's husband had died at the Battle of Hastings defending the Anglo/ Saxon king from William.

William wanted his knights married to the conquered as a way to further solidify the Norman dominance over the Anglo/Saxons. Harold, however, was unable to father a child, a necessity if he was to keep more than a temporary hold on the lands and estate of Oswin. A clever ruse was concocted between Iseult and Harold who took the orphaned child of an Oswin cousin in as their own child. Rand Oswin became Rand d'Auffay until the death of his adopted father when the rolls show his name was changed to Rand Oswin.

Through the centuries, the two families were neighbors, of a sort. In the country, they lived within twenty miles of each other but in London, their townhouses were on the same street. However, in these long years, there had never been any intermarriage. The Oswins and Farrs were simply too dull for each other. The men got on well together, but the women of the family, while appreciating the fact their husbands were not spendthrifts, drunkards, gamblers, and didn't chase women, looked for something more exciting in a marriage partner either for themselves or for their children.

Now, it was the turn of Rand Oswin's wife, Laura, to bemoan the fate of the girl who would marry a Farr.

xxxxx – Present Day

Melody looked up from her computer keyboard. The desk she was using was piled high with stacks of files and papers, but they were all in neat piles. Her eyes went to the screen in front of her as she read the last words written in the narrative. Something in the back of her mind was niggling her, but she wasn't sure what it was.

The revelation was odd. Somewhere in one of these mounds of stuff she had seen that name before and not in the same context as it was just used. Looking over the stacks she found the one she thought might be relevant.

At the desk near her, Arthur was deep into his project. The soft click of Melody's computer keyboard had become part of the background noise against which he worked. Shuffling papers, the scratch of a pen, and other such noises were the price he paid for having her in his workspace. Today, however, the sounds had stopped and their absence caused him to lose his concentration.

In the beginning, when Melody had first come to him as his ward, it was almost impossible to work in the same room. She was always asking questions and disrupting his train of thought, not to mention the introduction into his old style library of a computer in the form of Melody's laptop! He had been firm with her about the questions, he would answer them, but not until the end of the workday. The computer had eventually proved to be a good idea and he purchased one, as well as a larger desk, for her to use.

The quiet finally stretched into a longer period of time than he was accustomed and he looked up to see what was the problem. Every time he looked at her his mind remembered her as she had looked when she entered the Houston charity ball wearing the fairytale dark blue dress. She'd looked more like a princess that night than any of the ones living in Buckingham Palace. The most wonderful thing was that every day she was working at the desk next to him in the family library.

A smile crossed his face as he took in the sight of her. Her chestnut-brown hair with the subdued mahogany highlights, the large dark eyes, and the creamy skin. She was beautiful, not in the mode of a professional beauty, but the kind that would last a lifetime.

Arthur wanted to marry her and with her help, keep the ancient lines of the Farr family going into the future, but there were others who also wanted to make her their wife. At the mere thought of his rivals for her hand, his smile turned into a frown. Best not think about that right now, he wanted to know why she had stopped her work. "Are you having a problem?" he asked in a sympathetic voice. "Is there something I can do to help?"

Melody realized Arthur was speaking to her. She blinked to clear her mind. "It's just something, well, I can't quite put my finger on. It has to do with the French connection to the Farr line. Actually you could include the Oswin line. Just recently I read a letter or journal" she shook her head in exasperation, "and it relates back to the d'Auffay line, but I can't find it."

Arthur was intrigued. The d'Auffay murderers were something that the Oswin and Farr families shared. The two half-brothers had come with that bastard, William when he invaded England but they had not been able to pollute the Anglo/Saxon line of either family. What would Melody have read that made any but the most fleeting of mentions of the French?

"Melody, don't worry about it. I'm sure it will come to you," he soothed. Looking at his watch, "look, it's almost eleven and Nedda will be in shortly with the cake and sherry. Why don't you go freshen up and perhaps the item you're looking for will come to you. Oh, and don't forget, tonight we are having dinner after you go to evening services at the church. Would you like to have a curry?"

The redirection had seemed to work. Melody smiled at Arthur. "I don't think a curry would be very good that late, perhaps just a cold supper here would be better. If you want I can tell Nedda when she serves lunch." Getting up from her desk, "I'll be back in a few minutes." And with that, she left the room.

Melody knew what Arthur was doing and he was right, maybe if she wasn't looking so hard, it would come to her. While she was looking in the mirror over the sink in her bathroom, the answer came to her and she knew where to find what she had thought missing. However, how to prove the connection between the two families? Was the girl "from the d'Auffay family of Normandy" the same family and should she even try? It would probably take a trip to France to clear the questions and was it really that important?

Back in the library, the cart had arrived with the sherry decanter, two glasses, and a cherry cake. This was a tradition which went back to at least the Victorians and perhaps even earlier. The cake was different from an American cake in that it was not as sweet. It went well with the sherry and would assuage Arthur and

Melody's hunger until luncheon was served sometime after one in the afternoon.

Another tradition in Arthur's house was the fact 'business' was not discussed during the eleven o'clock break. If Melody had questions or wanted to talk about something she was doing concerning the Farr family genealogy, there were times when she was allowed such leeway. She would investigate her query further before asking Arthur more about it that evening after church.

She did, however, step out of the room after Nedda came for the cart to call Alfred in London. "Melody! I'm surprised to hear from you at this time of the day, is everything alright?" Melody could hear construction noises in the background and guessed she had called while Alfred was at a job site. She could hear the concern in his voice and worried she might have upset him.

"Oh, I am sorry about disrupting your day, but I was wondering when you would be back down for a visit? I have something I want to talk to you about and I am just calling to check." As soon as she said it, she realized he could get the wrong impression and that was exactly where he went.

"Why Melody, my dear, have you decided to accept my proposal? I can be there by the next train if you have! Just give me the word!" The excitement in his voice was palpable and Melody was sorry she let him have a false hope.

"No, Alfred, I just want to talk to you about the d'Auffay part of your family. I'm sorry to have made it sound personal, I shall be more careful in the future. I'm still thinking seriously about your proposal."

Alfred was very let down but he didn't want to let Melody know how much. "Don't let it worry you. Look, I'm about at a stopping point here and a few days of country air will do me good. I can be there by the time you get out of church. Will Arthur be taking you this evening? I can meet the two of you for dinner afterwards. Just text me the details and I'll see you both this evening."

Before Melody could tell him goodbye, he had rung off. She looked at her cell phone for a moment and then went back into the library. Arthur was putting a book on the shelf and turned to see her when she came in. "So, ready to get back to work?"

Melody nodded in the affirmative, "yes, but I just talked to Alfred and he'll be here this evening after church. Do you mind if I ask him to supper after church?"

The days when such a request would have upset Arthur were gone. He and Alfred were resigned to the fact they were competing for Melody's hand and knew she might discount either or both if they kept up the spat which had existed between them. During their visit over the recent Christmas and New Year's Holidays, they saw there was another competitor for her affections and a truce had been called. Now, Arthur just smiled and gave his approval for Alfred to join them.

xxxxx

Melody's life in Houston, her hometown, had revolved around her home, church, and school. With the death of her father, it had been just her mother and Melody, but Gina Russel, her friend from college, had become close so her family didn't really feel so small.

Having attended every church service, special event, and outreach program the church sponsored, Melody, her mother, and then Gina, were usually the first people called when the church needed something done. Now, Melody was in England, her mother was gone, and Gina's work kept her traveling to distant parts of the world. The little church in the English village was almost, but not quite, like the church at home. St. Alban's would never mean as much to her as St. John's.

Coming out of the Wednesday night service with Lord Arthur Farr, her cousin and guardian, Melody felt there was still something missing. Could she ever think of this church, Farr

Cottage, and a life with Arthur as her husband as being 'home'? Arthur took her arm and guided her to the car for the short drive to the Cottage.

The great stone hulk of Farr Cottage loomed in the headlights as Arthur drove up the long drive. Parked near the front door was the old Land Rover Alfred kept for the times when he was in the country. It looked as if he had just arrived. Nedda, the housekeeper had the front door open and light streamed out into the growing darkness.

The nip in the night air belied the fact spring should have been taking hold of the countryside. Alfred waited for Arthur and Melody to exit the car before going inside to the warmth of the lounge. Nedda's husband John took the car and Nedda announced that dinner would be served in half an hour.

For supper after church, Melody did not 'dress' for dinner but wore her church outfit for the meal. The three, Arthur, Alfred, and Melody, went to the lounge for a drink.

"Alfred, I have been checking on Major Lord Roland Farr and have found something to which I need to find answers." Melody didn't catch the look Alfred gave Arthur and so she continued on. "It has to do with this great-granddaughter of a 'niece of Napoleon' that he courted."

Alfred gave Melody an impish smile, "I'll try to answer any questions you may have. What do you want to know about Jillian?"

With a frown, Melody was quick to correct Alfred, "Oh, it's not really Jillian I want information about, but the d'Auffay family." Seeing the questioning look she received from both Arthur and Alfred, Melody knew she needed to make herself better understood.

"Both of you have told me about the d'Auffay half-brothers and their conquest of each of your family lands and estates during or just after the Norman Conquest. I understand that, what I find interesting is what happened after? Didn't the d'Auffay family in

Normandy question what happened to the assets the two men collected? Didn't they wonder where the loot was?"

Arthur jumped into the questioning. "What does that have to do with Jillian Percy?"

Melody smiled, "I'm getting to that. First I want to find out about the d'Auffay part of this." Turning to Alfred, "Arthur, as a historian understands, but it would have been expensive for a family to outfit a knight to follow William on the Conquest. When you figure the cost of at least two battle chargers, the armor, weapons, a page or servant to look after the knight and his things, well, it would have been a big investment. For the d'Auffay family to have sent two sons, well, that would have been a very heavy lift. They would have wanted a very big return on their investment."

"The same thing happened during the Crusades. European nobility had too many sons, not enough action to keep them occupied, and they sent them off to the Holy Land to make their, and by extension, the family's fortunes. The d'Auffay family would have inquired about what had happened with the two sons."

Alfred looked at Arthur. "I don't know about your family, but there is no record of anyone ever asking about the d'Auffay that darkened our door. What about you?"

Arthur was surprised; Melody had opened a question that had never been asked. Had anyone tried to claim the Farr estates for the d'Auffay family after the death of the older of the two half-brothers? In his entire search through the family's history he'd never seen any indication of it, but what brought it up now? What sparked this interest in the d'Auffay family?

Arthur turned to Melody. "No, no, nothing in our family records would indicate anything like what you're asking. Why, have you found something?"

Melody addressed both men, "when Marcel du St. Dinard, Marguerite's grandfather took her and her mother out of France, he brought the family documents. Marguerite's mother died on the way to live with her great-grandfather Angus MacLardie. After old Angus died and Marguerite married Jo Bannister, she had the papers with her when he bought the old Lovell house next to the Farr house in Mayfair. These papers have been passed down since then and ended with Jillian Percy."

"My French is not that good," Melody chuckled, "my Spanish is better, but what I read, indicated the du St. Dinard line had some d'Auffay included."

The two men looked at each other. Alfred was the first to speak. "I wonder if the 'spirit' of the d'Auffay's has finally taken its due? We slipped an Oswin in to be a surrogate son for a sterile d'Auffay and" turning to Arthur, "your family had a son already cooking when Henry d'Auffay wed and bedded your family's lass."

Turning to Melody, Alfred requested the question he and Arthur needed to have asked. "How do the d'Auffay and du St. Dinard families intersect? I mean, what do the documents show?"

Melody took a sip of her drink before continuing. "The du St. Dinard family had lost their lands and estates just before the father of the last Louis to sit on the throne prior to the Revolution died. Louis XV had actually done the family a favor, the fact the du St. Dinard family was no longer considered part of the aristocracy saved them from the fate of most of the rest of the titled class in France. At first reading, the documents make it look as if the problem was simply the brother of Marcel had fiddled with the king's mistress, but it was more than that."

Both men urged her to continue. "The father of Marcel, when he was a boy, had petitioned, along with his father, the 'return' of some estates in Normandy which they claimed belonged to them. This claim was based upon the marriage, in the 1400's of a girl, as the assertion states, "the orphaned daughter of the house of d'Auffay, recently returned from her family's estates in Cyprus."

The two men looked at each other. Arthur broke the mood. "What does Cyprus have to do with it? I thought we were talking about the d'Auffay and du St. Dinard families?"

Melody thought about what he had said. "The Normans had been part of the Crusades and when Cyprus was taken, a son and knight from the house of d'Auffay established himself there. The island was actually held until the Venetians took it in the mid-1400's which is when this girl is supposed to have been sent back to France as a bride. Her family lost their estates and she was the ward of the last governor. He arranged the marriage for her."

"The claim the du St. Dinard family was making was based on those facts." Melody continued. "The French crown, however, was having none of it. It seems the family of a former king's mistress's family already occupied the land of the d'Auffay family."

The men were both silent, lost in their own thoughts. Melody, however, continued on with more. "I think there would be records in the church or town hall that would confirm some of this, both on the d'Auffay side and the du St. Denis side. I would like to take a week or so and go to France to have a look. I also want to request you both have a closer look at papers or anything else that might have a bearing on either of the families. I want to make sure I have all of the right questions to ask."

Alfred spoke first. "I can look again. My family didn't keep the kind of stuff Arthur's did, but I think there must be a historian gene in his family that just lives for that kind of thing. A trip to France sounds wonderful, but remember, you and Arthur are invited to Beryl Somersby's official engagement party in London next weekend. You promised you would go and it would be a shame if you missed it."

Melody chuckled, "don't worry, I'll be there. I have some work to do here before I would go and Arthur hasn't given me permission to travel." Turning to her guardian/cousin, "you will say I can go, won't you?"

Arthur was taken by surprise at the request. LT Chadwick, Melody's trustee, best friend of her late father, and family friend, had entrusted Melody to Lord Arthur's care. He should go with her, but a project for the Home Office was due in a couple of weeks. Maybe he could work it out. Addressing his ward, "I think it might be fine. I could join you a few days after you get there. Let me make some travel arrangements for you and we shall see how it all comes together."

Melody beamed, "thank you, cousin. I'll be sure to be ready to leave from London after the engagement party!"

xxxxx

Alfred's London house was still not completely finished but his room was far enough along for him to stay there while Melody and Arthur lived just down the block in the Farr family's London home. The old cook, Mrs. Jones, and her niece Angie would look after them until Melody left for France and Lord Arthur returned to the Cottage to finish his project.

The party for Beryl and her fiancé Ian MacDougal, would be a big affair. Beryl Somersby's parents no longer had a country estate, but their London home was large and the party fit perfectly. The house was not far from the Farr London home and while Arthur, Melody, and Alfred could have walked to the festivities, Arthur insisted on taking them in his antique Jaguar.

Many of the guests were new to Melody, but the circle of friends Alfred had introduced her to on her last stay at Farr Cottage and also when she was in London greeted her warmly. A couple of young men tried to get close to Melody, but Arthur and Alfred were having none of it; they had staked a claim on her time and wouldn't budge.

One person in the group was not as pleased to see Melody as the others. Maude Harbison was Beryl's best friend and now that Beryl was engaged, she was no longer a threat to Maude's campaign to get Alfred to marry her. That is if she could get the American girl out of the way.

Maude had introduced Beryl to Ian MacDougal in hopes of making it easier to snag Lord Alfred and with Melody back in America, the way was clear for her. That was until Melody returned. Now, watching Alfred and Lord Arthur dancing attendance on Melody, Maud's fear that she might lose Alfred and anger at Melody, merged. Melody had to choose Arthur and leave her Alfred alone.

The evening started with cocktails in the drawing room, moved to dinner in a beautiful Edwardian dining room, and then to the beginning of the party. Several people who had not been at dinner had been invited for the official announcement and celebration of the couple following the meal. Champagne was passed to everyone and a toast drunk to the engagement. Beryl's father, a man well into his sixties, shed a tear as he handed his little girl into the arms of the big Scot.

Maude, however, enjoyed none of the festivities. The entire evening was a trial of watching her future husband at the side of the American girl. She smiled, but it was a false expression that hid her growing inner rage. Maude did see one bright spot, during the evening when she overheard Lord Arthur talking about a trip Melody was taking to France to do some work on the Farr family history. Maybe, if Melody was gone long enough, it would give Maude a renewed chance with Alfred.

Beryl saw none of the problems her friend and maid-of-honor was experiencing. She was so taken with Ian her mind didn't register the snide remarks Maude made about Melody or Arthur. Her brother, Nicky, was a good friend of Alfred's and did the refurbishment of all of Alfred's real estate holdings. When Alfred and Arthur returned from America after the Christmas holidays, he regaled her with stories Alfred had told him about the beautiful estate Melody lived on, the staff she employed, and the whirl of parties they had all attended. But, like anyone in love, her attention was on Ian and the chatter mainly passed her by.

The party started to breakup in the wee hours and the revelers returned to their respective houses to sleep off the food, drink, and fine time. Alfred left Melody and Arthur at the front door of the Farr house and tottled off to his place just down the street. Melody would be catching the train to France in the morning and Arthur was going back down to Farr Cottage for a couple of days.

xxxxx

The French trip was very fruitful. The church records in a village near Bernay, France told much of the story of the d'Auffay family. The information was enough to ask the right kind of questions of the main depository of chivalric history in Paris and while she had intended to comb the church records in du St.-Dinard on this trip, a call from LT Chadwick sent her to Paris for a few days. There would always be time to get to the du St.-Dinard part of the family.

xxxxx

LT's call was a surprise. He had told Melody he would be busy in the Asian basin for several weeks on business and the implication was it might drag on into several months. However it worked out, she was glad to hear from him and meet him in Paris.

She had heard about the Paris Ritz Hotel since she was a girl. Her mother was a Hemingway fan and had several of his stories and books in the library. Her father, however, didn't see the fascination. As far as her father was concerned, the only notable thing Hemingway did was liberate the bar at the Paris Ritz from the Nazis near the end of WWII.

LT had two suites at the hotel, one for himself and an executive assistant, and one for Melody. The assistant was there temporarily to finish some contracts and then head back to the office in Houston. LT liked Paris and from the looks of the people around him, Paris liked him.

A gorgeous redhead named Lilith hovered near him when he came to greet Melody at the train and didn't seem to leave his side. Melody wasn't sure who or what she was but it was LT's life and since he was currently single, it was none of Melody's business. The morning of the first day, however, Melody found out just who Lilith was.

Each country or region has their own laws when it comes to security, personal bodyguards, and weapons. France is no different, but if someone is going to travel in the country and needs the services of armed security, it is just easier to use local professionals. Lilith was a bodyguard, spoke seven languages, and looked more like a rich man's plaything than a security professional which made a great cover.

At breakfast in LT's room the first morning, Lilith arrived with some international newspapers for LT and suggestions of things Melody might like to do or see. LT apologized to Melody for putting her in Lilith's hands while he finished his business with the assistant, but assured her it would only be for a day or two tops. Then he explained who Lilith was and recommended that Melody take her and go shopping or sightseeing.

"I wanted someone who would blend in with you and two lovely ladies out for a day of shopping or sightseeing in Paris won't draw undo attention." LT turned to the bodyguard, "Melody is my goddaughter and she means a lot to me. Please take good care of her."

LT looked at Melody, "I still don't understand why Arthur or someone else wasn't with you in that little village. You shouldn't be traveling alone, not with the problems going on in Europe right now. I'll have to talk to your guardian about his responsibilities."

Melody came to Arthur's defense. "Pinky, he was in Bernay with me for a few days, but he does have his own work and had to present something at one of the ministries. I was the one who told him to go on without me. There was just so much to see and one of the priests at the church, an older man who was the caretaker of the documents I was studying, was on sabbatical. I had to wait for him to return. Please don't be angry at Arthur about something for which I was responsible."

Lilith raised an eyebrow, "Pinky?"

LT laughed, "I used to have strawberry-blond hair when I was younger, but now my hair is white. Melody's father was my best friend and he used to call me Pinky. Melody is the only person, besides my brother, who still uses the term." Lilith answered with a simple smile.

"So, what will you be doing today?" LT turned back to Melody, "I'm sorry it's a weekend or you could go to the archives for the records you're wanting, but since we will be here for a few days, Lilith can take you there on Monday morning. Today, however, is a different story, any ideas?"

"LT, it's Paris! I have more ideas of what I want to see than time to see them all!" Turning to Lilith, "LT's right about the archives, that will have to wait until Monday, but what about the Louvre or the Place des Invalides where Napoleon is buried?"

Lilith smiled, "it is strictly up to what you want to do today. I am at your service. My recommendation would be to see both. No one can see all of the Louvre in one day, but this quarter they are having a special collection of items on display from the time of Napoleon I and the Directorate. It would fit quite well if you saw the collection at the museum in the morning and then this afternoon, the tomb of rose marble. We'll have lunch between the two."

Melody was nodding her agreement and LT agreed with the plan. "I will be able to get away for lunch about one, why don't I meet you both at Harry's? Oh, say about half-past one?"

The program for the day was agreed and LT slipped away to his work and Melody and Lilith began their day.

xxxxx

Harry's New York Bar was a Paris landmark. In 1917 a young black man arrived with the American Expeditionary Force to fight in the "War to End all Wars." A native of New York, he was treated like a second-class citizen by the white troops, but then so were the other 'colored' troops. The commander, General John Pershing, had gotten the derogatory nickname "Black Jack" while in charge of black regiments on the frontier. Being black was something Harry couldn't help, and being treated badly was just something he had to accept.

The white American units spent the first few months being trained into a world-class army by the French. However, the black troops, in a bid to take the pressure off the slaughter in the trenches, were interspersed with white French troops on the front lines.

Harry was dumbfounded. He had always known he was just as good as any white boy, but back home in New York, in the training camp, and on the transport over, he knew his place. Black men didn't live too long thinking they were the same as a white man. In France, it was all different.

In France he was just another soldier. He learned French quickly and spent his days and weeks slogging through trenches. The rats, rot, and blood treated him the same as anyone else. During the rare moments they had down-time, he drank with his French buddies, shared women with them, and on Armistice Day, laughed, cried, and got drunk with them.

When the ships prepared to leave France with the American forces, Harry didn't go with them. He loved France and France loved him. Paris was a mess, but it was still one of the greatest cities on earth and it welcomed Harry with open arms. Harry found a job in a bar, a lovely girl to keep him warm, and life was wonderful.

During the 1920s, Jazz was fueling the sound of the Harlem Renaissance. The jazz greats also found loving audiences in Europe but especially Paris. Harry had his own bar in a rented space and in the basement, he put a rinky-dink upright piano on a small stage with just enough room for a few musicians, a singer, and little tables were crowded into the room for patrons.

The big names of American jazz would finish their sets at the fancy clubs; Harry's basement was where they would jam into the early morning hours. When the milk trucks started their rounds, the patrons of Harry's would finally go home.

The current owner of Harry's was a great-grandson who had never known a day of hardship in his life. He had visited New York, but it was no longer the same racist city his great-grandfather Harry had left. Rarely did he come to the bar he owned, he had managers to look after it and smoking was not allowed within the building.

Sitting under the fading red and white striped awning, Melody, LT, and Lilith were having a glass of wine while they waited for their sandwiches. LT had taken Melody inside while he recounted the history of the bar, its original owner, and a couple other stories he thought she would like. When they left the main bar to descend the stairs to the jazz room, the smell of cigarette smoke still hung in the air. Along the walls, pictures of young black men and women, plus a few white ones too, were signed and framed. The best of American Jazz hung on the walls, forever young, happy, and safe in an accepting country.

Upstairs in the main bar, business cards from visitors were stuck between the glass top and the oak bar while row upon row papered the wall behind the bar, and there were still thousands in storage because there was no more space. Harry's was the place to visit if you were an American in Paris, but for the locals and people from other countries, it was one of the best places for cocktails and hotdogs.

When Harry first started in business, the cocktail was just beginning. He had worked in a bar in New York where they copied those made by other clubs, but also made signature drinks of their own. After the war, Harry plied his trade at making mixed wonders for the locals and he was a hit. It served him well when he opened his own place.

Harry, however, missed only one thing from his hometown, besides his family. Baseball: Harry was a Yankee's fan and went to games when he could afford to do so. He couldn't sit in the main seats, those were for white people, but he could stand in certain parts and he really yearned to go to a game. Once he had the bar up and running, he decided if he couldn't go to Yankee Stadium, well, the next best thing was the kind of hot dog "red hots" they had at the games.

Over a period of several months, Harry looked for a sausage that would make a suitable stand in for the hotdogs he remembered from his hometown. A small butcher shop not far was able to recreate something very similar. Harry's new wife made the mustard and Maurice's bakery supplied him with fresh rolls he could split into buns. The whole endeavor had only been meant to be for Harry's enjoyment, but his wife and Jean-Paul, his new bartender, encouraged him to offer the American treats to customers.

The jazz club in the basement consumed quite a few of the hotdogs each night, but the sandwich was not an instant hit in the main bar. It was more than a year before the first customers began to come for just the hotdogs. Harry's had cool jazz every night in the basement, cocktails in the bar, and a sandwich which was a little bit of home to foreign travelers.

Melody enjoyed the tour and she and LT also ate the hotdogs. "I love this, this city is known all over the world for their cuisine, but we sit here scarfing down hotdogs; amazing." LT motioned to Melody and Lilith, "do you want this last one?"

Both young women shook their heads. LT put plenty of the house mustard on his sandwich and chased it with his drink. "Oh my," he said as he sat back in the metal café chair, "Tonight I have a lovely dinner all planned and right now it even pains me to think about it!"

Melody laughed, "Mrs. Bellamy would be appalled at how you abuse your diet." Turning to Lilith, "Mrs. Bellamy used to be LT's cook, but when he moved into his penthouse, he sent his staff over to my home in Houston. She used to watch what he ate and made sure he didn't gain weight."

"Mrs. Bellamy is still looking over my food, she gives Latrell my menus each week and it seems to work just fine." LT sighed, "I do miss having the big staff, but I think most of all, I wish I had my own outdoor kitchen so I could barbeque when I want."

Melody looked surprised, "but, I thought you were using the one at my house!"

LT chuckled, "I do girl, every chance I get, but enough of that, Now it's time I got back to work and the two of you still have some places to see here." He stood, kissed his goddaughter on the cheek, and left them to get a taxi.

xxxxx

Lilith, Melody, and LT left the Ritz by the back door, but instead of getting into a cab to go to dinner, LT led them down a narrow sidewalk about two streets over and one down. The night was cool, heralding the height of spring, but comfortable. As soon as they turned the corner to the street where the restaurant was located, the aroma of garlic wafted toward them.

The café was small but crowded. LT had made reservations and even then, it was necessary to wait five minutes at the bar. There was no menu to speak of, the wines available were good but nothing exceptional, and the fare was simple. A small table opened up and the three took their seats.

LT, in a slightly conspiratorial manner, leaned over and whispered in Melody's ear, "If you find you don't like what they serve, we can get something in the Hemingway Bar at the Ritz or room service, but I think you'll enjoy this."

Melody looked around at the other tables. At each place, in various stages of emptiness, sat strange pieces of crockery; dark green with white holes, the small ones had six holes, but the large had twenty-four holes. Baskets of fresh French bread sat on each table, and dishes of rice, mixed vegetables, and salad plates were also evident. The smell, however, was heavenly. Garlic, butter, and parsley permeated the air.

The main fare at the café was escargot, snails. In many places they were served in the shell, but in this restaurant, each snail was placed at the bottom of a hole in the special made casseroles, with garlic, parsley, and butter put on top to seal it in during the cooking. The dishes came hot from the kitchen and the fresh bread was used to get every drop of butter and juice with the snail. A glass of white or rose' wine helped to wash it all down. Melody was quick to put this café on her list of favorite places.

Over dinner they discussed the program for the next day. "If you would like, Notre Dame has services in the morning each Sunday, it might be interesting." LT said between snails. "And I thought in the evening we could take the Baton Mouche cruise on the Seine for dinner. If there is something you would rather see, please tell me."

Melody shook her head. "The Baton Mouche cruise sounds great, but I don't want to go to any services at Notre Dame. I do want to see the architecture, stained glass, and other artwork, however." Turning to Lilith she explained, "While I was in graduate school, I saw the painting of a half-clad woman called the "goddess of reason" in place of the altar at Notre Dame. You see, during the French Revolution there was a movement to replace Roman Catholicism with the cult of reason. Very disturbing, so I'll just go for the art, glass, and stone."

LT looked at her, wide-eyed, "Amazing the stuff you know. Moreover, the idea of turning a church into a "palace of reason" is just bizarre! It kind of makes you wonder about the French of that era."

Lilith simply smiled and explained to Melody, "LT knows my father and mother met when father was studying at the Sorbonne and mother tutored him in French. She was from an old Jewish family from Toulon and he was from a kibbutz in Israel."

She continued, "When father finished his degree in medicine they went back to the kibbutz where mother had four boys and a girl, me. One of my brothers lives here in Paris, but the others are all in the IDF, the Israeli Defense Force. When I had to do my national service in the IDF, I enjoyed the training and that is where I received the training for this job."

Melody looked at LT, that was the most Lilith had spoken since she had been introduced. LT took up the slack. "Lilith is being shy. I happen to know her father and she has as good if not better training than her brothers in the service. She did the advanced commando school so she really knows her stuff."

Melody was impressed. She had always felt safe wherever she went, but knowing she had a professional woman bodyguard to look after her was really something. However, was all of this necessary? She had Bellamy who was a former special operations guy, to watch over her safety at home. "LT, is all of this," and turning to Lilith, "believe me, I mean no disrespect for your expertise, but is it all necessary?"

LT sighed. "Melody, you buy insurance for your car, right? And your house, we have a ton of insurance on it, but we buy it to be covered in case something happens. You have security to keep anyone from harming you and if they do manage to get near you, it's good to know someone is there to help you out of a tight situation. No, we don't expect anything bad happening, but we plan for it anyway."

Putting his napkin on the table, LT got up and pulled Melody's chair out while the waiter did the same service for Lilith. Taking Melody's arm, "Enough of this, time we got back to the Ritz and a drink before bed."

xxxxx

The riverboat slid through the dark waters of the Seine as it motored through Paris. The dinner was not five-star cuisine, but it was good food and besides, the meal was not the draw. The boat, the music, and the sites of Paris from the water are what made the trip memorable. LT, Lilith, and Melody enjoyed the evening.

As the three headed back to the hotel, Lilith made arrangements with Melody and LT to meet them at the archives office in the morning. After seeing her charges to the hotel, Lilith left to spend the night in her own apartment. The job with the Americans would only last for another day or so and she needed to see if anything else had come up on her answering machine or email.

xxxxx

The archives, which held the documents Melody wanted were old, crowded, dusty, and the whole atmosphere was one of disorder. Perhaps what she was looking for wasn't here. Judging by the disarray, even if the documents were in this building, could they even be found?

Melody gave Lilith the names she was looking for, approximate dates, and all the information she thought pertinent from the churches in St. Dinard and Bernay. Now it would be up to the librarians in the archives to find what she wanted. A fee was assessed for the work it would take to find the items, more for making copies, and still more money to mail them to her in England. After almost two hours of waiting, Lilith came back to where Melody and LT were sitting, she handed them the receipt with a big smile, "And, they hope to have something for you in about 60 days!"

When Lilith caught Melody's frown she continued, "It would normally take up to six months for this kind of search to be completed since the records are not on computer but must be processed by hand. What you are looking for is from before the Revolution and in some cases, from the 1400s. I think 60 days is really very quick, at least for France it is quick."

LT took over the conversation. "Melody, why don't we take Lilith and have an early lunch. Is there anything else you want to do while you are in Paris or would you like to save it for your next trip?"

Melody looked at LT, "I suppose lunch would be nice, but can we go sit on the Champs-Élysées to enjoy the view?"

"Of course, what trip to Paris would be complete without it?" LT's grin broke the tension of the moment. "However, then I think it is time we left Paris. I want to get you back to England and I need to return to work. Tomorrow morning we will take the early train to London." Turning to Lilith, "it has been wonderful seeing you again and if you'll accompany us to the station in the morning, we'll say goodbye there."

xxxxx

The train pulled out of the Paris station. Melody and LT were ensconced in comfy seats where a steward served them drinks, a full three course meal, and chocolaty dessert. The two and a half hour trip passed very quickly for them.

As the buildings of Paris slipped past the windows and the outer suburbs gave way to verdant green fields and forests, Melody and LT had a chance to talk about her work. She brought him up to date on the part of the Farr family history which had triggered the trip to France and the meeting of Major Lord Roland Farr and Jillian Percy at the home of Alfred Oswin's ancestral country estate.

While Melody talked, he wondered if this was the connection between the two men that Alfred was always claiming made Arthur Farr and he cousins. LT hadn't divulged the results of the DNA test he had commissioned on the two men when they visited Houston. In his mind, there would be no need if Melody were to look elsewhere for a mate.

Changing the subject, LT asked Melody about her big celebration that was just a couple of weeks away. "Any plans for a party for your birthday or just a simple dinner with friends?"

"Oh, LT, I'm not really into much partying. With the engagement party Alfred, Arthur, and I just attended and the wedding being pushed up to this next month, well, that's enough for me."

LT smiled, she was a very steady and reliable person, not given to outrageous behavior, or risky pastimes. Just like her father and as he now realized, the majority of the Farr family line. "If you have a place at dinner that night, you might set one for Jeremy and me. We are supposed to meet up in Brussels and we would like to help you celebrate."

Melody beamed, "No one is more important to me than you, Pinky, if I have to disinvite someone to make it happen, there will be plenty of room for you both!"

zzzzz

LT stayed with Melody in London for a night and, at Arthur's insistence, two nights at Farr Cottage. Business, though, beckoned and early on the fourth day, Melody had to say goodbye to her trustee and old family friend. LT would be back, with Jeremy Higgins, for her birthday in five weeks. Until then, it was time to get back to work.

The marriage of Beryl Somersby and Ian MacDougal would happen the weekend before her twenty-ninth birthday. Since everyone would be in London for the wedding, it seemed convenient to have a dinner party to celebrate Melody's day on the Tuesday after.

Wedding Bells and Townhouses

Lady Grace Oswin moved among her guests at the impromptu house party. While it had originally been meant as a simple weekend gathering at Aldwin House, the addition of two more couples had quickly turned it into something more. Nothing, however, could ruffle the cool demeanor of either the hostess or her friend, Lady Annis Farr. Both women knew the purpose of the introductions of Major Lord Roland Farr to the young and eligible Jillian Percy. This was very serious business.

Lady Charlotte Percy and Roland's mother, Lady Annis, spent more than an hour having tea that very afternoon and invitations were extended for Miss Jillian and her mother to visit Farr Cottage within the next two weeks. The two people at the center of the discussions, however, were not included. Roland knew exactly what his mother was doing and for him to inject himself into the talks would have been unseemly. Miss Jillian, as the other half of the equation, would do as her mother and grandparents bid her to do.

Roland's mother watched him as he interacted with the younger people and especially Miss Percy. Her son was tall, slightly graying at the temples, and athletically built. Unlike many men his age, he had not allowed his body to go to fat but instead rode daily, ate within limits, and slept well at night. She did have to admit that the other men in the room were more socially skilled, conversant in the latest topics, and would be more tempting as a suitor for the young Miss Jillian.

The girl was very handsome, dressed fashionably, and didn't seem to have a serious thought in her head. She flitted from one admirer to the other, flashed her perfect smile, and engaged in conversation which was no more complex than the latest fashions, court news, and gossip. While she was not the ideal candidate for wife to her son, she or at least her family did have some attributes.

Jillian Percy's grandparents were getting on in years and her mother was a widow. The townhouse next to the Farr London house would be given as Jillian's dowry along with the funds to do the conversion to make the two houses one and any updating of the whole which might be needed to make it a suitable place for the happy Farr couple to live and raise a family. While Roland and his mother preferred the country estate, Farr Cottage, Jillian had never lived for long periods in the country and having the place in London might make her more comfortable in the marriage. The grandparents and Jillian's mother would occupy rooms in the newly fashioned home, but this was also seen as a plus.

xxxxx

Rand and Laura Oswin had added the additional guests. If his mother insisted he spend time outside of London, at least he could have some of their city friends as visitors. The Percy girl was adorable, but his mother had warned him her family was in negotiations with the Farr's for her to become Lord Roland's wife.

Rand didn't envy the girl. He was handsome in an older man kind of way, but Jillian was only in her early twenties and might not be happy with being the wife of a country lord, even if he was a Viscount. No, what little he had seen of Jillian had him convinced the marriage would not be a happy one and for that, he was sad. Speaking to his wife they both agreed it would be nice if, when the couple was in London, they make an effort to have them on their invitation list.

xxxxx

The visit to Farr Cottage by Jillian and Lady Charlotte was a success. The marriage would be a low-key affair because Lady Annis was still in mourning for her oldest son who had died making Roland the heir to the titles and estate. Normally, such a happy occasion such as a wedding would not go forward until a year had passed since the death, but Major Lord Roland needed a wife and he needed to work on having children immediately.

The grandparents of Jillian were also a concern. Her grandfather was bedridden and had been ill for the last couple of years. The doctor in Harley Street diagnosed him with a bad heart. Her grandmother, although currently in decent health, did not leave the house except on rare occasions. The wedding would be held at Jillian's family townhouse in London. Explicit instructions were given, by the grandfather, that if he should die before the marriage, the wedding should go ahead. He didn't want anything to stand in the way of the marriage.

xxxxx

Lord George and Lady Juliet Fitzwilliam were able to attend the nuptials. Lord George sat in a wheelchair during the ceremony and Lady Juliet watched over him and her daughter Lady Charlotte while young Jillian took her vows to Major Lord Roland Farr, Viscount of Gibbons. A sip of champagne and Jillian's grandparents retired to their rooms.

Roland Farr didn't like to travel by sea. Trains were alright, but he'd traveled enough in his life, he didn't find leaving his home and comfort a welcome event. The new Lady Jillian Farr, however, wanted a honeymoon and Roland relented to make his wife happy.

Jillian had envisioned two or three months in New York and some travel around America, but the thought of an Atlantic crossing did not sit well with Roland. He put his foot down and a channel crossing was made. The newlyweds were then able to travel around the Continent. The time away was also shortened from two or three months to four weeks.

The renovations on the two London townhouses were well underway when they returned and the new bride had to content herself with the quiet of the country. It wasn't nearly as bad as she had thought it would be, but possibly it was the presence of her grandparents and mother in Farr Cottage that helped her settle in to life in the Kent countryside.

The clear country air, hearty meals, and quiet seemed to boost the health of Lady Jillian's grandparents. Lord George spent more time in his wheelchair during the day than in bed so Lady Juliet and he spent many hours enjoying the gardens of the Cottage. One of the footmen from the London townhouse was assigned to push Lord George from one sunny spot to the next, adjust his lap-robes as needed, and fetch tea or medicines at various times.

Roland's mother, Lady Annis was convinced the quiet of the country would be more conducive to the new Lady Jillian becoming, "with child" but after three months of marriage, no sign of motherhood could be found. The maid assigned to care for the wife of the new Viscount gave Lady Annis monthly progress reports on the status of the couple's prospects of parenthood. Lady Annis had talked to the girl and Jillian's mother had also chimed in on the subject. Lord George, as the only male relative of Jillian, spoke to Roland about his "duties" as a husband and was satisfied with the young Lord's answers. All seemed in order, but nothing had 'taken.'

Mrs. Riley, the cook at Farr Cottage, was said to have some experience with herbs, aside from flavorings in dishes, but she did more in the way of simple remedies for colds, ague, and fever. The servants swore by her teas of sassafras root, ginger, honey, or mint. However, beyond that, she left the doctoring up to the local doctor. Lady Annis mentioned to Mrs. Riley if cook had a tea for her daughter-in-law it would be appreciated, but nothing was forthcoming.

Lady Annis contacted Lord Philip Phelps, a Harley Street physician who specialized in female issues, about the problem. She was counseled to wait until the marriage was at least six months along before starting to worry. His very blunt advice was to "let the couple alone, don't put pressure on them, and let nature have its way with them."

Jillian's grandmother wasn't so quick to give up on her grand-daughter. As the renovations on the London townhouses pro-gressed, it was necessary for decisions to be made about paint col-ors, wallpapers, fabrics, and furniture. All of the furniture from the two houses would be combined into the one home, but the fabrics and finishes had to be changed. Draperies and carpets could be moved about, but everything would need to be made to look like it all belonged to one establishment, not two places patched together.

Jillian had never been good at her studies, but she did well with art, color, and she had a flair for knowing what piece of fur-niture belonged with what other piece. Lady Juliet wanted her granddaughter to accompany her to London and help with the interior of the modified townhouses. Charlotte stayed to help her father. Roland had no interest in paint chips, fabric swatches, or things of that nature.

Lady Juliet had lived in the London townhome for most of her life and knew the Oswin family very well. Lady Grace Oswin had often come for tea or whist, but since Grace had preferred the country, the visits were rare. Lady Grace did, however, offer Lady Juliet and her granddaughter, Jillian, an invitation to stay at the London Oswin townhouse while they were in the city.

Rand and a very pregnant Laura greeted the guests with gusto. Ladies at this time didn't usually go about in society when they were as heavy with child as Laura. Being cooped up in the townhouse was beginning to wear on both her own as well as Rand's nerves. The only place it was still acceptable for her to venture at this time was church and since neither Rand nor Laura were very interested in the local church, Laura was stuck inside until well after the baby was born.

Lady Grace, upon finding her daughter-in-law was going to give her a grandchild had insisted Laura come to the Aldwin House for her pregnancy and confinement, but neither Rand nor Laura could have lived through that much time away from London. At least in town, their friends could visit. It was, however, in these later stages of her time when even visits were not welcomed. No, the idea of having houseguests made life for the expectant couple very happy.

The work on the renovations of the townhouses was reaching a fevered pitch. The outsides received a new coat of paint on the trim, the stone had been washed to remove the grime from the coal and peat soot, and the chimneys were all repaired and cleaned. Jillian was disappointed the town house had the two entryways which made it look like it was still separate establishments, but her grandmother assured her the cost to consolidate the front into one entry wasn't possible because of some kind of structural issue. Above the doorway of the Fitzwilliam townhouse, chiseled in stone, was the name of the original owners, Lovell. That also would have to stay.

Jillian and her grandmother spent most of their mornings in the new house with vendors who would supply the various items which were needed to finish the home. Luncheons and dinners were taken with the Oswins and most afternoons the women spent their time helping finish the items needed for the coming baby. Juliet saw the interest Jillian was expressing in all things 'baby' with Laura. However, she also saw the looks that Jillian and Rand would exchange at the dining table and in the lounge after dinner when the couple would play cards.

Every morning about nine, Rand would take one of the horses from the stable at the park and ride for an hour or so. On more than one occasion he invited his guests to accompany him, but their schedule of appointments always seemed to conflict with his ride. In the second week of their stay, Lady Juliet agreed that she and Jillian could use the fresh air and sunshine. While they rode in a carriage, Rand walked his horse at their side.

For three days the weather held and the ladies accompanied Rand in the carriage while he rode in the park. On the fourth day, it again looked like sun, but Lady Juliet could not accompany the youngsters to the park. Rather than keep Jillian from missing the fresh air of the park, she gave her permission for Rand to take her granddaughter riding.

Dressed in a black broadcloth riding costume, a tall hat with a green plume and with gloves, and boots dyed to match the plume, Jillian was a fashion plate on the grey horse Rand had brought her to ride. The horse was Laura's but she never rode. Even before her pregnancy made riding impossible, she did not like to ride but preferred a carriage while Rand rode beside her. For the next few days, the couple rode alone and the weather continued to hold, but on the fourth day, London weather did what was natural and it rained.

The pair was drenched by the time they returned home. Lady Juliet was at an old friend's house for lunch, Laura was in her bed napping, and the two were left alone. There were servants in the house, but since their presence didn't count except when needed, no one was there to stop what happened next.

Rand took Jillian to her bedroom and insisted she get out of her wet things. He knelt down and helped her out of her boots, stripped off her stockings, and helped her out of her soaked jacket. The white silk blouse she wore under the jacket was wet and plastered to her body. He insisted she step out of her riding skirt and take off the blouse.

Jillian stood in the middle of her room with wet clothes on the floor all around her. The fire had been lit and the room was warming. All she wore was her corset, chemise, and bloomers. Her inner clothes were still wet and Rand told her to turn around so he could undo the laces on her corset. Taking a small blanket from the chair, he wrapped it around her. "Here, cover-up and take those wet things off, come on, don't be shy, take them off or you'll catch your death of cold."

Jillian did as bidden. Rand gathered the wet garments and put them in the bathroom next to Jillian's dressing room. "Now, go in there and get one of you nightgowns on and I'll be back to help you dry your hair. Hop to it, we've got to get you dry as quickly as possible." Rand left the room while Jillian found a nightdress to wear.

Jillian put her dressing gown on over her gown and sat at the vanity table to take her hair down. The large hairpins in the back were getting tangled in the wet hair but the easy ones on the sides and top came out quickly. Jillian looked up when the door opened and she saw Rand as he came back wearing his dressing gown. He had a large towel in his hands.

"Let me get those for you," Rand said as he pushed Jillian's hands away. "You're getting them so tangled, you need to let me do this."

Rand ran his hands through Jillian's wet hair and extracted the last of the pins. With the big towel, he began to dry her hair, but told her it would dry faster if they sat in front of the fire. He put the pillows from the little sofa in the room on the carpet in front of the fireplace and led Jillian to a place on the floor. He brought a comb and brush but continued to towel dry the long, full tresses.

As the hair dried, he switched to using the brush. He sat behind her and the two talked while he worked. After several minutes he asked Jillian to turn and face him while he combed the front of her hair. The light from the fire flickered in her eyes and made them seem to dance as Rand continued to comb her hair. "Here, turn around and let me comb the back."

Within minutes, Rand was back to running his hands through her hair, across her shoulders, and down her arms. Jillian turned to face him and she could see what was in his eyes. She didn't object but allowed him to remove the dressing gown she wore over a diaphanous silk gown. Her curves, unencumbered of the corset, were soft and inviting.

The fire had warmed the room so Jillian did not feel a chill but the touch of Rand's hands on her bare arms sent shivers up her spine. She had never felt anything like this. He took off his dressing gown and the nightshirt he wore under it only reached to his mid-thigh. Tentatively, Jillian ran her hand over his calf and up his leg, stopping just above his knee.

Rand stood and pulled Jillian off of the floor. He picked her up and took her to the bed. Jillian didn't remember the covers having been pulled down, but the bed curtains were pushed aside when he put her inside. Rand got in beside her and pulled the curtains closed.

xxxxx

Jillian and Rand ate a hearty lunch with Laura. As late as it was in the pregnancy, Laura found it difficult to eat much because of the resulting heart-burn. He doctor had told her it was normal and to eat small meals consisting of milk puddings, soups, and bread. The three talked amiably through lunch and shortly after, Rand left for his club. There was no outward sign of anything untoward.

Lady Juliet returned in the afternoon and immediately saw a difference in her granddaughter. A look at the girls room and she knew something had happened. A smile crossed her countenance. Perhaps this trip to London was going to turn out more productive then she had hoped.

Once the line had been crossed, Rand and Jillian made good use of their time. Riding in the morning was an excuse for Rand to take Jillian to a small hotel for a couple of hours of fun. After everyone was in bed at night, Rand would slip into Jillian's bed and wouldn't leave until the hour before dawn when the servants were up.

Rand had taken to sleeping in the bedroom next to his wife's after she had found it uncomfortable to share her bed with a husband and a fast expanding tummy. For Rand, sneaking out of his room was no problem and he spent every night with Jillian.

Everything that needed to be done to finish the London townhouse had been done. Lady Juliet made her last inspection of the work and informed her granddaughter and her hosts at dinner that they would be returning to the country. The look on Jillian and Rand's faces told her everything she wanted to know. Laura was so into herself she didn't notice the look her husband gave the svelte young wife of the Viscount of Gibbons.

The next day, the luggage was taken to the station, the telegram was sent to have a carriage at the station when they arrived, and Jillian was near to tears to leave Rand. The night before neither she nor Rand slept but spent the night saying good-bye. Lady Juliet knew it was the perfect time to take Jillian home to reunite with her husband.

As Major Lord Roland Farr took his young wife to bed that night, Laura Oswin was in London laboring with a son. Rand had fleeting thoughts of Jillian, but they were quickly banished as dawn broke on a new day and he held his baby boy in his arms. Laura Oswin, tired and drained, glowed with the special aura of motherhood and Rand was even more in love with her than the day they had married.

Jillian thought of nothing but Rand. As her husband labored to fulfill his duty, it was Rand's hands that caressed her, his mouth that claimed her kisses, and his body that pushed her down into the bed. As Roland kissed his wife goodnight and rolled over to sleep, Jillian felt a tear roll down her cheek and wet her pillow. News of Rand and Laura's baby boy would reach them before the end of the week.

Eight and a half months later, Roland held his newborn son in his arms as Jillian slept, her long labor finished at Farr Cottage. The boy had the blue eyes of a newborn and a fuzz of chestnut hair on his head. While he looked more like his mother than his father, he was hailed by all as the future of the Farr family line. A note from Lady Grace Oswin to Lady Annis Farr arrived in the next week, congratulating her on the birth of Roland's son, "a week this Thursday past."

xxxxx – Present

Melody pushed her chair back and stood. Arthur had gone up to London on business and she was alone in the library they shared at Farr Cottage. If he had been at his desk he wouldn't have liked the interruption, but with him gone, Melody could pace the room, look out the floor to ceiling windows, or simply work late into the evening. Right now, however, what she had just read and the narrative written from it, disturbed her.

From the time she had first arrived at Farr Cottage all those many months ago, Lord Alfred Oswin had made the veiled claim that he and her cousin/guardian Lord Arthur Farr were related.

Cousin Arthur had always poo-pooed the idea and was hostile to Alfred in the beginning. The disdain in which Arthur viewed Alfred had changed as they both vied for Melody's hand, but the underlying claim to being blood relatives was still a sore point. Alfred often said the question could be settled with a simple DNA test. Arthur never acquiesced.

The boxes of letters, the diaries, and all the other bits of paper which Alfred had found of his family's from the time of Rand, Roland, and Jillian, combined with what she had read in the Farr family's collection pointed to the possibility that what Alfred had been saying was true. Or, at least, could be true. An entry in the journal of Roland on the birth of his one and only child cites the weight of his boy as more than 8 pounds, as weighed on the kitchen scale. For a first baby and one that was almost a month early, it was unusual.

Now, should she call Arthur and tell him what she had found? She reread the items, more than three times, just to fix the words in her mind. No, this was something best discussed in person, but Arthur would not be back to the Cottage until after Melody's birthday.

This next weekend was the wedding of Beryl Somersby to Ian MacDougal in London. Alfred and Arthur were invited to the wedding and the two were taking Melody as a guest. The following Tuesday was Melody's twenty-ninth birthday. The celebration was being done in the Farr London townhouse and LT was flying in with Jeremy Higgins. Arthur was giving the party and along with his business in London, was also working on the preparations for the event.

LT, that's it, she'll talk to LT. He'll know how to proceed. But, and she looked at her watch, would he be asleep, awake, in a meeting. With LT it wasn't easy to tell. She grabbed her cell phone and tried her luck.

A familiar voice answered the call. "Melody! How are you girl? Looking forward to your big day next week?"

Whew! Well, at least he wasn't sleeping and there was no background noise to speak of. "Hi LT, no, well yes, I am looking forward to it, but most of all, I'm looking forward to your visit and seeing Jeremy again. You are both still coming, right?"

LT laughed, "We wouldn't miss it for the world! I just talked to Jeremy last night and he will meet me in Brussels just like we planned. How is your work going?"

Melody hesitated. Well, she had called him for advice, she might as well go ahead. "Something interesting has developed. You know I have been working on the second older brother of my great, great-grandfather Richard Farr, Major Lord Roland Farr. Well, from the source documents I have, both those of the Farr side of the family and some given by Alfred from the Oswin clan, it seems Alfred might be right when he says he and Arthur could be related. Jillian, the very young wife of Roland had only one child, a boy named Charles Harold Farr. But, she may have had an affair with Rand Oswin, Alfred's great, great-grandfather."

"Since the day I met Alfred he has intimated there is a connection between the Oswin and Farr family lines but Arthur has always dismissed the idea, often being hostile when it is mentioned. What should I do about it?"

LT waited to answer. He had the one piece of information no one else had, the results of the DNA he had done when the two men came to Houston to visit Melody for the Christmas and New Year's Holidays. Should he share or wait until he would see her in person on her birthday? "I think you should wait until I get there. It's only a little more than a week away and from what you tell me, the birthday party is going to be just the five of us, Alfred, Arthur, Jeremy, you as the birthday-girl, and myself. No, wait until I get there. We can talk about it then." Quickly, he wanted to change the subject. "You still haven't told me what you want for your birthday, so come on, tell old LT what you want."

Melody pushed the familial question to the back of her mind and concentrated on LT's question. "I have everything I want. Just bring Jeremy and yourself, which is all I want. Funny, you're my godfather and except for Arthur, you are the only family I have. Just be safe and that is present enough."

LT chuckled, Melody was not the graspy, grabby kind of girl some of his ex-wives or girlfriends had been. Ask them a question like he had just asked Melody, and a whole list of expensive presents could have issued forth, but not her. "Okay, it will have to be a surprise then. The party is on Tuesday so we will be in sometime Monday afternoon. Take care."

Melody just had enough time to say goodbye before the line went dead.

So, the news would have to wait, but how would it be received?

xxxxx

The Somersby/MacDougal wedding was a beautiful affair. The nuptials were held in a church nearby to the home of Beryl's parents. The wedding supper and reception were in a hotel ballroom, but at a small hotel with a smallish ballroom. The MacDougals were there in force, kilts and naked knees aplenty, along with tartans from other clans who came down to London to wish the young couple well.

Melody, Arthur, and Alfred watched as the piper tuned up his bagpipes and piped the newlywed couple into the ballroom to begin the festivities. The tartan on the bag was the same as Ian wore at the church and Arthur told Melody it meant the piper was a member of the clan MacDougal.

The supper was tasty but cold and the toasts went overlong. After the requisite first dance by the couple, the bride and her father, and other meaningful traditions observed, the cake was cut, the bouquet tossed, and Beryl and her husband left for a honeymoon. Alfred had been cornered by Maude Harbison but broke away in time to join Arthur and Melody as they slipped away. Melody had church in the morning and she wanted to get back to the townhouse.

Arthur asked Alfred in for a drink and the three of them gathered in the lounge for coffee, and brandy, and to talk about Melody's birthday party. Melody was tired and soon left for bed. Arthur and Alfred stayed in the lounge.

Arthur refilled his guest's brandy and asked, "So, what did you get her, you know, for her birthday?"

Alfred thanked his host for the drink, "I haven't yet. What could she possibly want? She has everything a girl could need plus some. I mean, look at that setup she has in Houston, she could buy anything she wanted so what could I give her?" He took a sip of his brandy and shook his head. "What did you get her?"

Arthur was relieved to hear he wasn't the only one who couldn't find a present for Melody. "I got her the same thing you did. Now, what can we think of to give her? Maybe if we put our heads together …"

xxxxx

LT and Jeremy arrived at a close-in private airport in London on the afternoon of Monday and took a black taxi to the townhouse. Melody was at home, but Arthur and Alfred had left shortly after lunch and hadn't returned. Melody showed the men where they would be staying and told them to meet her in the lounge. She had hoped to have a chance to talk to LT alone, but as he and Jeremy were descending the stairs, Alfred and Arthur returned from their errands.

"Melody, take our guests into the lounge and I'll be right down." Arthur said, "I'm sure they might like a drink right about now."

Having everyone here was going to make it hard to talk to LT about what she had discovered. This wasn't something that should just be blurted out. No, she'd wait until she could get LT alone.

xxxxx

Alfred left to check on things at his own house before coming back for dinner. Sitting outside in her little car was Maude Harbison. He invited her in and took her coat.

"Maude, I've been invited to Lord Arthur Farr's this evening, but I have a little time. What can I do for you?"

Maude sat down in the salon. She looked around at the changes Alfred had been making to his townhouse. "Oh, I love what you have done with this room! It looks so stylish, did you have a decorator do this," she said as she motioned to encompass the room, "or was it something you had seen somewhere?"

Alfred stopped what he was doing for a few minutes. Looking around the freshly redone room he was happy with the outcome. He hadn't been quite sure of the mix of colors, but it had come off just super. "No, a friend of mine from near Aldwin House does this kind of thing all the time and he gave me a color pallet to choose from and it just seemed to work."

Turning his attention back to Maude, "Now, what can I do for you?"

Maude was getting more frustrated and angry as the conversation went on. Couldn't he see she was the only one of the group left for him to marry? Beryl was safely married to Ian and off on their honeymoon. Now it was her turn and Alfred just hadn't clicked to it yet. "Alfred, you know, I have been wanting to do some work at Milton Abbey, my family's country home. It hasn't been lived in since grandpa went, uh, well, since he went away. We don't have the townhouse anymore and I have that little apartment in

Baily Mews. Why don't you give me some pointers about what can be done to the Abbey?"

Alfred was beginning to feel a bit uncomfortable. "Maude, I, uh, right now I'm supposed to be at Arthur's for drinks and dinner and tomorrow night is Melody's birthday, but let me see, after that, maybe I can give you a hand. Would that we alright, I'll give you a call after Wednesday."

Maude stood up and took her coat from where Alfred had put it, on the back of a lounge chair. "Sure, sure. I have some things to do myself. I'll wait for you to call. Good night, I wouldn't want to keep you away from your American friend."

Maude left, got into her car and drove around the corner. In the rearview mirror she saw Alfred walk across the street, knock on a door to another townhouse, the one on the corner, and go inside. It wasn't too cold for her to sit outside and wait to see when he would get back. Besides, she had thought to bring something to drink and a packet of fish and chips for her supper.

This wasn't the first time Maude had watched Alfred's house. Once, when he told her he was going to his country estate, Aldwin House, as an excuse of why he couldn't escort her to a dinner, she didn't believe him and watched until she saw him leave for the station. She even followed the taxi he had called to take him to the train. No, she knew men couldn't be trusted to mean what they say so she was happy to just wait and keep an eye on him.

They had known each other for years, ran in the same circle of friends, and like other people of their class, wouldn't think of dating, well, seriously dating, outside of the group. Now, she and Alfred were the last unmatched pair and it was time for him to quit this infatuation with that American and settle down with her.

Maude was equally as well born as Alfred even if her family wasn't as well set as his. Milton Abbey, her family's ancestral home, was in need of repair, but without the money to do so, it was just sitting there. She could blame that on her grandfather, Lord William Merritt Harbison.

Her grandmother died at a young age, just after giving birth to her father, Robert. Grandfather never remarried, but spent considerable money on perky young ladies whom he had fancied loved him for himself and not his money. As her father got older and left for college, the gifts to the ladies got more fabulous until the last one walked out with most of the family jewelry, a couple of Holbins, and a pair of Restoration chairs.

Maude's father married a solid young lady from Leeds who did not have a title but did have a substantial fortune from her family. They redid the London house and left her grandfather to watch over himself in the country. At last, there were no more women, but there was also no more money. Lord William Harbison was broke except for the Abbey and the London townhouse. The deed had always remained in Lord William's name even though it was the money from her mother's family that did the refurbishing of the house.

It was a terrible fight. Father against son, son against father and all the while, Maude's mother pushing her husband to get the title to the townhouse or to get back the money she had spent. Maude was young when all of this was going on and most of the time she was away at school, but it was the main subject of gossip in London so news of it was bound to seep into her boarding school.

Before any resolution could be found, grandfather had a stroke. If he had died, the title would have passed to Maude's father, the Abbey might have been saved, but even if it wasn't, it was still in decent enough shape to sell, and the family would have lived in the townhouse. But he didn't die, he lived in a residential care facility for another ten years. The Abbey sat empty for those ten years and sank deeper into ruin. Maude's mother left, taking her fortune with her, and the townhouse had to be sold to pay expenses.

Maude finished her chips, but didn't have the appetite to eat the last of the fish. She wiped her hands on a moist towelette she had in her purse and thought about Alfred. Suddenly, she noticed the lights at the entryway come on and the door open. She sat up and strained to see Alfred emerge. When five people filed out, Maude studied each as they descended the stairs to the sidewalk in front of the house.

Alfred was the first down, then that horrible American girl, Melody, an older man she didn't recognize and a younger man who took his place near Melody that was also unknown to Maude and Arthur joined them after locking the front door. The group walked down the street in the opposite direction from where Maude was sitting. She speculated that since they were walking and were not going by taxi or car, they must be headed to the pub.

Maude wondered if she should 'drop in' at the pub. It might be nice, seeing Alfred with this odd group. But, would he remember she was in the same outfit, so possibly he would think she was following him. Hmm, she needed to think about this. If she did go, maybe she could find out who these other people were. They probably had something to do with Melody.

Oh how she hated that girl, woman, whatever. Things were going just fine for her until Melody showed up. Even the day she arrived, Melody was all Alfred could talk about. He should be concentrating on her, not this ward of Arthur's.

That was an odd thing anyway, a twenty-eight year-old woman needing a guardian? Absolutely crazy! When the word got out that this American girl was coming to stay at Farr Cottage so she could be the ward of Lord Arthur Farr, Viscount of Gibbons, people wondered what was wrong with the girl. Was she so ugly nobody would marry her, maybe she was poor and needed a place to live, and Sir Arthur was her only living relative who would take her in, whatever it was, it was unheard of in this day and age.

Alfred told her and the rest of the group at an informal dinner party about meeting her that first day. If fact, it was all he could talk about. Her chestnut-brown hair, dark eyes, beautiful face, and stunning figure. Pifft, men were so stupid about those things, so she wasn't a dog in the looks department, it just meant she was probably poor as a church mouse and needed a place to stay. But then she and Arthur came to the dinner party at Alfred's when the gang got to meet her.

Every guy there was smitten by her. This American girl in her dove grey silk charmeuse gown walked in and every man in the place, even the married ones, couldn't take their eyes off her. Really, you would think they hadn't seen a woman in a clingy dress before! What idiots!

Melody left London the next day and returned to the country but Alfred ran after her, like a dog chasing a bone. The best thing though, she left for her home in America after that and good riddance! Yea, well, until Alfred and Arthur both decided to spend almost a month in Houston with her over Christmas and New Year.

Maud's head started to ache again and she reached into her purse for the bottle of pills. She was having to take more and more of the pills since Alfred started hanging around Melody; that was another thing she could blame on the girl. She just didn't know what any of them saw in her. She wasn't exactly mousey, but neither was she very vocal. Humph, that was it, maybe she should go around to the pub and find out who those other men were, maybe one of them would take this American off her hands!

xxxxx — The Hind and Pearl Pub

The group settled into the large booth at the pub while Alfred went to the bar for the drinks and Arthur pulled an extra chair in which to sit. Jeremy joined Alfred and helped him carry the order. Melody, sitting next to LT, to whom she was aching to talk, but he gave her a stern look, glanced at Arthur, and she understood the subject was not to be discussed at the moment.

Up for a Monday evening, the pub was surprisingly only half full with patrons. These were the locals who lived within walking distance and often used the pub as a place to meet friends because their apartments were too small to accommodate several people at a time. Mayfair, the area of London where the Farr and Oswin townhomes were located, used to be the home of the upper-echelons of society. However, some of the homes had been chopped up into several flats, the stable areas or mews were turned into apartments, and some homeowners simply didn't like to entertain in their once great houses.

Melody was so happy to see LT and Jeremy. She was surprised how much she had missed them and felt a pang of homesickness as she listened to LT talk about fetching Jeremy from the airport in Brussels to make the short flight across the Channel. He continued, "My crew is really looking forward to the layover here, it seems they have been doing nothing but hauling me from meeting to meeting, but now, it's off for home. I'm getting anxious to get back," he turned to Melody, "but not before we celebrate your birthday."

Arthur was interested in LT's travels, "why all of the travel? Can't you do your business from Texas?"

"There are just some things that need to be done in person. I like to look somebody in the eye when I make a deal, especially one that means the future of Chadwick Holdings. I may be the chairman/CEO, but I answer to a lot of family members. I think some of the things that were accomplished on this trip will stand us all in good stead for many years to come. We've done some judicious branching out and made sure that not all of our 'eggs' are in one basket. I just like to know we not only own the eggs, but also the baskets."

Alfred and Jeremy returned from the bar with the drinks. For the next half-hour the conversation flowed and everyone had a relaxed time. A few of the older patrons had left but a couple of younger people arrived. Then when the door opened the next time, it was Maude Harbison.

Melody saw her first and for just for a fleeting second she thought she saw a strangely sour look on Maude's face before it was replaced with a slight smile. Alfred looked up and motioned for her. "Maude, fancy seeing you here. I thought you were going home. We were just about to leave but, you can sit with us for a few minutes."

Alfred pulled another chair up and Maude was introduced to LT and Jeremy. Hmm, Maude realized she was right, they were Americans, why couldn't they just take Melody and go home! She smiled at the group, "I was at home, but my flat is so small I just needed to get out for a bit. A walk down to the pub is always a good bit of exercise." Looking at LT and Jeremy, "are you staying long?"

Jeremy was the first to speak. "Oh, we're just here for Melody's birthday tomorrow evening and then I have to get back to work and so does LT. I'm a Marine and LT, well, he's kind of a business-man and an old friend of Melody's family."

LT looked over at Jeremy, "I take exception to the 'old' remark, seasoned maybe, but not old, surely." Everyone laughed. "And you Miss Harbison, how do you know Alfred?"

Maude's cheeks flushed a bit before she answered. "Gee, Alfred and I have known each other since we were children. We all run with the same group of people, gone to schools with each other, and are basically from the same kind of people. In fact, Alfred and I are the last singles in our group. Our friend Beryl was just married this Saturday last."

Arthur didn't want to get too deep into the social life of Alfred's group and thought it was time to get his cousin and guests home. "It has been nice seeing you again Maude, but our guests have just arrived today and will be tired. It's time we get home. Enjoy your nightcap!"

Maude saw them leave. Humph, sure, she would enjoy her nightcap, but tomorrow she had some work to do. From the looks of things. She would need to make things happen and happen to her advantage. Alfred had to see that she was the only one for him, but as long as Melody was in the way he wouldn't realize it was she and not Melody he should be with. No, it was up to her now, it was up to her.

Happy Birthday!

The morning of Melody's twenty-ninth birthday was rainy and overcast. The London weather had been fair for the last several days, but it was spring and rain was almost a certainty. Maude left the city early and headed south-east past the old Crystal Palace grounds and on into the country. Milton Abbey was just inside the border of the County of Kent.

For the past several months she had been coming to the Abbey at least every couple of weeks or so. As the gate to the property came into view, she pulled her little car over and stopped to look. The filigreed iron gate which heralded the entrance was in sad need of paint and repair. One of the stone posts had started to deteriorate but the heavy chain and padlock which kept the gate from opening was still firmly in place. No one knew where the key to the lock was located. Her father didn't have it, she had looked all over the house for it, and of course, grandfather didn't give it up before he slipped into a coma.

Pulling the car back onto the road, Maude followed the ivy and weed-overgrown wall to the other entrance to the Abbey. This dirt track was also unkempt, but it did serve to hide the fact it was still a way to get into the Abbey grounds. Since she was a child, Maude had known about the service entrance. Her grandfather never allowed trades-people or anyone he deemed 'beneath' him to come through the front gate. Maybe this is why Maude didn't mind the gate being locked, it represented her grandfather's evil side.

In the Middle Ages, water mills were used to grind grain into flour and were called gristmills and those used to saw trees into lumber were called sawmills. Located near a flowing water source, the mill owners took a portion of the item to be processed as their fee for doing the work. Most of the mills in England and Europe were owned by religious orders. The farmland around the monastery, abbey, friary, or convent was owned by the religious community and worked either by the members or by paid workers. The wealth of these institutions was enormous in the day.

In 1536, King Henry VIII, began the Dissolution of the Monasteries. The Reformation or break with the Catholic Church in Rome had been caused by the Pope's refusal to allow Henry a divorce from his wife, Catherine of Aragon. Part of the perks of this break was the approbation by the Crown of the religious properties in England. Monks, nuns, priests, and friars were put out on the road and the wealth of their communities flowed into the coffers of the King.

Milton Abbey had been an insignificant little place on the southeast side of London. Originally it was a sister of the one founded by Saint Eanswith in 630. She was the daughter of King Eadbald of Kent, the son of Saint Æthelberht, the first Christian King of the English. When the Danes destroyed the original Abbey, sisters who had escaped the marauders moved further inland. The fast flowing river was the perfect place to put a mill.

The Benedictine sisters of the Abbey had originally called themselves Saint Peter's Abbey of the Poor. However, the village that grew on the land they owned was called Mill Town and when the Dissolution came in 1537, the new owners, sycophants of the King, called it Mill Town Abbey. Through the years it simply became known as Milton Abbey.

The original buildings were mostly gone, time and a lack of use will do this, the mill was dismantled when the Industrial Revolution's steam powered machinery allowed manufacturing to be put anywhere the owners preferred. The main house, however, was rebuilt in the late 18th century when the next set of owners of the property took possession.

The Harbison family had been very close to the Regent of George III, the Crown Prince who would later become George IV. As Crown Prince, the son of the king had nothing to do but eat, drink, visit his tailor, and attend house parties. Even before the Prince of Wales was officially named Regent by Parliament, Lawrence Harbison was a friend and confidant of the future Regent and King. For his loyalty, he was given Milton Abbey.

The house was built in true Regency style and the Harbison family hosted the Regent several times. The bedroom he slept in was never used by anyone until after his Royal Highness and His Majesty George IV had passed and his younger brother, William IV, ascended the throne. When this happened all future chances of a royal visit were finished.

Maude's visits to Milton Abbey and the surrounding area had become commonplace. The locals were no longer surprised to see her and so she blended into the background with the other people seen most every day. Her visits to the shops, home-improvement store, or pub were as normal as for any other person in the village.

The service entrance to the estate was overgrown with weeds and Maude liked that because it helped to camouflage her passage. Since her first trip to the great house, she had been working toward something, but until recently, hadn't really known what it was. With Melody back in England and her future as the wife of Lord Alfred Oswin in jeopardy, she knew exactly what she must do and the plan for carrying it out was becoming clearer to her the more she worked at the house.

Like the front gate, the front door of the house was locked with a big padlock. The rear door to the kitchen, however, was one Maude was able to open and with the help of instructions she found on the internet and then a clerk at the local do-it-yourself store, she was able to change the lock and fix the window she broke to initially gain entrance to the house. Other work was done to further her plans.

Some of the furniture was still in the house, mostly things no one wanted, but Maude was able to find a couple miss-matched chairs to use at the big table in the old kitchen. A narrow cot was also put in the room. The old wood stove remained. In the winter, it was all of the heat or cooking facility she required. Most of the cabinets had been stripped out, the massive old stone sink was still there, and Maude used battery powered lanterns when she needed light. The house still had a pump to the well in the kitchen yard and with a self-test kit she determined the water was fine for drinking and for cooking.

Another room just off of the kitchen was the old butler's pantry. When the house was still in use by her grandfather, it had been lined with cabinets where the china, silver, and fine crystal was stored. Now, however, the finery was gone along with the cabinets. The five-foot by seven-foot room had a heavy door at one end and Maude changed the lock so it would be secure. She also drilled a hole in the door so she could put a viewer that gave her the ability to see all of the room. A single light bulb hung from a wire. Maude put a narrow cot in the room, a stool near it, and at the other end, a bucket with a roll of toilet paper.

Maude wondered about how to power the single light bulb in the room and found the solution in a camping catalogue. A solar panel, storage battery, and wire to make the connection was all she needed. She debated putting a small fridge in the kitchen but decided against it, whatever she would need was in the rows of cans, jars, and cases of bottled water she had stored in the kitchen pantry.

This would be her final trip to the Abbey before the big day. Everything was in place, the supplies were ready, the solar battery was charged, and she was confident everything would go according to plan.

Maude put her hand in the large purse she carried and pulled out the gun she had. It was one of the few things she could thank her father for keeping. Finding bullets for it had been difficult, but since it was a relic from WWII, they could still be purchased over the internet. She had taught herself how to use the gun and was pretty good at shooting soft-drink cans off the old stable fence. It frightened her at first, but after the first few times, it became much easier.

Replacing the gun, she pulled a jar of green powder from her purse. While she was investigating sedatives on the internet, it surprised her that most if not all of the ones for people were almost impossible to buy. A friend of hers, however, related to her a story about a medicine her dog was given by the vet and how it was the same thing people took but in a different dosage. The tip was all she needed to find a suitable replacement for what she wanted.

It was a good idea that she tested the powder though. The instructions on the bottle said the tablets could be ground into a powder to mix with the dog's food, which was fine, but it also said that she had to give the medicine by the weight of the dog. She figured that Melody was about 115 pounds so she went to the dog-pound and found a large dog that weighed about that much.

When she got the dog to the Abbey, she carefully measured the amount of sedative powder, mixed it in some food, and waited for the dog to go to sleep. The dog was very hungry and finished all of the food quickly. Within minutes he was asleep on the floor. In a half-hour he was dead.

Maude buried the dog in the deserted garden and set out to find another one on which to practice. She had to go further and it was a slightly bigger dog, but it would have to suffice. It actually took her four dogs to get the dosage right. The last dog lived, but unlike most English, she didn't like dogs so it gave her something upon which to practice her shooting.

She looked around the part of the house she used, checked everything twice, and left in time to get back to the city. Maude knew about the birthday dinner at Arthur's house tonight for Melody and wanted to park around the corner from Alfred's to make sure what time he got home. She didn't want him to stay overlong at Arthur's and if she was watching, it made her feel like she had some control over his actions.

Before she entered London proper she ran her car through a carwash to remove the mud from her tires and undercarriage. The rain had made it muddy and it just wouldn't do to track mud through Mayfair!

xxxxx – Melody Has a Birthday!

Mrs. Jones, the cook, and her niece Angie served a wonderful dinner for Melody's birthday, but now it was time for the guests to retire to the lounge for coffee, brandy, cake, and presents.

As Angie rolled in the cart with the cake, their Lordships, Arthur and Alfred, joined Jeremy and LT in singing a round of "Happy Birthday." Arthur instructed Angie to fill everyone's glass with champagne and he offered the toast. "To the loveliest ward a man could have, to your health!"

The rest of the company added their sentiments and hugs followed. Arthur started the gift-giving. "I know you have a great interest in Major Lord Roland Farr and he brought this to his mother, Lady Annis when he returned from India. I would like you to have it." Inside the velvet box he handed Melody was a gold and ruby necklace and earrings set.

"Oh my" Melody gasped. "They are beautiful! These will go with several of my gowns, but especially the red one I got in New York." Turning to LT, "you remember the one, I wore it to the dinner party you had for the businessmen in the suite at the Plaza."

"Indeed I do! It is a beautiful gown and they will go perfectly." LT smiled at the memory of the dress. The men who had been at the dinner still ask how Melody is doing and where she is.

Lord Alfred stepped forward with his gift, a large package which he cradled in his arms. "You have many lovely outfits and many times you have spoken about the lady, Louisa I think her name is, that makes your clothes. Well, take her this and let her fashion you something that is one-of-a-kind." As Melody opened the gift, she was surprised to see the material inside.

Alfred continued with his explanation of the contents. "A friend of mine designs fabric. Since the Farr family does not have a tartan, I asked him to design a unique pattern just for you. The place that loomed this from virgin Scottish wool, said there is enough there for whatever you would want to have made."

A kiss and hug for both Arthur and Alfred meant it was time for Jeremy to give Melody his gift. "I enjoy having you ride a motorcycle with me, but you need a proper helmet. This one is just your size and even has your name on it." Jeremy turned the shiny black helmet so Melody could inspect the back of it. There, in gold script and no more than a half-inch high was "*M. Farr.*" "Here, put it on and let's see the fit."

Melody eagerly put the helmet on and was surprised at how light it was. "How did you get one that is not as big and heavy as most helmets are? This one feels like the riding helmet I used to wear as a child or nothing more bulky than a fur hat."

"It is made with the same kind of material the new flak-vests are made from for the military. It will keep your brain protected if you fall but will also stop a bullet, uh," he quickly added, "not that you would need to stop a bullet or anything that dangerous." He glanced at LT who was smiling at Jeremy's discomfort. "This helmet is based on the same technology as the specialty helmets made for certain members of the military. Anyway, Happy Birthday, I hope you like it."

Melody took the helmet off and gave Jeremy a kiss on the cheek. "I love it! When will you take me motorcycling again so I can wear it?"

Jeremy stopped his nervous fidgeting. "The next time I visit, I will try to come for a longer stay. How does a motorcycle trip through the Midlands sound to you?"

"Sounds great to me," Melody said, "and when it's warmer, it'll be just the right time for us to do that."

LT watched the other two men as Melody was talking. Both Alfred and Arthur realized their presents had just been upstaged by their rival from America. It was time for LT to give her his gift before things got out of hand.

"Before I give you this, I think some explanation is in order. Several years ago, your mother and father were in New York with my wife, Celia, and I. While your dad was doing some business for the bank and I was working on an energy deal, your mom and Celia were out shopping. About the third day we were there, the wives wanted your dad and I to go with them to Tiffany's. Now usually there is only one reason why a wife would want to take her husband to a jewelry store and that is because she wants to buy something that is more expensive than what she usually buys or she wants him to see something he can buy her for a special occasion." LT took a sip of his brandy before continuing.

"While my wife was showing me an outrageous bracelet, your dad was looking around at some of the display cases. He pulled your mom over to one and told her he wanted to get a particular item for you." LT chuckled, "your mom was a very practical person and told him you were too young for something like that."

LT pulled a box out of his tuxedo pocket and handed it to Melody. "I think you are gown up enough for this and in a way, it's what your father picked out for you. I hope you wear it with all the love it represents."

Melody hugged LT and kissed him on the cheek. "Oh thank you for this! I know I'll just love it!" She opened the Tiffany-blue velvet box. Inside was a gold chain and a simple gold 'tag,' much like the dog tags worn by soldiers. A diamond was embedded in the tag and near it, in script, was her name, birthdate, and the words "Happy Birthday from Mom, Dad, and LT." Taking it from the box, she noticed the large clasp and commented on it.

LT fidgeted a bit before answering. "I had them put a very strong clasp on it because we wouldn't want it to get lost or come undone." What LT didn't tell her was that embedded in the clasp was a micro-miniature tracking device. Her safety was paramount and whatever he could do to add to her security he would do. He was, however, a bit upset when she took the chain and tag off and put them back in the box. "Aren't you going to wear your gift?"

Melody laughed, "Oh LT, I will, but it needs to go with the right outfit. I don't think it was intended for me to wear all the time. It needs a nice turtle-neck sweater to really show it off. All of mine are at Farr Cottage and when I get back there, I'll wear it often." She noticed his sad look. "I love it and it means a lot to me that you gave it to me for my birthday."

It was time to break the mood in the room and Jeremy provided the distraction by stepping out for a few minutes. While he was gone, Arthur announced the fact he needed to retire early. "I have a presentation to give in Edinburgh tomorrow and I'm taking the early train. So," looking at Alfred, "I will walk you to the door." Alfred shook LT's hand and gave Melody another hug and kiss.

Arthur led Alfred to the front door to say goodnight, but Alfred still had something to say. "A ruby necklace? Really Arthur, giving Melody some of the family heirlooms is a bit over-the-top, don't you think?"

Arthur flipped on the outside light. Turning to Alfred he replied, "You were in Houston and certainly must have noticed, she could have anything she wanted. I don't think an antique bit of gold and rubies will tip the scales in my favor. The Farrs of Houston have done very well and"

Before he could finish, Jeremy had joined the men in the foyer. He had intended to say goodbye to Alfred but heard the exchange. "The best thing the Farrs of Houston have done is Melody and I would ask you both to remember that." Wanting to diffuse the tension he said, "I will be leaving with LT in the morning and probably will not be seeing you both for a while." He shook their hands and turned to go to his room.

xxxxx

At the end of the street and just around the corner, Maude sat in her darkened car. When the outside light came on she was sure Alfred would be out soon. That cow's birthday party would finally be over and things could get back to normal. Maude was sure that with Melody out of the way, Alfred would be at her door begging her to marry him.

Maude waited to see her intended and was slightly surprised it was taking so long. But, alas, the door opened and Alfred turned back to speak. Maude was too far away to hear, but soon he was out of the door, across the street, and entering his own townhouse. She waited until the light at the Farr's went out and also the one at Alfred's before she started her car and went back to her own apartment. She needed her sleep; tomorrow was a big day.

xxxxx

Arthur left the townhouse before anyone else was up and about. Mrs. Jones, sleepy after being up so late the night before with the birthday celebration for Melody, had made Sir Arthur coffee and enough breakfast to get him on his way. Mrs. Jones would finish her work in the kitchen and her niece would do the rooms and tidy up before the end of the day. The last person out of the house would be Mrs. Jones and she would lockup.

LT was awakened from a sound sleep at just past five by Jeremy. Jeremy had to leave to return to his outfit. A panicked commander had called for his special unit to oversee the securing of an oil-field which had just been 'liberated' from ISIS control. ISIS was known for sabotaging well-heads and/or blowing them up before retreating so it was imperative Jeremy get back to his day job.

LT had considered waking Melody before he left, but decided to let her sleep. LT slipped a note under her door to tell her of the need to leave before she was awake and needed to say goodbye in a note instead of in person. He would call her later. LT felt bad about the fact he hadn't talked to her about their Lordships but there just wasn't the time or the opportunity. He would make some time for her and see where things were and what he needed to tell her on the phone.

Both men had traveled with little luggage and it made it convenient for them. LT called a 'radio taxi' and Jeremy went to the kitchen to thank Mrs. Jones for the wonderful meals. By the time Jeremy finished, the cab had arrived to take LT and Jeremy to the small South London airport where the plane was waiting to take them back to Europe. Jeremy would meet up with his group in Brussels and take a military transport from there.

xxxxx – Maude's View

Maude watched as the taxi arrived to take the two American men away. It was very early and she had been at her 'station' watching for most of the night. If Alfred was on time, he would be leaving to the renovation project he and Beryl Somersby's brother had going over at the East End lofts.

Just past seven, Sir Alfred locked his front door and left. He had a car garaged one street over and in the opposite direction from where Maude was parked. She checked the items in the car she would need. She had three bottles of water in a small cooler which had a small piece of wax on the plastic tops. They needed to be marked so she didn't drink one by mistake. It wouldn't do for her to knock herself out and miss the chance to finally be rid of Melody.

xxxxx – Melody

Melody stretched and looked at her watch. Oh, my! She hadn't expected to sleep this late! Rushing through her bathroom, shower, and dressing routine, all she could think about was seeing LT until she saw the envelope on the floor near the door.

So, she would have to wait to talk to him and she understood why they had to leave. But, it would've been better if he had woken her. As it was, she was going to be late for her train if she stopped to pick up her boots from the boot maker in Knightsbridge.

Melody left her room and heard Angie humming as she walked past the room Jeremy had used. The wires coming from the girl's ears told Melody she was 'dancing to the music' and probably wouldn't hear her.

The sound of Mrs. Jones rattling around in the kitchen blended with the 'goodbye' that Melody called to the Farr family's old cook. The taxi Melody had called was waiting in the street as she pulled the heavy front door behind her. Melody picked up her purse and the carryon she usually carried. Once inside the cab, she told him the address in Knightsbridge and settled into the back seat.

xxxxx – Maude's View

The taxi had just pulled up in front of the Farr house. Maude started her car and left it to idle while she waited for the person she was expecting to emerge. Although the minutes crawled by for her, a look at her watch told Maude she had only been waiting for Melody to appear for less than five minutes when the door opened and the American girl came down the steps.

Maude was careful not to follow to close, but the busy London traffic made it hard to keep them in sight. Ah, yes, Sir Arthur's boot makers. She had followed him and the American to the shop only a few days ago. So, she was picking up something before going to the train, this might be easier than she had thought.

The taxi refused to wait and Melody took her carryon and her purse with her into the store. The little car Maude drove fit perfectly into the slot by the door and Maude got out to wait for her prey to emerge.

Kidnapped!

The boot maker insisted Melody try on the boot he'd fixed for her. She'd ordered the pair made and during the last fitting, found a problem with the right one. The adjustment was made and it was now perfect. The boots would be delivered to the Cottage in a couple of days.

Looking at her watch, Melody saw how late it was. She still had to find a taxi to take her to the station. There would be plenty on the main road which was half a block to the left. As Melody left the store, a familiar person was just getting out of her car.

Maude was able to watch as the American girl prepared to leave the store. Better to let her think she had just arrived so Maude opened her door to give the impression. Putting a smile on her face and steeling her resolve, Maude waved at Melody.

"Hi, fancy seeing you here!" It was all Maude could do to be genial. "Where are you headed?"

Melody smiled at Maude. "I'm on my way to find a taxi. My train will be leaving without me if I don't get to the station on time."

"Oh, let me take you. I can get you to the train in no time. Now is not the best time to try for a taxi, the traffic is too heavy and they don't like to stop." Opening the passenger side door, Maude said, "Get in and let me put your bag in the back."

For a moment, Melody hesitated. Maude had been Maid-of-Honor at the wedding of Beryl Somersby just this last Saturday and she had been introduced by Alfred. "I suppose it will be alright, but I'm not putting you out of your way, am I?"

Maude nodded in the negative, "Oh no, but we need to go." Taking the carryon from Melody, Maude stowed it in the back of her car. It would take a trip of its own after she'd disposed of the American.

Melody closed the door and buckled herself in. The ride to the station shouldn't be too long but the traffic was heavy, just as Maude had told her.

At the first stop light, Maude took a bottle of water from the console between the two front seats. "Care for some water? It seems we are having one of our warm spring days here in London."

Melody paused before taking it from her but then took the bottle, opened the seal on the top, and tasted it. "Mmm, it tastes like cherry. I love cherries and you get such nice ones here in the market. I didn't know they made flavored waters here. It's good." Maude smiled as she congratulated herself for putting just a hint of cherry flavor in the water to cover the taste of the sedative.

Melody took several sips from the bottle, put her head against the window, and looked over at Maude. "All of a sudden, I, feel, so, tired ..." Maude caught the bottle before Melody let it slip from her fingers. At the next stop light, she put a lid on the bottle to keep it from spilling. Besides, she might need the sedative in the days to come.

xxxxx

Angie finished the last bedroom, bathroom, and the lounge shortly before lunch. Her Aunt, the cook Mrs. Jones, had spent most of the morning making breakfasts that no one ate and then cleaning the kitchen so the house could be closed until the next time Sir Arthur and his American cousin came to stay.

Mrs. Jones looked up from the refrigerator as Angie came into the kitchen. "Are all the rooms done, the linens ready for the laundry, and the sheets put back over the furniture in the grand parlor?"

Angie nodded in the affirmative, "I've even closed the drapes in the bedrooms. I know how Sir Arthur gets on you about things like that." Looking at the sandwiches her Aunt had made for their lunch, "didn't anyone eat bacon this morning, or didn't you want to throw this out?" Angie bit into a wonderful bacon and tomato.

"I don't know where Miss Melody was, she never came down for breakfast. Did you see her or see when she left?" Mrs. Jones had finished clearing out the fridge and was starting to eat her sandwich. "She usually eats a good first meal and has more than one coffee, but this morning, nothing."

Angie continued to eat her lunch. "I heard them talking last night, when I was serving at dinner, that the two American men were wanting her to go with them, but she wanted to finish some work she had at the Cottage, you know, Sir Arthur's place in the country." Taking another sandwich, Angie continued. "Sir Arthur wanted her to stay but he had to leave very early this morning. I didn't see the girl, maybe she went with the other Americans."

Mrs. Jones poured some lemon squash into Angie's glass and took some for herself. "Maybe so or she might have gotten the train, but either way. Finish up so I can wash this and close the house. I have the cutest little cap I'm knitting for your sister's baby and I want to finish it before the tyke gets too big for it." The two women laughed and thought nothing more about the American girl.

xxxxx

Maude drove to the outskirts of London and turned down a quiet street. Getting out of the car, she opened the passenger side door and made sure Melody didn't actually fall out. By pushing on a handle, the back of the seat reclined and anyone looking into the car would not see Melody. To make sure she wasn't seen, Maude put a light blanket over Melody. The carryon which Melody had been carrying had gone into a luggage locker at the train station nearest to the Mayfair townhouse. Maude had also put Melody's purse in the locker along with the cell phone she always had with her. Maude took the battery out first, but there was nothing else to tag who Melody was.

The plan was to drive to the Abby, enter by the back way, and put Melody in the room she had prepared for her. When she adjusted the back of the seat she realized she hadn't thought about how to carry Melody's dead-weight into the house from the car.

A blue tarp used to keep some building supplies from scratching the interior of her car would have to do. Maude would roll Melody from the car onto the tarp, pull her into the house, and then into the room. It would be hard work, but anything was worth doing if it meant she would finally have her Alfred.

Passing through the village of Milton did not cause any notice. The villagers had seen her enough times that she had just become another part of the everyday background of life. No one really noticed the postman or police, the same with the other people in the town. Maude even smiled at the crossing guard at the local school.

xxxxx

Maude sat at the kitchen table with the lantern lit, eating a packaged meal. It was hard work getting Melody into the house but finally, she was tucked up on the small cot. Maude took her shoes, jacket, and the belt she was wearing, covered her with a thin blanket, and put a protein bar next to a bottle of water. According to her calculations, the woman should be waking up within the next half-hour.

xxxxx

Melody didn't exactly see the light, but the brilliance of the source penetrated her closed eyelids. Her first impression was that it wasn't the sun because there was no heat coming from it, just illumination. Her head hurt and the brightness did not help. Slowly, she tried to move her head but it screamed pain at her and she stopped. Next, was the attempt at assessing her body and its condition.

When Melody had been a child, one of the first ponies she had, had thrown her and the instructor at the time told her never to just get up without checking herself over first. Since that time, Melody had taken more than one tumble from a horse, jumper or barrel-bender, and every time she followed the same advice. Her initial assessment was that she had a raging headache, was very thirsty and hungry, and that her body was sore all over. She also was mildly chilly, her jacket was gone, and her shoes were missing.

Ever so gingerly she raised her hand to her eyes and shielded them from the light as she opened her eyes and took a look at her surroundings. The ceiling was high, the source of the light was a single bulb, the room was very small, and there were no windows. He watch was also gone so knowing the time of day was out of the question. The walls were white and freshly painted because the odor of paint still hung in the air. Melody had no idea of where she was or why.

From her feet to her head, she moved first one part of her body and then another until she was sure nothing was broken and it was safe to get up. Next to the top of the cot where her head had been was an unopened bottle of water and a protein bar in the wrapper. Before she could think about the food and drink she needed to stand up and try the door.

The floor was cold stone and the door didn't budge. She tried the handle, knocked on it, and even shouted. For some reason, Melody had the sinking feeling that whoever had put her in this room was not going to answer her or let her out. Being proved right on that score didn't add to her sense of comfort but also didn't make her panic. At the foot of the cot she spied a bucket and a roll of paper. She needed to relieve herself and it looked to her like this was all the 'facilities' she would be allowed.

On the other side of the door, Maude stood on a low stool and looked through the spy-hole. She hadn't wanted the possibility that Melody could see someone looking at her, so she had made it just high enough to put it out of the American's reach. Watching her, Maude was surprised Melody had not panicked when she first woke up and found out she was not on a train or in the comfortable surroundings of Sir Arthur's country estate.

Seeing the way things were working in the room where she had Melody, she decided to put a camera in on the next sleep cycle. The one she had was actually a low energy consumption model which would usually be a part of a home security system. She could have it on intermittently or all the time and watch the feed from her phone. The solar generator she had installed for the light would power the camera.

As Maude watched, Melody sat on the cot and examined the bottle of water and the protein bar. Try as she might, Melody was unsure about what was happening to her. Unbeknownst to Maude, the medication she had put in the water had several serious side effects. Disorientation, short-term memory loss, and other, as yet un-manifested symptoms could arise very soon.

Melody removed part of the wrapper from the energy bar and took a small bite. It tasted just fine and reminded her of just how hungry she was. Melody looked at the bottle of water and saw that the cap was sealed and nothing looked odd. Opening the bottle, she downed half of it rapidly. She was so thirsty! Putting the remainder on the table, she ate the rest of the power bar. Before she could finish the water, however, Melody slumped sideways and was deep asleep.

Maude waited for over a half-hour before opening the door. The first thing she did was put the girl straight on the cot and covered her. The room did seem a bit chilly to her so she got another blanket from the ones she kept in the kitchen on her bed. Next, the soil bucket had to be replaced with a clean one. Finally, using a mid-height step ladder, she pealed the back off of the sticky part on the back of the camera, pushed the wire through the same hole as the one the light bulb used, and she removed the unused water and empty wrapper from the little table.

Closing the door, Maude checked the feed from the camera on her phone. It showed the entire room and could be zoomed in to look at Melody's sleeping face. The last thing she did was put a fresh bottle of water on the table, another power bar, and locked the door. Melody would not be going anywhere for quite some time but Maude had things to do in London and wanted to get back to her apartment. Getting in her car, she thanked the Lord for the rain that was falling hard enough to wash away the marks where she had drug Melody from the car to her prison.

Maude knew it wouldn't be long before that cow, Melody, would be missed and she had to keep suspicion away from herself. Alfred had the idea he was in love with the American and if he knew Maude had taken her, well, he might not be happy with her. No, she needed to show herself in London and a couple of girls, sisters, she had known in school were providing just the right place for her to do that.

June and Maggie were not close friends from school, but their invitation to a dinner party was just the perfect cover for her other activity. Maude had RSVP'd the day before and even recommended they ask Lord Alfred to dine with them. That would have been wonderful, but June told her they would pair Maude with a cousin of theirs from South Africa. Normally Maude wouldn't have gone to one of June and Maggie's parties, but it was all that was available. She would just have to endure the cousin.

When Maude reached her apartment she only had half an hour before she had to be at the dinner party. Opening her door she found the mail on the floor. She sorted through it as she climbed the stairs and most of it was just junk or bills. A post card from Tenerife she knew was from her father and it was tossed on the sideboard to be read later. The only envelope she was interested in was the heavy vellum one from her mother's bank in Glasgow.

Maude's mother and father divorced and while her father was sent packing with nothing, her mother wanted to make sure Maude had a little something to take care of her school and the basics of living. Every quarter a letter arrived from her bankers informing her of the amount to be credited to Maude's account. And, every quarter, a post-card arrived from her father.

Maude's grandfather had dissipated the family fortune on younger women over the years since his wife died but Maude's father did exactly the opposite. He lived the life of an aging gigolo on Tenerife where he 'allowed' lonely older women to pay for dinners, a pair of gold cuff-links here and there, a new dinner jacket, and in one case, a widow from somewhere in the United States called Peoria bought him a new car. Maude grimaced at the irony.

Showered and dressed for dinner, Maude checked on her 'guest' at the Abbey via her phone. The blankets over the sleeping form had not moved. It would take two hours for dinner, another hour to get to the Abbey and Maude calculated she should be there in plenty of time to watch the cow wake up, eat, and drink more of the sedative, and return to sleep. Oh Alfred, she thought to herself, soon you will be mine, and that girl will not take you away from me.

xxxxx

Lord Arthur Farr was not happy. He called Melody several times and the calls had all gone to voice mail and now the blasted thing said her mailbox was full and could take no more messages. He had been in meetings from the time he arrived in Edinburgh until the dinner last night. By the time the talk had ceased and the last brandy was served, it was late and he was tired. He would call Melody in the morning. He started in the early morning trying to call and now, late in the afternoon, he couldn't reach her.

The phone at the Cottage rang and rang before Nedda picked up and said hello. "No Sir Arthur, she's not here. John went to the station yesterday morning but she wasn't on the train. He waited but then called me and I told him to come back, if the girl arrived she could either take a taxi or call for someone to get her. I didn't think it was necessary for John to lose a whole day of work just to wait on her."

Now Arthur was worried. The evening of the birthday dinner there had been some discussion of Melody leaving with LT Chadwick for a few days, but it wasn't like Melody to go off and not tell him. He was, after all, her guardian for another year and he had a responsibility. "Okay, I will see if she is with the estate trustee. If you hear from her, have her call me. Bye."

The next call Arthur made was to LT Chadwick. He didn't know exactly where LT was, but supposed he was still in Europe somewhere. Surely if he was going to take Melody back to the United States he would have told him or left a message at the Cottage.

None of the numbers he had for LT answered and he left messages at all of them. There was still another day of presentations after this one, but thankfully, today was almost finished. Arthur went back into the meeting room to continue his work.

140

xxxxx

LT was at 30,000 feet for part of the time Arthur was trying to reach him. Not until the plane landed and his phone worked again did he find the multiple messages that Melody's guardian had left for him. Immediately, he called Arthur and his call went to voice mail. LT didn't know what Arthur wanted, but something wasn't sitting well with LT.

More than five hours later, Arthur and LT finally had a chance to talk. "I just wanted to speak to Melody, she didn't go back to the Cottage and I wanted to know when she would be back." Arthur hurried on, "I was surprised she decided to take you up on your offer of going with you and Jeremy, but I guess you were very persuasive."

LT didn't know what Arthur was talking about, but he was even more worried than before. "Melody isn't with me; she is supposed to be in England, at Farr Cottage. Are you sure, I mean did you check? I've been trying to call her but her phone's voice mail is full." The hair on the back of LT's neck started to bother him and he didn't like it.

Arthur waited to answer. "No, no, I talked to the housekeeper and Melody didn't get the train from London. I've tried calling the townhouse, but there is no answer." The full impact of what he was saying was beginning to sink in. "I'll call Mrs. Jones and ask her or her niece Angie when they last saw her and what she said, uh, maybe she changed her plans and didn't tell anybody."

Quick decisions were forming in LT's mind. "You talk to them and then get onto the police. Ask them if they can look into this. I'll be there in a few hours. First, let me give you a number that will always find me."

LT repeated the number a second time. "This is the office in Houston. They can do a patch through to the plane and let's pray this is just a silly misunderstanding. I've got plans to put into action and I'm sure you have calls to make." Almost before Sir Arthur could say goodbye the line went dead.

xxxxx

The vibration of the phone and its soft trilling sound made enough of an impression on Lilith that she and Jacque stopped what they were doing. Finally, Lilith answered, ready to dismiss whoever was interrupting her fun. "Hello?"

"Lilith, LT, go splash some water on your face. Melody is missing and I need your services." LT's strong voice and business-like demeanor made a chill run up Lilith's spine.

"My phone is a cell so keep talking." Lilith was headed to the bathroom, more for the privacy than out of need. "You kind of caught me doing something other than sleeping so give me the facts, I'm awake and listening."

"The last time anybody is sure they knew where she was, it was on Tuesday evening, at her birthday dinner in the London townhome of her guardian, Lord Arthur Farr. He had to leave very early in the morning on Wednesday to take a train to Edinburgh, a guest of mine had to get back to his unit so we left early also, and everyone assumed Melody was still asleep." The more he talked about it, the more concerned he became. "She was supposed to take a train about mid-morning to the country house of her family, Farr Cottage, but she never arrived and there is no indication she ever got on the train."

Lilith listened intently to LT and didn't interrupt or speak until he finished. Finally, Lilith starting asking questions about the police, if any threats had been received, plus several other items. LT answered with as much information as he had. "The local police aren't looking at this as anything more than a twenty-nine year-old woman going off to be by herself without telling anyone. I know she wouldn't do that and so far, the people in England haven't gotten them to understand otherwise." LT had someone who might help, but that would be a call for later in the evening, European time.

Lilith agreed to meet at the de Gaul airport in two hours. "One thing, I know England has pulled out of the EU, well at least they voted to do so, but what are the reciprocal agreements like for security people?"

Lilith reassured LT. "I've had clients travel all over the EU and never had a problem. The Brits haven't changed on that score and probably won't for some time. Don't worry about it, as long as your airplane crew doesn't mind the hardware, we're fine."

For the first time since he found that Melody was missing, LT laughed. "Lilith, they're from Texas, they will welcome the hardware." He quickly reverted to his somber tone. "I'll see you in a couple of hours."

A knock on the door took LT's attention away from making his next call. LT had left a message for Jeremy which LT assumed Jeremy would receive somewhere in the 'sandbox' where he and his unit were supposed to be headed. LT was surprised to find Jeremy, duffle bag in hand, standing in the door.

"Where is she and what is being done to find her. I mean, how could she be missing? All she had to do was get on the train to a sleepy little village and take a car or taxi to Farr Cottage." Dropping his bag on the floor, he turned a warrior's face to LT. "She is my future wife and we have to find her."

LT brushed the comment aside, "What are you doing here, I thought you were on your way to oversee an oil field? I put you at your base for just that purpose and now you're here? You need to …"

Jeremy interrupted, "I have people who are trained to carry on without me. This is a family matter, my future family matter and whatever you have planned, I'm in. The Colonel, my boss, understands that fact, well he did after a little explanation, and he's good with me being here. What you need to do now is tell me what the plan is and what I can do to get her back safe, and sound, and how I can deliver 'consequences' to whoever took her."

LT grunted. "Calm down, if it's okay with the Marines, then of course I want you in on this. It's just that right now, I don't know what 'this' is or who all is involved. I do need to make a very important phone call so take your stuff, put it on that company plane parked outside, and oh, you might want to change. I think the English authorities might get a bit miffed at a battle-dressed Marine showing up at one of their airports."

Jeremy reached for his bag, mumbled a thank you to LT, and left for the plane.

LT pulled a note from his pocket with a U. S. phone number. Marty, the man he was about to call, was a friend. He wasn't as close as Melody's father had been, but he had known Marty for years. Marty graduated from Texas A&M as a petroleum engineer the same year LT was finishing his business degree from Harvard. Marty went to work in the oilfields and on oil rigs while LT did an internship in New York which had been demanded by his uncle Silas.

All these years later, Marty had climbed through the company he worked for to become the CEO five years ago and in two years, when the current Chairman was due to retire, Marty was slated to take his place. Well, that was until a friend of theirs from New York called late one night and asked Marty to serve his country as the Secretary of State. The next day Marty was on the way to New York and the company he had served for so many years started looking for a new CEO.

LT sent a congratulatory note when he was named and then a Texas fruit basket when he was sworn into office. Now, he needed to talk to him, not to wish him well, but to ask for help to get his god-daughter back.

A very proficient but familiar sounding voice answered the phone, "Secretary's office may I help you?"

LT was happy to hear Marty's secretary from Houston on the phone, "Milly! This is LT Chadwick, how do you like Washington?"

He could almost hear Milly smiling on the other end of the call, "Why Mr. LT, it's cold and miserable, but the boss needed me so here I am. How can I help you?"

LT sighed, "I need to talk to your boss. It's kind of important and I know I don't have an appointment, but could he fit me in?"

"No problem, his last appointment just left. Good to hear from you." LT heard the click of the call being transferred.

The next voice he heard was Marty's. "LT you old cowboy, how are you? How's the weather down in Houston?"

LT began to tell his friend what was going on. "Old Charlie's girl? My, my. So you think a little nudge from the American Embassy might help? Look, give me about twenty minutes. We just sent a new ambassador to London last week and he should be easy to find. You probably know him, Larry Ward, he was over at Shell for years. I'll have him call you." The line went dead.

LT sat and looked at his phone. Sir Arthur had been unable to get the British police to do anything. Melody was twenty-nine years old and sane. Also, it hadn't been forty-eight hours yet. The excuses just rolled out and nothing was being done. The vibration in his hand alerted him to an incoming call.

Larry Ward's soft Texas drawl was unmistakable to LT. For the next four minutes LT briefed the new ambassador to the Court of St. James. Larry asked some questions then told LT to wait until he could get the British liaison officer on the line. Ambassador Ward would call back in a few minutes. "Charley Farr wrote the first mortgage on a house for me when Linda and I got married, in fact, his bank also did my car loans until he sold the Farr Bank to that big city bank several years back. Give me a few minutes to find Glenn Hapworth, the liaison. I'll get back to you." Before LT could respond with a 'thank you', the line went dead.

Humph, again LT sat with his phone in his hands. He looked at his watch and calculated how long he still had to wait for the jet to be ready to leave to pick up Lilith in Paris before flying into Biggin Hill airport. The waiting was the worst part of this whole affair. Not knowing what had happened to Melody or where she was weighed heavily on him, but the inactivity in trying to find her, having to depend on others to help only made things worse.

The phone started vibrating before the familiar trill began. LT answered before the first few notes of his ringtone had started playing. "LT, Larry, I've got Glenn Hapworth on the line with us and he has some questions for you. I'm going to leave you two to talk. I'll keep apprised on this end, but call me when you get here and if you need something. This is a good number to call or use the first one I called on, that's my private number. Don't worry, we will try to do what is necessary to get Charley's daughter back to you. Bye." LT heard the line click and knew that the American ambassador to Britain had signed off.

LT told Glenn Hapworth the same information he had imparted to Larry but Glenn asked some questions Larry hadn't thought of asking. The back and forth lasted for about five minutes before Glenn also clicked off with a promise to start the ball rolling with the local police. "Call me when you get to London and I'll give you an update. Goodbye Mr. Chadwick" The clipped British accent of Glenn Hapworth made his conversation sound all businesslike and in a way, comforting for LT.

Two final calls would complete the preparations to leave for Paris. The first was to a friend at an oilfield services company in Houston. "Mitch, this is LT, what do you have going to London today, tonight, as late as tomorrow?"

Mitch Lotrell leaned back in his custom made leather chair. "Well, hello to you too LT. As for what I have going anywhere, most of my business is currently in the opposite direction. Why do you ask?" As LT told him about the missing daughter of Charley

Farr, Mitch sat up straight and started taking notes. "Gee, LT, this is bad. Uh, if you can have your guy at the West Houston airport in, oh, say, forty-five minutes, I'll get one of my crews to spin up my G6. Will that work?"

LT breathed a sigh of relief, "You bet, I'll get John Bellamy there and Mitch, please keep this between you and me. I don't want a lot of people knowing that Melody is missing." LT got the needed assurances of silence from Mitch and rang off. It was time for the last call and the trip to Paris and London.

The phone on the other end of his cell rang twice before the familiar sound of his old butler answered. "Farr House, Bellamy speaking." Before LT could speak, Bellamy was greeting him. "Hello Mr. Chadwick, when did you return to the office?"

"John, I'm not calling from the office. I'm in Europe. Miss Melody is missing." Bellamy had been surprised when his former employer used his first name, but the news that his current employer, Miss Melody Farr was missing gave him a partial answer as to why LT had used his familiar name. For the next three minutes LT explained what he knew, what steps, well, most of the steps he had taken to find her, and requested his presence. "You're former special ops and like Marines, you guys never retire. Can you put your game face on one more time for me and Miss Melody?"

Without hesitation, "I will be at the airport in thirty minutes. I'll see you in London, Sir. And, we will get her back, that's the job I signed on for, to keep her safe. …I'll be there." The line went dead. LT shoved his phone in his pocket, opened the door to the general aviation office where he had parked the jet, and sprinted to the open door of the plane. A steward took his coat while the co-pilot closed and locked the door. Before LT was in his seat the plane began to roll toward the runway where they would take off. Within minutes they were wheels-up and putting a small Eastern European country behind. ETA for Paris' de Gaulle Airport was an hour and fifty minutes.

Jeremy was sleeping on the sofa across from LT's desk. Like any military man who has seen action, Jeremy had learned to get sleep when he could, in order to be as ready and alert as possible when he would be needed. LT leaned his head against the window and prayed. "*Melody, we are on our way, just hang in there until we find you.*" He whispered.

xxxxx - Maude

June and Maggie's dinner party was such a bore and the cousin from South Africa was even worse than she imagined. Maude managed to leave before the two hours she'd allotted herself and thought it wouldn't hurt to go back by her apartment. It might be necessary to prove where she'd been and a little noise, at least enough to wake a neighbor or two, might be just the thing.

Maude stayed a bit longer than anticipated at her apartment, but when she left, she'd brought an extra blanket and the foresight to stop at the ATM at the bank to withdraw some funds. Finally, she was headed out of town and soon, left London behind. She knew the back entrance to the Abbey and didn't need to hunt for it in the dark.

With all of her things in the kitchen, she checked on Melody. The medicine should be wearing off and Maude was ready for her. While she had been asleep, Maude had put an extra blanket on Melody, changed the waste bucket at the foot of the bed, and put a fresh power-bar along with a 'doctored' bottle of water on the night table.

The camera she had put in the room made it much easier to watch Melody. For more than an hour and a half, Maude waited for Melody to waken. Finally, the cow began to stir.

She looked terrible. *Humph, you should see her now Alfred. She looks like she's been drunk for weeks. Her eyes were sunken and had dark circles, that mahogany-brown hair was filthy and straggled.*

Look at what your 'beautiful' girl has been reduced to, her true self, and I saved you from her. Maude refocused her attention to what Melody was doing.

xxxxx – Melody

Melody sat up very carefully. Any sudden movement and her head felt like it would explode. She had a terrible thirst, the light was hurting her, and her hair hurt. The clothes she was wearing were all twisted around her and tug as she might, could not get them straight. Her clothes also hurt her skin.

She still didn't know where she was, but now she didn't know if she didn't know or if she just forgot where she was. Maybe she had even forgotten who she was. She did know she had to use the restroom and then remembered the 'toilet' was a bucket at the end of the cot.

Trying to move was agony. She was bruised from head to foot from being dragged in from Maude's car, but then, she didn't know that was the reason for her pain. Melody only knew she had to get to the bucket. Once that was accomplished, she shakily made her way back to the edge of the cot.

Thirsty, hungry, still chilly, and head pounding, Melody tried to think. While she worked on thinking, she tore open a bar of food and ate half of it in one bite. The water was still sealed when she opened it and Melody downed most of it. She finished the power-bar, and started to drink what was left of the water. This time, the bottle hit the floor and the remainder spilled. Maude would get it after Melody was safely out.

xxxxx – Maude

Wow, it didn't take near as long for Melody to go back to sleep as the last time. Maybe the sedative had a cumulative effect she didn't know about.

It didn't say anything on the package it came in and the dogs she had tried it on couldn't tell her. Maude simply passed it off and went in to the room where Melody lay, slumped over from a sitting position.

Maude finished cleaning the spilled water, emptied the waste bucket, and put a fresh power bar and bottle of water in the room. With Melody seen to, Maude could look after her own comfort. She was sure no one could see any smoke coming from the chimney attached to the old stove in the kitchen. She would be sure to douse any flames before the sun came up, but tonight the warm stove would take the edge off the spring chill. Tomorrow Maude would go to the village and see if any of the papers said anything about the American cow being missing.

xxxxx – London

The jet carrying LT, Lilith, and Jeremy barely came to a stop before the door opened and the three exited the plane. A lighted SUV was sitting on the tarmac and a customs/immigration official was in attendance to stamp passports and examine luggage. Before the legalities were out of the way, LT was on the phone with the American ambassador, Arthur, and a Detective Chief Inspector (DCI) Applegate.

DCI Applegate had the most news. "Mr. Chadwick. At the request of the liaison at the American Embassy, we have examined several hours of camera recordings from around the residence where Miss Farr was living. I will meet you at the home of Lord Arthur in about forty-five minutes to show you what we've found. There is also a ping on the GPS locater frequency we were given. We're awaiting a magistrate to give us the order to open a locker at the train station where we believe it is being stored. I will see you shortly."

LT looked at the phone in his hand. So, finally, someone might have news of Melody. But, as usual, it wouldn't be made available to him until more time had passed. He supposed, perhaps unreasonably, the best news would have been that she had been found and was waiting for them, alive and well, at Arthur's house in Mayfair. Time was of the essence and it was slipping away from them.

During the drive to Arthur's, LT filled in the rest of the people about the phone call he'd had with DCI Applegate. It was the first lead they'd had and with the photos, might lead them to where she was. Lilith was quick to point out that London had more cameras per street than any major city in the world. "My friends laugh that in London, you can't blow your nose without the people who monitor the cameras catching a cold. The cameras are all over."

The group arrived at the townhouse only minutes before DCI Applegate and Police Constable (PC) Scott. The young PC was weighed down by stacks of pictures and files, but took no time at all spreading them out on the dining room table. When everything was ready, DCI Applegate began the presentation of what they'd learned.

"This street doesn't have any cameras on it. This isn't unusual for Mayfair since most of the residents don't like them and have been successful in keeping them out. Where we do have cameras is most of the rest of the City. The first shot we have of Miss Farr is her as a passenger in a radio taxi on Wednesday morning. We've been in contact with the company and they're in the process of talking to the driver." The DCI nodded to the PC and another picture was handed around. "The picture shows her leaving the taxi near Knightsbridge."

Arthur broke in, "That is near my boot maker. She was supposed to pick up her boots last week but there was a problem with one of them. They were sent to my country home and arrived yesterday."

The DCI thanked Arthur for the information. "We weren't sure where she had gone from the taxi so that will help us fill in some of the missing parts of where she might be. The next picture shows nothing, but actually it shows us a lot. The taxi is gone and so is Miss Farr. It simply means the taxi didn't wait for her. We need to find out how she moved on from where you," pointing to Arthur, "think she had gone; the boot maker's."

A phone rang in the distance and Angie, Mrs. Jones', niece came in. She asked for DCI Applegate and showed him where the phone was located. He returned within minutes. "That was the station. The taxi driver confirmed he had picked up a lady matching Miss Farr's description on Wednesday morning, taken her to Knightsbridge, and she paid him off. He left her and didn't see her again. So that answers some of our questions. Also, the magistrate has given the order to open the locker at the station and I have a constable there now. Whatever he finds he'll bring here."

The briefing droned on. A young, uniformed constable arrived with Melody's carry-on bag, purse, shoes, and jacket all secured in police evidence-bags. The DCI looked through the bags and found the GPS signal had come from the clasp on the tags LT had given Melody for her birthday. Her phone had been in her purse with the battery removed. The mystery of why she couldn't be reached or the ability to track her by her cell phone was at last answered.

DCI Applegate cleared his throat. "This," he motioned to the items laid out on the table, "indicates the disappearance of Miss Farr is not casual, but appears to have been premeditated, perhaps even criminal. I don't know why you," pointing to LT, "would have felt it necessary to put a GPS tracking device in her necklace, but as it turns out, it didn't matter. She is not with the necklace and the tracker hasn't helped us find her."

LT took the floor. "DCI, I'm thankful for what you have done already, but …"

The DCI held up his hand, "This is only the beginning." Turning to the constable, he told him to take everything to the station and have it sent to the forensics department. "I want the fingerprints and any other evidence by morning." Focusing on LT and the rest of the people gathered in Lord Arthur's dining room, "I will leave a PC here to monitor the phones in case a ransom demand comes through. The photos from several cameras should be ready in the morning along with other information."

Applegate looked at the people gathered, waiting for information, "I'll be here no later than nine in the morning. Get a good night's sleep, you'll need it." With that, he left.

Arthur and Alfred had a few quite words in the corner, and then Arthur told LT and the others what had been said. "When Melody didn't arrive at the Cottage, I asked Alfred to try and trace her steps from here to wherever she might have gone. He showed her picture at the train station, but got nothing. Then, he went to the country, to our local train station, and they said she hadn't arrived." Looking over at Alfred for support, "he then had an idea that maybe she had gone back to France, to the places in Normandy where she had been a few weeks ago. He showed her photo at the churches, hotels, and train stations there, but nothing. They remember her from before, but nothing recent. He just arrived just before you did. I wish he had brought better news."

Arthur turned back toward the darkened window. Alfred looked at some of the photos on the table, and everyone else just kind of milled around. No one wanted to go to bed or leave; it would mark another day without Melody.

Finally, LT slapped the table. "I should never have let her comeback here! She would have been safe in Houston, in her own home, with Bellamy, and her staff!"

"LT, don't be so hard on yourself." Alfred tried to sooth the American man. "You know Arthur is her legal guardian and she was supposed to return here. Why, look at him, he is just as distressed as the rest of us."

"Alfred, don't." Arthur said softly, continuing to look out the window.

"But you know I'm right. It's in the will her father left. She had to …"

"Alfred! Just … just drop it LT must know what he is saying." Turning from the window, Arthur looked LT in the eyes. "You do know something, right?"

Alfred looked from Arthur to LT and back to Arthur. "What's this …?"

LT cut in. "Yes, but now might not be the time."

Alfred came to stand between Arthur and LT. "I think if you know something, we should be told."

Before LT could begin, Arthur stepped in. "Alfred!" Arthur said a bit too harshly and then in a softer tone, "Alfred, I think what LT knows and has not said yet is that I am not truly Melody's guardian." Then raising an eyebrow to LT, "Am I right?"

LT nodded.

"Nonsense. You are the only Farr male relative she has and … and … oh. Oh!" Alfred trailed off.

Arthur looked straight at LT. "When or how did you find out? Houston?"

LT nodded again. "The water bottles from the ride from the airport to Melody's that first day. The DNA took a few days, but it is unquestionable."

Arthur looked down then stood tall, squared his shoulders and faced Alfred. "What LT is referring to is what you have been trying to tell me for years, but, I didn't want to acknowledge."

Turning back to the window, Arthur continued. "Since Melody went missing, I have been reading over the work she was doing after she returned from Houston. I thought, maybe, there might be a clue or something to what had happened to her." He shook his head as if in disbelief. "She figured it out. I don't know how, probably from the journals those damn women always were writing in. Uh … anyway… it seems a young bride of an old man was expected to conceive a child and when the old man either wouldn't or couldn't do the deed, she turned to one of your ancestors to get her with child."

Alfred was white. "I, uh, I knew it was a rumor in the family, mostly from the servants. I, uh, just, uh … whew." Alfred sank into the nearest chair.

LT stepped in to the silence. "Right now, this instant, the only thing we should be thinking about is Melody. Now, DCI Applegate will be back in the morning and we all need our sleep. Alfred, I think Arthur probably has a place where you can stay if you don't want to be alone in your house." Arthur nodded and Alfred left the room with Jeremy. Lilith also went to find her room.

By two in the morning, everyone except for the PC that DCI Applegate assigned to the front of the house, was asleep. Near four, a black taxi arrived with Bellamy and his wife, Mrs. Bellamy. PC Drake had been informed another member of the security team would be arriving from America, but he was not expecting that person to bring his wife. After some discussion, Lord Arthur was summoned to explain the facts about the Americans that were requesting entry.

The Bellamys were both able to sleep in the small jet that flew them from Houston to London. Arthur, however, showed Mrs. Bellamy to a room and gave Bellamy a brief rundown of the situation. While Mrs. Bellamy was able to grab a couple more hours of sleep, Bellamy spent his time in the dining room with the security photos, pictures of the things from Melody's carry-on, purse, and other items from the locker, as well as a pot of strong coffee.

xxxxx – Maude

The ringing of the alarm pulled Maude out of a fitful sleep. Looking around the darkened room, it took her a few seconds to catch her bearings. This wasn't her small, cozy London apartment but the cold kitchen of the old family estate. Maude checked the remains of the fire and put the embers out by scattering and dousing them with water.

She checked the camera feed to see if Melody had moved and found the cover over her was in the same condition as when Maude had slept. By Maude's watch, Melody should be waking in the next three hours. That should give Maude enough time to go into the village for the early papers from London and get back before Melody awoke.

Before leaving for the village, however, Maude wanted to put the blue tarp on the floor. Melody had been having difficulty getting back on the bed before passing out from the sedative and Maude had found it hard to push her into a reclining position on the cot. If Maude's plans were to be carried out as she wished, tonight would be the last night Melody would spend in the Abbey. If she slept on the floor, it wouldn't make any difference.

Blue tarp in place, Maude left for the village, and bought three papers, the *Times*, *Guardian*, and *Daily Mail*. She was also able to get some fresh hot buns from the bakery. Along with a bottle of milk, she had enough to keep her fed and busy for the day.

As Maude pulled into the cobbled yard near the kitchen door, she happened to notice the old hay-trolley near the barn. *Hmm*, she thought, *I wonder if I can use that to move the American cow from the house to the car?* The only way to know was to measure.

Maude dumped her purchases from the village on the kitchen table and grabbed a tape-measure. She checked the size of the pantry door opening, the same on the kitchen, and then was outside looking at the cart. It had rubber wheels, which were dirty, it squeaked loudly when moved, and would fit through both doors with ease. So, change of plan, now it was from the cot Maude had to move Melody and not pull her across the floor. When Maude checked the height of the trolley with the height of the back of the car, it would make moving the body so much easier.

The first look at the papers didn't indicate anything about the woman being missing. Surely Melody had been gone long enough for people to notice. Hadn't she? You'd think she would be missed by somebody, well at least Arthur, her guardian, would have noticed her missing. Maybe not. Perhaps she was going someplace that morning besides Farr Cottage, but then, wouldn't someone know she wasn't where she was supposed to be?

Maude looked at her watch and then at the sleeping figure in the old butler's pantry. Melody should be waking within the next half hour and Maude wanted to be ready for the show.

xxxxx - London

DCI Applegate arrived to a very busy house. The addition of the two Americans, employees of Miss Farr was noted. Bellamy, LT, Lilith, Jeremy, and their lordships had spent more than an hour after breakfast looking over the items in the dining room, almost as if one or another of them would give someone of the group a special insight or other into what had happened to Melody.

Sir Arthur had called his solicitor in the night to request a dawn consultation. The highly unusual meeting lasted for only a few minutes before the lawyer scurried off to his office to do as Lord Arthur had bid.

At breakfast, which had been before seven, Arthur finally had to tell the rest of the group what he'd found out about his relationship with Lord Alfred Oswin and the Oswin family.

"I was looking over some of the work Melody had done on the second oldest brother of Richard Farr, Melody's great-great-grandfather." Arthur began, "Roland married Jillian Percy and it was from her family this second townhouse came from, in her dowry, and the funds to merge the two houses, together, literally. Roland had been a major in Her Majesty's forces in India when his brother, the Viscount of Gibbons, Lord Harold Farr died of pneumonia."

"Roland was called back by his widowed mother, Lady Annis Farr, and she arranged for the bachelor head of the family to marry. He was in his late forties or early fifties when he married Jillian. She was in her twenties. The couple produced a son. But, and this is where the connection between the Oswin and Farr families happens, the true father of the son was not Major Lord Roland Farr, but Rand Oswin."

Arthur continued. "Melody combed through the journals, diaries, and letters of the Oswin and Farr ladies of the time. It is in the journal of Jillian's grandmother that Melody found the key to everything. It seems the grandmother was intent on making sure the couple produced a child. After Jillian and Roland had been married for a little more than six months, she decided it was up to her to make sure Jillian had a child and if it meant coming to London and putting her in with Rand Oswin, well … then that is what needed to happen." Arthur took a long sip of tea.

"Rand Oswin's wife, Laura, was pregnant with their first child and, as was accepted at the time, sexual relations were often curtailed during the final months of a pregnancy. Jillian and her grandmother, Lady Juliet Fitzwilliam, came to London to oversee part of the renovations of this house. While in London, they stayed with Rand and Laura Oswin in the Oswin London home, just down the street. Nine months after they were in London, Jillian produced a son." Arthur sighed. "This is where the connection is and I'm sorry," he nodded toward Alfred, "for not listening to you all these years."

It was time for Alfred to take over the story. "All I ever had were the rumors of the family's servants to go on, nothing solid. There was a young woman who would later be called Nanny Young. She had been hired to work for Rand and Laura Oswin a couple of weeks before their first child was born. At the time, she was not the baby nurse, but an assistant to the baby's nurse. Nanny Young stayed on with the family until long after the Great War." Alfred sipped his tea and continued. "Supposedly, she had seen Rand and Jillian, who, as Arthur has said, was a guest in the house while the Farr townhouse was being refurbished. Later in her life, Nanny Young passed the story on to a housekeeper who passed it on to the cook who worked for my parents."

Alfred put his hand on Arthur's shoulder, "I don't know if you remember, but when I was about seven, and you would have been, oh, maybe sixteen or seventeen," Alfred went on, "you and your family visited my family for part of an afternoon. I overheard cook and the housekeeper talking about how alike you and I were. I asked cook about it later and all she said was it was normal for cousins to look so similar, "even if we were distant cousins." From then on, that is how I always thought of you."

A sudden commotion at the door of the breakfast room focused everyone's attention back to the present. DCI Applegate and another plainclothes police woman came in. Applegate introduced his sergeant to the group. "This is Sergeant Russell, she has spent most of yesterday, and last night putting together what we think might have been the crime committed against Miss Farr." Turning to the woman, "You may begin your presentation when we all move into the dining room. The photos and other items are there from last night."

Everyone stood around the dining table, intently watching the presentation. Sergeant Russell began by laying out the stack of photos she had been working with. With some she had an explanation of what or where the shot was taken. "We looked at the cameras from the area around the boot maker's, the station where the purse and other items were found, and one car was at both places within the time frame we were interested in examining." Looking at Lords Arthur and Alfred, "this street does not have any cameras controlled by the local authority, but one of your neighbors does and they are due to return from holiday later this morning. As soon as we can get their permission to see the footage they might have, it may show this same car on the street."

Addressing the group as a whole, "This is not a crime of chance; nobody just happened upon Miss Farr and decided to kidnap her. No, it was studied, planned, and so far, has been very well executed." Turning to the DCI, "Sir, would you like to continue?"

The DCI nodded. "The person or persons who have taken her knows her, knows a lot about her, and watched her. We need to see any film from the camera of your neighbor down the street. Trying to tag one car going in or out of London, or even anywhere inside of the city is almost impossible without an idea of where to start looking." Looking at the intent faces, "Any questions or comments?"

Lilith spoke up, "You said you might have a picture of the car, what can you tell us about it or if you have a picture from one of the cameras, let us see it."

The Sergeant pulled some picture from the group on the table. "As you can see, no one is inside and the car was parked in a way we don't have the license or tag number. The photos are in black and white so color is not definite. I've poured over footage of traffic in and out of both areas but could not find the car."

DCI Applegate cleared his throat. "The list of guests at the recent wedding Miss Farr attended has been examined. Some of them didn't know who she was, had never met her before, or even been introduced; each has been cleared. A second group, those you," nodding towards Alfred, "told me met Miss Farr at a dinner you gave last year, they have also been contacted, for the most part, and cleared. A couple of those, the bride and groom from the wedding, are out of the country, and another two haven't been reached." The DCI pulled a small notebook from his pocket, opened it, and flipped to a page. Reading from the page, "A Mr. Derrick Warren and a Miss Maude Harbison aren't at home and don't answer their phones. The company Mr. Warren works for has been contacted to determine if he is out of town on business. Miss Harbison was seen at a dinner party on Wednesday evening but has since been away."

Closing the book, the DCI put it back in his pocket. Turning to where Lord Arthur and Lord Alfred were standing, he addressed them in particular. "One or both of you either know or have some connection to the person or persons who have taken Miss Farr. I asked you last night to rummage through your memory, try to remember places you may have taken her, or people who may have been introduced to her that we have not checked. Have either of you come up with anything?"

Arthur shook his head but Alfred was looking at the photos on the table, particularly the two of the car outside the train station and the bootmaker's. Something in the back of his memory told him it was familiar but not who it was or where he had seen it. "I just don't know, that car, I've seen one like it, but I'm not sure where. Oh, I know there are thousands of this same make and model running around London, but someone, or somewhere, but …" Alfred trailed off, lost in thought.

The Sergeant walked out of the room. Within less than a minute she had returned and shared a confidence with the DCI. "Well, Mr. Warren is accounted for. His office just called to tell my Sergeant he is in Hong Kong on business and has been out of the country since the day after the wedding. Miss Farr was at her birthday dinner this past Tuesday so that rules him out. I've told my officers to get a warrant for the apartment of Miss Harbison."

Alfred shrugged, "Maude? I just don't see her being involved. She's been a part of this group I've hung out with since, oh, some of them since school," he simply nodded in disbelief. "She was the maid of honor for Beryl, the girl that got married last weekend. Hmm, I …" His voice trailed off.

"Lord Alfred" the DCI began, "People can show you one side of themselves and still have another you know nothing about. Think of the people who commit crimes and when their friends or family find out, they can't believe that "such a nice, quiet person" could have done such a thing."

"However, right now, this is where we are at in the investigation. My Sergeant is going to accompany the officers when the warrant comes to open the apartment of Miss Harbison and I will be at the office. If you have anything else, anything that might be possible in this case, call anytime." The two officers left.

xxxxx – Maude

Maude finished cleaning the waste bucket, replaced the protein bar, and bottle of medicated water in the cell where she was confining Melody. Glancing around, she was looking forward to getting the American girl out of her ancestral home. The smell in the room was bad enough, but Melody had been unable to make it to the waste bucket in time and soiled herself. Maude removed the dirty clothes, cleaned the cow, and put some second-hand clothes on the sleeping body.

It took quite some time to do all of the work, and she still had to burn the clothes she had taken off her captive, but at least this would all be over soon. Maude put the dirty things in the fireplace and would burn them in the night so no one would see the smoke from the fire. If the fire was still not out by morning, so be it, she would be far to the north by the time anyone might see evidence of burning coming from the chimney.

Maude made some tea, took a meal packet from the shelf, and settled in to read the rest of the papers. Half way through the *Daily Mail*, Maude dropped her fork. *Damn, well this is going to change things up a bit.* The article she was reading was the weather report for Budgies Neck. Rain had been forecast for this evening, but they had changed it and now it wasn't going to start until after nine in the morning.

Budgies Neck was a one lane village about three hours north of London. For fifty-one weeks a year the place was an un-noticed spot on a forgotten road with a pub, small shop for staple grocery items with a post office over it. The bus didn't even stop there but rather one kilometer down the road. However, one week out of the year, this week, that all changes. Romany and Travelers, Gypsies who have lived on the edges of society in Britain for centuries all bring their caravans (RVs and travel trailers) to the Neck for one of the biggest horse fairs in England.

Maude's grandfather had taken her and her parents to the fair one year when she was very small. Maude remembered the big open fields where the Gypsies set up their camps, the horses they had brought with them to buy, sell, and trade, and the carnival like atmosphere of the entire place. Beyond the fields, woods ringed the outer limits of the area and that is where she was going to dump Melody.

She needed rain however, to carry out her plan. Maude had watched the detective shows and movies on television. She knew to wash the room where she was keeping her prisoner with bleach to remove the chance DNA would convict her of kidnapping. Maude was using a blue tarp to move her in the back of the car and to get her from the cot in the cell to the car. She needed the rain to wash away her tire tracks or at least obscure them enough to confound the police if they ever found where she had dumped Melody's body.

Several years after that first trip with her grandfather to the fair, Maude had gone there by herself. With all of the people in the village and surrounding area during the week-long event, she could drive Melody from the Abbey to Budgies Neck, go down one of the many forest tracts with her car, and dump Melody. With the American cow dressed in tattered second-hand clothes, un-washed, no identification, and appearing to be affected by drink, people would think she was just a homeless alcoholic. It might take weeks for her to be "found." That is, IF she lasted that long out in the elements.

The sleep/wake cycle Melody was on meant Maude would have to keep her until after the morning waking and feeding, let the cow go back to sleep, and then move her to catch the rain. Plus, Maude would have to try and adjust the level of the medication to maybe have Melody wake earlier in the morning, preferably before sun-rise. Maude just didn't want to be moving her out of her house during daylight on the off chance someone might see her and begin watching what she was doing.

Maude put her newspapers down and got to work on another bottle of water for the cow's medicine. Perhaps just diluting the bottle of water she had already made would be enough. Too bad she didn't have a dog to test it on, but there wasn't time and she didn't think any of the local animal shelters or pet hospitals would give her one on such short notice.

xxxxx – London

Lord Alfred left to get a shower and change of clothes, Arthur, LT, and the people he had brought sat and looked over the photos on the table, talked, and waited for the DCI to either call or bring more information. The group didn't have long to wait.

Sergeant Russell arrived only moments before the DCI. The family who lived at the end of the street returned from vacation and was more than happy to share their surveillance video with the authorities. The items taken from Ms. Harbison's apartment were interesting but no full on pointers led to Melody.

The still photos of the car sitting at the end of the street nearest Alfred's showed a shadowy figure, but no clear face. A partial license plate number was all they had to go on and that was being run through the proper office. Results were expected shortly.

Nothing was taken from Maude's apartment, there was no proof a crime had been committed, but pictures of almost everything in her flat had been made. A postcard from her father, letter from a Scottish bank, bills, adverts, and other items were found in the waste basket. Nothing of interest was found in the fridge, drawers, cabinets, or closets. A couple of photo's hung on the wall, one of her and her family when she was a child, and one of her and her grandfather in front of an old country house, were all that was evident. It was a small apartment without much that was personal to Maude.

"We will," began the DCI, "dig out the plate number on the car, but that could take a good bit. Do any of you see anything here that might mean something to you?"

Everyone milled around looking at the new evidence. No one recognized anything. The DCI and his Sergeant left but promised to keep everyone informed if things changed.

As the DCI's car pulled away from the curb, Alfred was just crossing the road to Arthur's. Everyone was in Arthur's dining room with either a cup of tea or glass of sherry when he arrived. "I just saw the coppers leaving, anything new, or the same?"

Arthur showed his newfound cousin the pictures the Sergeant had laid out. Alfred looked over the ones from Maude's apartment and commented on the photo of her with her family. "Poor girl, this was probably one of the last happy times in her life. Once her grandfather was put in the care facility, her family disintegrated. Such a shame." Next Alfred looked at the still photos from the security camera down the street.

"You know," he said, "this is just at the end of my block, but the end I rarely pass. When I leave my house it is either to get into a taxi or walk to the pub. The pub is near the park so I always just walk there. Still … there is something about this picture. Hmm."

LT, Arthur, and the rest let Alfred think without interrupting. If he had some idea, it was best not to disturb his thoughts. "Hmm, it's just … well, it's right there but … dra …" his voice trailed off. The anticipation in the room was palpable. Then, the color drained from Alfred's face.

"Oh … No! No!" The photo of someone sitting in a car dropped from Alfred's limp hand and fluttered to the floor. Alfred backed up and sat down, hard, in the nearest chair. He was ashen. He raised his eyes to the group and tried to speak.

Arthur handed Alfred a small glass of brandy offered by Bellamy. Arthur mouthed a thank you to Melody's butler.

It took almost two minutes before Alfred could speak. Some of the color had returned to his face, but his hand was still a bit shaky. "Uh, I'm sorry, but … well, it's quite a shock, but I think the person in the car is Maude Harbison. Now, I'm not saying she is the one who took Melody, but that is her car and I don't know why she would park outside my house like that, but … well … I'm almost sure that is her car."

LT had his cell phone out and was dialing the DCI. It rang twice before a precise voice answered. "Applegate."

"DCI, Alfred Oswin has just looked at the photos of the car parked at the end of the street and he is sure it is Maude Harbison's with Maude sitting inside." The rest of the people in the dining room could hear the call since it was on the speaker. "She may need more looking at after all."

Applegate was way ahead of LT. "My office just called to inform me the partial number matched a car owned by Maude Harbison. I'll be at Lord Arthur's in fifteen minutes." The line went dead.

The group at Arthurs turned their attention to the photos taken of the contents of Maude's apartment. Bellamy laid them out from 'contents of trash basket' to 'pictures on the wall'. Jeremy, Lilith, and Bellamy went over each photo, looking for the one clue that might tell them that Maude had Melody. For Maude to park on the street where she could watch Alfred's house was one thing, but making the leap to being Melody's kidnapper was quite another. Photos of Maude's car were laid next to the photos of the suspected kidnapper's car near the train station and bootmaker's.

Alfred knew Maude better than anyone in the room. He had been friends with her and the group they ran with for more than twenty years. Once the initial shock of finding out she had been stalking his home had subsided, Alfred was all business about how he looked at the possibility Maude had Melody. "I just can't believe she would want to harm Melody, I mean, why would she do that? What would she want with someone she doesn't know?" Shaking his head, "I just don't see it."

DCI Applegate walked in with more photos and his sergeant followed with more papers and began informing the group of what they had. "The apartment was given another look, but nothing has turned. This time, though, we weren't carful to put things back but looked deeper than just opening drawers and taking pictures of papers, we brought the lot out with us."

Arthur picked up a piece of paper from the ones laid on the table. "Sergeant, when you were in her apartment, did you see any dogs or that she had a dog?"

"No, your Lordship, why?"

"Because, she has a receipt from a shelter in the South of London, Crystal Palace area, for a dog, mixed breed, 113 pounds, named "Bubbles." Awfully big dog for an apartment." While Arthur was talking, others were riffling through the stack.

A total of five receipts were found for large dogs, all bought in the last two plus months. Lilith, Bellamy, and Jeremy glanced at each other. Jeremy and Bellamy left the room and talked quietly. Lilith joined them. Bellamy was the first to speak. "You noticed all of the dogs were chosen for weight and nothing else," he observed? "Breed, age, house training, nothing else seemed to matter but the weight. I'll give you my last dollar she has Melody."

Jeremy knew there were a lot more questions to ask. "Hmm, yes, 105 to 120 pounds. I think we're talking about a test animal. Poison or sedative, but where has she got them?"

Lilith reached into a satchel she was carrying. She extracted Bluetooth type earpieces from the bag and handed one to Jeremy and to Bellamy. "This will give us two way communication and it's encrypted."

Turning it over in his hand, Bellamy looked for the listen/talk switch. "Sleek, you must shop at some of the places where I used to get my stuff." He put the device in his ear and tried it for volume. "Staggered prep?" The other two nodded. "I'll be down in five."

Bellamy bounded up the stairs to his room. Lilith looked at Jeremy, "You might as well get your game-gear on too. I'll monitor the briefing until you get down." Jeremy followed Bellamy.

Within a few minutes the men returned to the foyer, dropped their kit bags on the floor near the door, and went into the dining room to relieve Lilith so that she could get prepped for action. The look on her face told them nothing of import had turned up while they had been gone.

Bellamy and Jeremy were dressed very much alike. Both had comfortable, rubber-soled boots on that were tough but silent. They each had a Kevlar lined jacket on over dark sweaters and dark pants. Nothing the men wore would make noise, reflect light, or cause alarm. At night, they would be a hole in the darkness. When Lilith joined them she was attired the same way.

DCI Applegate received a call from an inquiry. "Well, she is nowhere to be found. The last we know of Ms. Harbison was when she made the withdrawal from the ATM. It was not her regular branch, but more toward the south and east. Hmm," the DCI rubbed his chin. "She keeps leading toward the south and east, but until the local constable gets back about the Abbey, there is nothing else in that direction."

Earlier, the DCI's sergeant had been tasked with the inquiry about the Abbey. The local constable's office in Milton had been notified and requested to send an officer to the Abbey. However, the more experienced local officer, PC Jerri Morley, was suffering from morning sickness and sent a rookie, PC Jenkins to do the check. Jenkins, newly assigned to the Milton station, was unfamiliar with the countryside and the people. He had never seen Maude Harbison and got lost, briefly, looking for Milton Abbey. What he found, and reported, was that the gate was locked, the lock was rusted and showed no signs of having been touched in the last few months, and there was no activity near the gate.

Before the Sergeant had finished the report, Lilith was on her laptop looking at maps and aerial photos of the Milton area. Google Earth and Live Maps is a wonderful open source, but it would have been more useful if the photos and maps had been made in the late fall or winter. The old estate had masses of trees around the perimeter and the Abbey itself. The back was in shade or shadow or simply obscured by foliage. The wall marked the property on the two roads, Abbey Lane that ran by the front gate and the perpendicular lane that marked the edge opposite the river called St. Joseph's Way.

St. Joseph's Way was the more promising. By following the wall Lilith could see where it seemed to disappear into a line of trees. It was forest beyond that. Was there an opening in the wall obscured by the trees? Only by seeing it in person could that be ascertained. Jeremy and Bellamy were looking over Lilith's shoulder at the computer screen and nodded their agreement.

"DCI?" Sir Arthur queried with a receipt in his hand. "Did you people find a drill in the apartment of Ms. Harbison?"

Flipping through the pages of inventory, the Sergeant shook his head. "No your Lordship, no drill. Why?"

"This receipt is for a cordless drill and it's from," Arthur looked closer at the paper in his hand, "uh, Jackson Ironmonger's and DYI shop in Milton."

Lilith, Jeremy, and Bellamy gave a slight nod to LT. The four headed out of the room. Lilith was the one to speak. "LT, we think this Maude must be at the old Abbey. We're going down there to scout the place." Looking to the others, "I think if we find Maude, we will find Melody." The two other security experts nodded in agreement.

"I think you may be right. I'll talk to the DCI." LT walked back into the room before the others. "DCI, my people think the Abbey is the place to look. They are going down there."

"Mr. Chadwick, I tend to agree with your people's analysis, but I must insist they have a suitable police presence with them." Turning to the three private security people standing by the door, he said. "My government and my superior all want to give you as much cooperation as possible, but Maude Hargrove is a British citizen, the Abbey is English soil, and you will be under our direction. Understood?"

Jeremy, Lilith, and Bellamy all nodded. "We need to get moving. It will be dark soon." Lilith said as she turned to get her kit bag from the foyer.

LT, Arthur, and Alfred joined the DCI in his car and Lilith, Jeremy, and Bellamy rode with Sergeant Russell. Lilith was used to driving London's streets, but she couldn't skirt the speed limits like the DCI or the Sergeant. The sun was just going down when the little group stopped at the Milton police station. DCI Applegate asked the men to stay in the car while he notified the locals that they would be working in their bailiwick. If backup was needed, it wouldn't do to make the locals angry.

xxxxx – Maude

Everything was ready for the morning. The American cow had been so drowsy Maude had had to force half of the bottle of water down her throat. The protein bar was uneaten and would stay there until her final meal. The last half bottle of water was also beside the cot for the morning.

Melody hadn't opened her eyes and Maude said nothing to her so there was no way she would know who had made her drink the drugged liquid. Maude had been careful not to let Melody know who had taken her or where she was, but after the first two or three bottles of water with the sedative in it, the woman didn't seem to notice much of anything. Just getting to the waste bucket and back onto the cot before she passed out was all she could manage and she didn't always do that well.

The last of the mess was cleaned up in the old Abbey kitchen, the fireplace was filled with papers, soiled clothes, and food wrappers to be burned. Maude wouldn't start the fire until after dark but this time, would not need to put it out before dawn. Maude would have Melody moved to the back of her car and they would be on the way to Budgies Neck.

Maude finished her meal, put the packaging in the fire to be burned with the rest, and looked over her travel route one last time. She didn't want to have to manage a map while she drove and getting lost was not an option. With Melody drugged and stuffed in the back of her car, she was not looking for any problems.

The alarm on her cellphone was set for midnight. She wanted to get some sleep and then finish her preparations before she had to deal with Melody one last time. A soothing cup of tea while she started the fire in the kitchen fireplace helped her relax enough to drift off to sleep. Tomorrow was the day when all of her problems would go away.

xxxxx – Outside the Abbey

The cars were parked on St. Joseph's Way. The lights were all off and the darkness was moonless and deep. Sergeant Russell spoke softly with DCI Applegate while the Americans whispered with Lilith. Their lordships stood by themselves.

"Arthur, I still find it hard to think that Maude would have hurt Melody. It's just not like her to do something, anything, which would harm another person." Alfred was careful not to let his voice get too loud. "All of this," he waved his hand at the police and the others waiting to help find Melody, "it just doesn't seem real. I'm just praying this nightmare is just that, a nightmare and we'll wake up."

Arthur patted Alfred shoulder. "Applegate was right, you know, it's so hard to know what people will really do. She must be sick or something. Melody wouldn't hurt anyone so she couldn't have seen her as a threat. I want Melody back, but I really hope Ms. Harbison is not the one who has taken her."

"I would also like to think this is all just some kind of mix-up and Melody will come back to us just as she was the night of her birthday. I have also prayed that she is unharmed and will be here in any moment." Arthur and Alfred walked a little way down from where the cars were parked. A slightly acrid smell floated on the air and caused Alfred to start sneezing. Arthur gave him his handkerchief.

After the sneezing subsided, Alfred turned to Arthur, "Why do you think she did it?"

The question caught Arthur off guard. "What do you mean? Maude?"

"No," Alfred continued. "Why do you thing the grandmother of Jillian Farr pushed her into Rand Oswin's arms long enough for her to get pregnant? Why do that? I mean, it was Victorian England and unless you were the Crown Prince, such things were unheard of in society."

"Hmm, not really. From what Melody was able to glean from the diary and journals of Juliet, the grandmother, it must have seemed logical to her. Her mother had escaped from France during the time of Napoleon. Her mother was only a child then and the whole thing must have been traumatic. The mother, Marguerite, would have related all of that to the grandmother when she was a girl. And, if it meant the substitute of one man for another to get the girl pregnant, then, I guess she could rationalize doing it." Arthur had looked at that part of the story very closely himself. It still left him wondering at the desperation to keep the marriage from being barren. The grandmother must have worried that if no child or children were forthcoming, perhaps the Farr family would have looked elsewhere for a better wife for Roland.

"You realize," Alfred added, "if Roland wouldn't have had an heir, the title and estates would have gone to Melody's family line. I think, and correct me if I'm wrong, that the next son, Edward, the vicar, had only girls and a wife who was unable to have more children." Alfred nodded toward LT, "I think the godfather of Melody didn't miss that point either."

"Alfred," Arthur began, "I have been aware of this since first reading the work Melody has done. LT's job is to look after his goddaughter and the only thing I can really think about now is that we find Melody so she can be looked after for many years to come."

Among the group of Americans, Jeremy had quietly slipped into the darkness. LT moved over to where the Police officers were standing in hopes of keeping their attention on anything other than the missing Marine.

Jeremy's dark attire blended into the darkness. One of the best pieces of equipment he had with him was his night-vision headpiece. With it, he could see where the grass and fallen leaves had been crushed by the wheels of a smallish car. The wheel base was a dead giveaway and the depth of the depressions made by the tires showed it was not a heavy vehicle.

He stayed out of what little light there was and moved within the shadows. Jeremy listened for the sounds of dogs or even a dog, but none was evident. Coming around a broad bend in the tract, the smell from the fireplace was getting heavier. Buildings, a barn, and other service structures could be made out in the darkness. His foot hit one of the cobbles and he froze.

The soft ground had been his friend as long as he made each footfall carefully. Now the surface had changed and he had to adjust his approach. Quietly, purposefully, he took each step and waited before the next. A loose cobble and he could make a noise which might be heard.

On his left, the great stone house of the Abbey rose into the dark. Sideling up to the corner, he took a mirror from his belt. The unbreakable plastic was first used at knee height to check for surprises around the edge of the building. Seeing nothing, he brought the mirror up to eye level and looked at the back of the house.

A soft light spilled from three windows. One of them seemed odd until he realized it was cleaner than the other two. *Hmm*, he thought, *whoever is in there must not have had a key. Looks like they had to break a window to get in and then replaced it.* People either wash all of the windows or none of them, not just one.

Thirty-five minutes from the time he left the group, he returned to give his report. DCI Applegate was not amused. "We have laws in this country and you just broke a number of them! Now I have requested a search warrant for the property, but until it arrives, I don't want to see you or any of you," motioning to Lilith and Bellamy, "private security people going onto that property. Do you understand me, I don't want to SEE, any of you do that!"

LT had his phone out and was punching in the number to the American Embassy's Liaison. Turning to the DCI, "I can help speed up that search warrant." Moving his attention back to the phone, "This is LT Chadwick, what help do you need to get a search warrant signed right now?"

The DCI was being sucked into the whirlwind that was LT Chadwick and his determination to find his god-daughter. Applegate turned just as Arthur and Alfred were moving toward the path taken by the security people. "No you don't! I may be pressed to allow these foreigners to run about the countryside without obeying the rules, but your lordships are British subjects and I can bloody well stop you! Stay put!"

Arthur and Alfred moved back toward the police car. The shapes of Lilith, Jeremy, and Bellamy had long since merged with the darkness. In the far distance, a siren could be heard coming from the village but abruptly stopped as it came within earshot of the Abbey. The local police came for backup with the siren silenced and the blue lights still flashing. The DCI motioned for the lights to be turned off. The road was again in darkness and the wait for the signed search warrant continued.

Jeremy took the lead. He had been down the tract before and was familiar with where things were. The three did not speak, but used hand signals which each could see with their night-vision gear. The earpieces were also used to transmit a series of clicks which each of the specially trained operators knew by heart. Survival on a mission depended on muscle memory and being aware of where each of your own people was and what they were doing. Everyone knew their lives depended on the teamwork they had learned on mission after mission in some very unfriendly places in the world.

Lilith held the middle position and Bellamy brought up the rear. Depending on what they would find when the time came, each person in the group could take whatever part was the most efficient. There was, of course, no guarantee this was the place or the person who had Melody, but the bits and pieces of information on Maude and the absence of the dogs, was enough for them to put a lot of confidence into the idea they would find Melody at the end of this path.

Nothing had changed since Jeremy had made his initial reconnoiter of the Abbey. The smoke still curled from the chimney, a little less than before, but it was still there. The smell had not improved, but it would take some time and a good breeze to dissipate. At the corner of the house, he motioned for everyone to stop. Carefully Jeremy peaked around the edge of the worn bricks. Nothing had changed.

A soft glow spilled from the windows and the doors to the shed were closed where the car was parked. But something didn't feel right. It took a few seconds for him to notice the door to the back of the house was ajar. It had been closed when he had been back here before. His hand signals told the others to be alert. Getting close to the ground and moving in the shadows along the wall, Jeremy made his way slowly toward the open door.

Maude was slowly getting back to sleep. The fire in the big fireplace was good for burning the items she wanted to be rid of, like the soiled items of Melody's, but this late in the spring it was too warm to be in the same room while the fire burned. The smell was another matter. The stench of the burning waste was almost more than Maude could bear. Sleepily, she had opened the door to the kitchen before lying back down on the cot and pushing herself to sleep. She knew the next day would be long and the more sleep, the better it would be for her.

Jeremy moved cautiously and at times he stopped to make sure he wasn't making any noise that would not blend in with the normal night sounds. The last few feet to the door and he was almost on his stomach. The muscle control he had was tremendous and the adrenalin his body produced in these situations helped give him the power he needed. Before looking in the door, he stopped again to check for any noise that might alert someone to his presence. Watching him, Lilith and Bellamy were amazed at his abilities.

Slowly Jeremy raised his head and looked into the room. His eyes swept the scene and he lowered himself from sight. In that brief moment his mind registered everything he had glanced at and processed the information. He had seen the large old table, two mismatched chairs, an ancient stove, fireplace, and the cot with a sleeping or reclining figure. The figure had their back to the door. In one part of the room he saw a door with a padlock on it, a couple of peep-holes drilled into it at different heights, and some wires running from a set of batteries. On the table were a closed laptop and a cell phone that laid on top.

The door with the padlock was of the greatest importance. Something was in there that the person in the cot wanted to keep secure but also needed to keep watch over for some reason. Jeremy pulled back from the door, inched his way to the corner of the Abbey, and turned to join the others. LT had notified the group that a warrant was signed but hadn't yet arrived.

The three retreated to a spot where Jeremy could give his report. The information was given, via earpiece, to LT. As LT listened, he could see a blue glow emanating from the police cars that were speeding from the next village, Fletcher's Pond. It was from this town, larger than Milton, where a magistrate had been rousted from his bed and directed to sign the search warrant.

DCI Applegate ordered the three people who were already on the grounds to return to allow the local police to serve the warrant. Jeremy exchanged a solemn look with Bellamy and Lilith. Jeremy said. "I don't like this. The police haven't any idea what we've seen. Who knows what's in that house or what she'll do. If Miss Harbison does have Melody, well, that to me says Melody is in danger. We need to be in there."

Lilith shrugged, "The local police will always want to take the lead in something like this. All we can hope to do is make sure they have the best information we can give them and backup when they need it." She motioned toward the road, "Let's go and see what we can do to help."

xxxxx – Maude

Maude's cell phone played a melody signifying it was time to wake up. She still had some work to do before it would be time to move the American. It took a few seconds for her to remember she was the one who had opened the door. She smiled to herself with the memory of getting up to allow a breeze that helped to take out the smell and bring in the fresh night air. Maude stretched and took a bottle of tea from the ice chest near the cot. It wasn't the same as having a cup of tea, but it would have to do until she got on the road.

The camera feed on her phone gave Maude a good look at the girl sleeping her drugged sleep. As usual, the cow hadn't moved since the last bottle of dosed water. The one she'd given the American that morning was lighter so she woke sooner, earlier in the evening. However, the one Maude had mixed up for Melody to drink that night was a heavier dose so she could make it until Maude had dumped the woman in the woods. She would have to start moving her in another hour and it was necessary to have her completely out. From the sleeping form, it looked like Maude had given her enough.

The ashes in the fireplace were almost out and except for a few scraps of charred cloth, it would be impossible to know what had been burned. Maude stirred them with a poker and looked around to see if anything else needed to go on the fire.

A quick check on her phone confirmed the weather report for Budgie's Nest was still for rain. Maude smiled. She could dump Melody in the woods and no one would know who she was. Hump, just a homeless drunk or junkie. No identification, no money, and the way she looked now, no one would want anything to do with her. Maude was just taking out the American trash.

xxxxx

Jeremy drew a brief diagram of the grounds he had seen, the room where someone, probably Maude was asleep on a cot, and the door with the padlock. DCI Applegate thanked him and started giving orders to the police officers who had come from Milton and Fletcher's Pond. Turning back to the people LT had brought to find Melody. "You can come with us, but stay back and don't get in the way. We can handle this; you just need to let us do our jobs. Understood?"

Lilith, Bellamy, and Jeremy nodded. "Good. Sergeant, did you call for that ambulance?" Sergeant Russell gave a slight nod. "OK, I think we're ready. Is everyone in position?" The police from Milton were over the wall and moving toward the Abbey from the front. One officer would stay there to guard the door in case it was used as an escape route. The others would advance to the left side of the door from where the light was coming and the ones from Fletcher's Pond were advancing to take a position on the right side of that door. All would signal when they were ready.

LT, Arthur, and Alfred moved to the edge of the wall and the path that led to the back of the Abbey. Jeremy, Bellamy, and Lilith were behind the police and spread-out so as to be in position if case they were needed.

No one is really sure where everything went wrong, but before the officers from Fletcher's Pond could get to the back door, the Milton police woman who was not standing at the front door, collided with a bucket near the rear door. The metal bucked went skidding across the cobbles making a terrible racket. The noise alarmed Maude. By the time the officers tried to open the now closed back door, Maude was armed and she'd fired a shot through the door to warn anyone who was trying to enter.

British police are proud of the fact they do not have to carry weapons to do their job. There are special armed units of the force who do have guns and each officer is supposed to have access to a weapon and know how to use it, but they are not, as a rule, carried on their persons or in their cars. A person shooting at an officer is not normal in the countryside, although, in London, it is not unheard of. The Milton and Fletcher's Pond police didn't have any guns and neither did the DCI or his Sergeant.

The addition of a gun changed things for DCI Applegate. He decided to try talking to Maude. Jeremy had seen a cell phone on the table in the room and Alfred was asked for the phone number he had for her. Being a part of the circle of friends, the DCI thought Alfred might have a better chance with talking Maude out of the Abbey than an unknown police officer.

Alfred used his phone to call Maude. He put it on speaker so everyone could hear. After several rings, Maude answered. "Alfred? … Alfred? … Is that you?" The voice was a bit shaky and unsure, but was definitely Maude Harbison's.

"Hi Maude. Yes, this is Alfred. Uh, Maude, … we, uh, I'm worried about you. What are you doing in this old place?"

"I'm, uh, I'm doing something for you, I mean, us. But, but you can't be here now. I'm not done." Her voice was becoming a little louder and more manic, "uh, you have to go away now and take whoever is here with you. I'll be back in London later tonight when I'm finished. You go away."

Arthur leaned over the phone and blurted, "Where is Melody? Do you have her? This is Sir Arthur Farr and I want to know where Melody is."

Maude half shouted, "Melody, Melody! Is that what this is about? Alfred did you bring these people here just to find out about Melody? I'm, … I'm, … go away!" The line went dead. The gathered group looked at each other. The DCI asked Alfred to call again. This time, the phone rang and rang and rang. Maude didn't answer.

Alfred laid the phone down. "Uh, look, let me go to the door and talk to her. Maybe we can end this without anyone getting hurt. We must find Melody and I think Maude is the only one who knows where she is."

"This is very dangerous," Arthur, visibly shaken, said. He put his hand on Alfred's shoulder, "let me go with you. Maybe we can convince her to give herself up. If nothing else, at least she's going to be arrested for having a gun and firing it at people."

DCI Applegate looked from Alfred to Arthur. "I shouldn't let you do this, but since you're the only one available to us whom she knows, well, OK, but don't stand in front of the door. Stand off to the side. My people will be right there. If you can get her to open the door to talk, we might be able to get her into custody without further incident. I have sent for some armed officers, but it will be several minutes before they come. Just be careful!"

Their lordships' moved toward the door with a couple of constables as guides. Bellamy, Lilith, and Jeremy were opening the lock on the front door so they could make their way in behind Maude. The great rooms of the old Abbey were deserted and almost completely devoid of furnishings. The house was dark but the night-vision gear made moving from room to room easy.

Near the back right side of the house, a door led to steps that would take them down to the old kitchen where Maude was armed and keeping the police out. A small aerosol can was used by Jeremy to lubricate the hinges of the old door to make it open quietly. Three quick blasts did the trick and without sound. Once open, the trio could hear Maude talking to someone. Silently, they moved down the short flight of stone steps and stood just beyond the weak light of the lamp Maude had placed on the big table.

At the rear, Alfred was trying to get Maude to open the door. "Maude, open this door. You know you're going to have to come out, why not do it now? Everyone has been worried about where you are. The police have talked to our friends, they even called your mother in Scotland and your father in Tenerife. So it's time to stop this and open the door."

The back and forth continued for another few minutes. Maude finally opened the door just enough to see outside. Speaking to no one in particular, Maude said, "Take the police away. All of you; just leave! I'll be back in London tonight and" addressing the remainder to Alfred in particular, "I would like to see you tonight … or … or anytime."

Arthur was getting impatient. He had been standing on the opposite side of the door from Alfred but, in his estimation, the conversation was not going well. Without thinking he stepped out of the semi-protected place he had occupied and said very forcefully, "Where is Melody? Do you know where she is?"

The trio at the foot of the stairs in the kitchen heard Maude's manic shriek and two rapid fire gunshots. Cat like, Lilith was across the room, had Maude pinned to the floor, and the gun out of the woman's reach. Bellamy and Jeremy came in just as the constables came through the back door. Outside, Arthur took one step back and then another before crumpling to the cobbles.

Paramedics from the emergency services hovered over the body of Sir Arthur Roland Farr, Viscount of Gibbons. A plastic tarp was placed over his body until the proper police attendant could remove the remains.

Inside the Abbey, Jeremy and Bellamy took the key that hung on a nail near the locked door. Opening it, the smell made both men take a step back. They could see, on the cot, something that looked like Melody's hair but the rest of the form was covered in two thin blankets. Constables and the DCI elbowed the pair aside as they went in to see if the woman was still alive.

Alfred came through the kitchen door as Melody was being taken out on a stretcher. Everyone turned to look at Maude when the air was rent by her loud cackle, "The American cow isn't as pretty now, is she Alfred?" The look Alfred gave to Maude made the color drain from the face of the unfeeling abductress.

LT looked at the state of his goddaughter as the emergency workers put her into the ambulance. The Americans and Lord Alfred were taken to the local hospital in the DCI's car. LT spent his time on the ride making arrangements for a private doctor and nurse to accompany him and Melody on the jet to Houston. First, however, it would be necessary to determine if Melody was going to live through the next several hours.

Aftermath

"**M**ISTER CHADWICK," DCI Applegate said forcefully without raising his voice. "I can't allow you to take this woman out of England. She has to give evidence! I have to question her! Taking her out of my jurisdiction is just not going to happen!"

LT Chadwick stood his ground. "Look, Applegate, she can't speak to anybody right now. The doctor isn't even sure she is going to make it through the next twenty-four hours." LT motioned toward the critical care unit where Melody was being taken care of. "You heard what he said, if Maude Harbison had been able to give Melody one, two maximum, more doses of this dog sedative, Melody would never wake up. As it is, she still hasn't come out of the sleep induced by the last dose."

LT spent the time from the rescue of Melody at the Abbey where Maude had held her on his cellphone with a doctor. He then notified the liaison at the American Embassy, spoke with the ambassador for three minutes, and spent the rest of the time trying to arrange for Melody to be taken back to Houston. It was the efforts to move his goddaughter that had upset the DCI and set off the problem of what would happen to Melody if she survived the next couple of days.

Bellamy was also on the phone. His job was to arrange transportation from the small regional hospital where they were currently treating Melody, back to London for the team. Jeremy and Lilith had all ridden with either the DCI or his detective sergeant (DS). Now they needed to find their own way back to the London house. Alfred was at the morgue with Arthur's body and would stay with it until he accompanied the Viscount, by train, back to the Cottage.

LT spoke with one of his cousins at St. Luke's Anglican Hospital in Houston. After informing George Harris of the circumstances, Dr. Harris was all business. "LT, you need to get her over here ASAP. I know of a great doctor in London who can take care of her until that can happen. Dr. Li is the best in her field. I'll get onto her but you get Melody to London and then, as quick as you can, get her here. I'll call back in a few minutes, as soon as I get things setup with Dr. Li."

While LT was on the phone, he didn't take his eyes from the small window high in the door of the room where the medical staff was working on Melody. After each call he resumed praying for his goddaughter and then plowed ahead into the next call. It was during one of these prayer preludes that his phone vibrated in his hand. He recognized the number of his cousin, Dr. George Harris.

"LT, OK, I have it all set with Dr. Li. She will be calling the doctor where you are shortly and making the arrangements to move Melody to London. She will be going to a private hospital and will probably be moved by air-ambulance. I'll start making plans for taking over her care here. If you need a doctor and nurse to travel with you to Houston, just tell Dr. Li and she can set it up for you. Bring the jet into Hobby Airport and we'll have a crew waiting for you to bring her into the hospital." George paused. "And LT, get here quickly."

The line went dead and for a few moments, LT just looked at the phone in his hand. A movement out of the corner of his eye pulled his attention back to the door to the room where Melody lay. The same doctor who had talked to him initially exited the room with his cellphone in a gloved hand. He nodded at LT as he walked past and stood in a corner of the waiting room while he took the call.

If what Cousin George had said was right, the call the doctor was taking was probably from a Dr. Li in London. It was a short call. The doctor slipped the phone into his pocket, peeled off his glove and stopped to talk to LT.

"It seems," nodding toward Melody, "your goddaughter is to have the services of the esteemed Dr. Li. That was her on the phone. I told her what I had found so far and she is sending a helicopter to us to take Miss Farr to London. If you would like to ride with her, there will be enough room."

"Doctor, I hope you don't mind, but she is the only child of my best friend. He died several years ago and she is not only my goddaughter, but all I have left of my friend."

The doctor shook his head. "Oh, no, I don't mind. I am at the limit of what we can do for her here. I'm glad she is going to be in such expert hands." Looking around the room, "I need to tell the DCI we are moving her. The helicopter will be here to get her soon and I need to let him know. Excuse me, I see him over there." The doctor hurried down the hallway were Applegate was deep in discussion with his DS, Russell.

LT's gaze returned to where Melody lay. He motioned for Bellamy, Lilith, and Jeremy to join him. His explanations to them were interrupted for only brief questions. Bellamy would be taking Lilith to the station after they reached the London house so she could get the Chunnel train back to Paris. Jeremy was heading back to his base to have a talk with his Colonel, and Mrs. Bellamy would be leaving for Houston to prepare the house for Melody's homecoming.

At the mention of homecoming, LT winced. He hoped and prayed that Melody would be going home, but now it would be a miracle for her to survive the next few hours. Everyone standing in the circle around LT knew it would be touch and go, but no one wanted to think it would come out badly.

xxxxx

The private air-ambulance settled onto the roof of the exclusive hospital where Dr. Li would see to Melody's care until LT could get her to Houston. The two nurses that rode with his goddaughter showed the economy of movement that marked them as experts in their field. LT hung back and tried not to be in anyone's way. After the stretcher was taken from the helicopter, LT jumped to the roof and ducked under the slow-turning rotor blades.

While the gurney carrying Melody was moved down a long corridor, LT was shown where he could wait for news. LT wasn't good at waiting, especially not on something like this, but nothing he could do would make things better or worse. He had done all he could in getting her here, now he needed to let the doctors do their work.

A little gray-haired lady in a nursing-sister's garb came to ask him if he wanted any tea. The pained smile he gave her was returned by a warm smile. "You just sit here and I'll bring the tea. Everything always looks better after a cup of tea, trust me on that."

Alone in the waiting room, LT sat with his thoughts. Just before the chopper picked up Melody to bring her to London, Alfred had come to see LT. Everyone else, except for the DCI and his DS had left. Alfred could barely speak.

"LT, I … uh …" words failed the young man. LT put his hand on his shoulder and Alfred looked him in the eyes. "I am so … uh … so very sorry for what has happened to Melody and … well, uh, and poor Arthur. I just feel it is all my fault."

LT shook Alfred's shoulder. "Now you listen here," the older man said sternly, "Maude is the only one who is responsible for what she did, both to Melody and to Arthur. Don't try to make it out that it was something you did or didn't do because that is placing the blame where it doesn't belong. Nobody, and I mean nobody thinks you are the one who should take responsibility for what she did. No one."

Alfred nodded his head. "Thank you for that. I, uh, well, I will be taking Arthur back to the Cottage. I talked to the Vicar and we'll probably do the funeral in a couple of days. I want to stay close to Melody, but, well," his voice trailed off.

LT could see the pain in the man's face. "Don't worry. I'll keep you posted as to her condition. You take care of Arthur. Let me know when the service is and if I can, I'd like to come. Can you please do that for me?

Alfred nodded, turned, and left.

The clatter of the cups on the tea cart jolted LT from his thoughts. The lady was back and it looked like cake was going to be part of the tea. "I'm Sister Agnes and while we wait to find out how your goddaughter is doing, we can sit and have our tea. The kitchen had a lovely cake ready for us. Can I serve you some?"

LT began to relax. Whatever this woman did at this hospital, she was excellent at taking care of people's fears. Before he realized what was happening, Sister Agnes had given him a second cup of tea and a third piece of cake. Tummy full and the relaxing effects of the tea had finally taken hold. Sister Agnes left him covered in a light blanket with the lights dim.

xxxxx

Dr. Li peeled off her plastic gloves, raised the level of the lightening in the waiting room, and stood in front of the sleeping form of the large, white-haired American. *So, this is the man that*

governments and hospital administrators on two continents listen too,
Dr. Li cleared her throat rather loudly.

LT quickly came fully awake. Before him stood a tiny Eurasian lady in a doctor's white coat. The name tag said her name was Dr. Li. Dr. B. Li.

Dr. Li backed up as LT stood to his full height in front of her. "I'm Dr. Li. And you, must be Mr. Chadwick. We need to talk about your goddaughter."

LT's attention was completely engaged. "Please, just call me LT. What about my goddaughter?"

For the next twenty minutes the doctor explained Melody's condition. LT tried to keep his questions to a minimum, but when Dr. Li got too deep into medical terminology he didn't hesitate to ask what something was or the implications of the treatment. "So, what you're telling me is for the next three days" LT started to say.

"At least" Dr. Li interjected.

"Mm yes, at least three days, you want to put Melody into a drug-induced coma. While she is in this coma, you're saying you are going to try cleaning the stuff Maude gave her out of her kidneys, liver, and brain by using a combination of medications, mechanically washing the blood with dialysis, and letting the body, primarily the brain, heal itself? But isn't part of the problem now the fact she isn't waking up? Why would putting her under be any different than what is already happening?"

Dr. Li looked up at the tall man. "Mr. Chadwick, uh, LT, her kidneys and liver can't handle the medication she was given. I have to help her get that out of her body and the best way to do it is with the dialysis. As for the need to put her in a controlled coma, let me explain it this way." Dr. Li paused before she continued.

"The medication this woman gave your goddaughter is for use by vets to sedate dogs, cats, or even large animals. It all depends on the doses given. The police tell me they found several dogs, large ones, about the size of Melody, buried on the property where she was found. The woman tested this drug on the dogs and from what the forensic vet told me, she over-dosed all except the last one. I don't know exactly how much of this medication was given to Melody. What I do know is her body needs to be cleansed of the drug and allowed to heal. This treatment is how that will happen."

LT started to interrupt but Dr. Li was not finished with him. "I don't mind your camping here, I understand that, but there are other things you should do to keep yourself well. I knew Arthur, if I could get away to go to the funeral, I would, but …" the doctor shrugged as she looked around the ICU. "Go say goodbye to him for Melody, for yourself, and if you would, for me. I will be on the phone with you if anything changes and I'm sure, you can't keep yourself from visiting her at least three or four times a day."

LT nodded. "When can I take her back to Houston?"

Dr. Li smiled. "Ah, yes, your cousin George told me you would want to know that. If all goes well, and that is a big IF, sometime next week. She can recover in Houston, but as George said, if I didn't treat her here, he would have to bring me there to do this treatment. I am only one of a handful of people in the world who do what I do." As she turned to go she smiled, "you're lucky to have me."

LT watched as the diminutive doctor left the room. Pulling out his cellphone, he dialed his cousin George at the hospital in Houston. The two men spoke for several minutes.

"George, what did she mean by that? "We're lucky to have her." Why, what is it she does that is so special?"

"LT, just that. She is originally from Hong Kong. Her father was in the British Foreign Service when the colony was still under colonial rule. In the late 1970s, before the handover to the Chi-Coms, the family moved back to England. Her mother was a very accomplished surgeon, but she was Chinese and the family was afraid the British government might limit immigration of native-born citizens of Hong Kong."

George continued. "Barbara, uh, Dr. Li, did her undergraduate work at Oxford and her medical training in Edinburgh. About five years out of her residency, she married a Brit who wanted to live in Hong Kong. They moved there, but it was very different than the colony she had left. What she did find, was a doctor who was working on addictions. She spent her time there studying under him. When her marriage ended, she returned to London, opened her practice, and I have been trying to steal her for the last ten years."

LT was alarmed. "Hey, hey, wait! What does what happened to Melody have to do with addiction? Explain that!"

George clucked his tongue, "calm down, I'll explain. The medication Melody was given can have the same effect as narcotics. She was given high enough doses for several days, kept from food or drink that might have alleviated some of the effects, and even now is in danger. We don't know if she is addicted, but she might, actually very well might be, and we need to clean the drug out of her and heal the addiction center of the brain. Just let Dr. Li do what she does best and trust me. What she said was true, if Melody was here I would have to send for Dr. Li to treat her."

"Go get some sleep. You've been short on any meaningful rest for days and need to take care of yourself. Dr. Li will call if Melody's condition changes. You staying at the hospital and worrying over her like an old mother hen is not going to make this go any faster or change the possible outcomes." George was worried for his cousin. The Harris family was a part of the pool of beneficiaries who depended on LT Chadwick to run Chadwick Holdings so besides being a doctor, he had a personal interest in LT's health.

"Dr. Li told me she knew this guy where Melody was staying. Are you going to attend the funeral? If so, you need to think about that and your other duties." For the first time, George's mood lightened, "besides, I don't need to send two ambulances to Hobby, one for Melody, and one for you."

"OK, ok, got it." LT broke in. "Let me go look at her again and I'll go get some sleep. I also want a decent cup of coffee. Do all hospitals make a mess of it?"

Dr. George Harris laughed at his cousin. "We do that so people don't hang around any longer than necessary. I'll talk to you soon. Dr. Li said she would have someone give me updates. If you need me though, you have the number. Bye cuz!" The line went dead.

xxxxx

The black taxi pulled up in front of the Mayfair home of the Farr family. As he paid the cabby, he looked at the front door and saw the black wreath that hung there. Before LT's foot landed on the top step, the door opened to reveal Bellamy.

"Good morning Mr. LT, how is Miss Melody?" Bellamy asked as he greeted his former employer. "We have all been so concerned about her."

LT gave Bellamy a full rundown on the condition of his god-daughter and Bellamy's employer. "So, it is going to be a few days before we can move her to Houston. Is there any chance there is a cup of coffee in the house?"

Bellamy nodded. "Mrs. Bellamy has breakfast ready for you. I called the hospital about twenty minutes ago and they said you had just left the hospital. She wanted to make sure you had a decent meal."

LT looked at Bellamy, "I thought you had put Mrs. Bellamy on the plane back to Houston? Wasn't she going to get things ready at Farr House for Melody's homecoming?"

Mrs. Bellamy brought a plate of eggs, sausages, and bacon into the breakfast room, put it at the place set for LT, and turned to address his concerns. "Mr. LT, the girls, Glen and Paul, can take care of the house. I am better used here and at Farr Cottage for the funeral of his lordship. Who else will feed you?"

Sitting down at the table, "Okay, okay, I surrender. Really, I'm glad you both stayed." For the next few minutes LT filled in both Bellamy and Mrs. Bellamy about the condition of their employer. "It may be some days before we can take her back to Houston. And," nodding to Mrs. Bellamy, "you're right, I think you will both be needed at this house and Farr Cottage. We also need to pack Melody's things so they can be sent home. Thank you both for staying."

The food, coffee, and a chance to decompress were beginning to take their toll on LT. He was barely able to keep his eyes open as Bellamy poured him a second cup of coffee. In the distance, the chime of the front door bell could be heard.

Seconds after going to answer the door, Bellamy returned with a silver salver holding an expensive looking linen business card. "Sir, a Mr. Smyth, solicitor, to see you."

LT picked up the card, read it, and put it back on the salver. "Bellamy I need some sleep. Can't this wait?"

Bellamy handed the card back to LT. "Sir, he said he was Lord Arthur's family solicitor and needed to see you, urgently."

Resigning to the fact he would have to see the man, LT put his napkin down, and directed Bellamy to show the gentleman into the study. "Oh, and bring us some coffee, I need some to keep from sleeping."

Mr. Smyth was a balding gentleman of at least 70 years of age. His suit was carefully tailored, wore nothing flashy, and spoke in a modulated tone. He reminded LT of vanilla pudding. It must have been the yellowish-white fringe of hair below his shiny pate.

"Mr. Smyth, my name is LT Chadwick, what can I do for you?" LT shook the man's hand and sat down at the desk across from the visitor.

"Mr. Chadwick, my family has been solicitors to the Farr family for the last five generations. With the death of Lord Arthur Farr, there are some things I need to do to fulfill my duties and that of my family's firm." The man reached into his briefcase and extracted a file.

Bellamy entered the room and LT held up his hand to stop Mr. Smyth from continuing. "Mr. Smyth, please, call me LT and would you like some coffee?"

The guest nodded to Bellamy and continued on with his task. "Yes, uhm, LT," the solicitor opened the file on the desk. "Early last week, Lord Arthur called me, urgently, and asked me to come see him. He wanted to inquire about the titles and estate he holds in trust for the Farr family. It seems some information Miss Melody Farr was developing might prove he did not have the Farr family bloodline he had always thought himself to possess. I left here and told him I would look into the matter for him. On Saturday morning last, he call very early and informed me he was sure he was not of the Farr bloodline. He said you had done a DNA test when he and Lord Alfred Oswin were visiting in Houston." Smyth looked up from the paper from which he was reading.

"May I ask, sir, why you would have done this?" Smyth looked LT in the eyes as if to challenge him.

"Well, Melody Farr is my goddaughter and the daughter of my best friend. Since her father died, I have looked after her and her mother. After her mother passed away I've tried to watch over Melody. I am also the trustee of the estate her father left her." LT took a sip of coffee. "Both gentlemen, Arthur and Alfred, were interested in her as a marriage partner. There was some talk that the two men may be related and I wanted to know if it was true. I was and always will look out for the best interests of Melody."

The last was said a bit more forcefully than he intended, but he was tired, worried, and didn't see the point in the conversation. Mr. Smyth, however, returned to his papers. "No problem, perfectly understandable."

"During the meeting on Saturday morning, I was told to bring some papers I had been asked to prepare that changed the will of

Sir Arthur, except for the personal bequests, and before ten that morning, they had been signed and stamped." Again Mr. Smyth looked up from his papers. "Will you be attending the funeral and reception at Farr Cottage?"

LT shook his head. "Mr. Smyth, right now the only thing I am sure of is that as soon as you leave, I will go try to get some sleep. I haven't had much these last few days. My goddaughter is still not out of the woods and as soon as she can be moved, I will take her back to Houston. This is all I know. Anything else, well, that is all open to change."

Mr. Smyth gathered his papers. "Mr. Chadwick, uh, sorry, LT, I will be reading the bequests at Farr Cottage after the service at the local church. The rest of the will can be left for another day, but please don't wait too long. Decisions will have to be made."

LT reached over the desk to shake the man's hand while Bellamy waited to show him to the door. "What decisions? What does it have to do with me or Melody?"

Surprised, the man turned. "Because LT, Melody inherits everything and I would suppose that until she recovers, you will be acting on Lady Melody Farr's behalf."

<h1 style="text-align:center">Futures</h1>

The private jet touched down on the runway at Hobby Airport in Houston at mid-day, taxied to the general aviation area of the field, and was met by an ambulance sent by St. Luke's Anglican Hospital. LT's cousin, George. Dr. Harris was at the hospital waiting for Melody, the private nurse from England, and Dr. Barbara Li. LT and the Bellamy's were met by LT's car and driver. Melody, still in a drug-induced coma, was unaware of anything going on around her.

Dr. Li and the nurse rode with Melody. LT would stay at the hospital while he sent his car to take Bellamy and Mrs. Bellamy to Melody's home, Farr House. LT wanted to see about getting Melody settled in her room, talk to George about her condition, and possibly learn what would be happening with his goddaughter.

The flight into Houston was difficult for LT. He could usually nap on a long flight. In business, it made sense to use the time either to work or sleep. Many times he had gotten off a plane, attended a meeting that had to be conducted in person, and then returned to his plane for the trip home, all in the space of less than a day. Yes, sleep had never been a problem before.

Two rows of seats were removed from the plane to accommodate the gurney that Melody had been secured to while in the hospital in London. There were IV's, a breathing tube, and other things attached to her and she had to be kept from accidently pulling something out or loose. The nurse sat with her and Dr. Li checked her almost every half-hour, but from where LT was sitting, he could look at her all the time.

She had never, in all the years he had known her, looked so helpless. Even as a baby she had been an impish little girl with her full head of curly chestnut hair and the twinkle in her eyes. Now, her skin had a grayish pallor, the hair was lank and lifeless, and she seemed to sink into the sheets and blankets that covered her.

While he watched her, the last few days replayed in his mind.

The funeral had been very well attended by staff, friends, and people with whom Arthur had worked in various ministries. Of course Alfred was there and treated the whole affair as if it had been his brother who had been shot and not a newly discovered distant cousin. At the last moment, Jeremy was also able to attend.

Alfred and Jeremy had been in contact with LT several times a day from the time Melody was first taken to the hospital. Both men worried over the woman they loved and wanted to be kept apprised of the situation on an almost hourly basis. Alfred had spent the better part of one day arranging the service for Lord Arthur which kept him busy for a time and Jeremy was in meetings with his Colonel once he returned to his base of operations. Just as the service was starting in St. Alban's Church, Jeremy slid into the pew next to LT.

The surprised look on LT's face was soon relaxed when Jeremy mouthed the words "we'll talk later." As the Reverend Charles Paxton intoned the service, the eulogies were given by Alfred and a don from Oxford who had been good friends with Arthur. The interment was in the family vault. The condition of Melody was the only thing on LTs mind.

LT had not expected to return to the Cottage for the reception, but Alfred had insisted. Mrs. Bellamy spent the time during the funeral packing up Melody's things at the Cottage. Bellamy secured her work from the Library and saw to any other items she had brought with her. In going through her papers, Bellamy noticed a large brown envelope from France, and simply added it to the stack of documents. The information Melody had requested on the d' Auffay line had arrived.

The solicitor, Mr. Smyth had come down from London to read the bequests. He buttonholed LT and insisted he sit in as Melody's executor. The interested parties left the rest of the guests to the cakes, tea, coffee, and brandy to spend a few minutes learning what they had been bequeathed by their employer.

Nedda and her husband John were given a modest sum of money and the free-rent of one of the cottages on the estate for as long as they wished to live there. The couple knew the cottage and were happy to take advantage of the bequest. Lily, the day maid, was given a sum of 500 pounds sterling for each year she had been employed at the Cottage. Her eight years of service netted her a tidy sum. Mrs. Jones, the retired cook from the house in London was also awarded a sum of money and the continued rent-free use of the apartment above the garage where she currently lived. Her niece Angie was given a thousand pounds.

After the bequests were read and each person had left. Mr. Smyth again tried to speak with LT. "My work is done here. Our firm has been the solicitor for this family for generations, but you might wish to go with new people. I can give you recommendations if you like." The man said as he packed his briefcase.

LT stood before him. "Is there some reason why your firm, uh family, would not wish the relationship to continue?"

Mr. Smyth stopped what he was doing, thought a moment, and looked LT straight on. "No, but what we wish is not important, it is what Lady Melody and you, as her agent, would like.

What if, hmm, we agreed to stay on, temporarily of course, until Lady Farr is again able to make decisions for herself and with your counsel, a more permanent judgment can be reached?"

LT smiled, "That sounds good to me. Let's leave it at that." He offered his hand to the man, they shook, and LT asked him to have a brandy before he left.

Smyth shook his head. "Thank you, no, I don't drink. I will send your office a copy of the will and any other items that may be of interest and you can always reach someone from the firm." Taking the overstuffed briefcase, the man turned, and left.

Jeremy saw the door to the study open and the lawyer leave. Before LT could get away he wanted to talk to him. Grabbing a glass of wine from a passing server, he headed in to give LT some explanation for his attendance at Arthur's funeral and wake.

LT had been surprised to see the young man. Jeremy had left his unit as they were about to go into the field so he could help find Melody. He was only gone from his base for a few days and as soon as Melody had been found in the Abbey belonging to Maude Harbison's family, he had returned to his outfit. That was less than a week ago and here he was, back in England. LT was getting concerned the Marine captain would run into trouble with his job and his commitment to the Marine Corps.

The first part of their discussion concerned Melody and what Dr. Li was doing about her care. "We will be leaving for Houston in a few days. Dr. Li assures me the treatment is going along well, but I don't see any change. They haven't woken her yet from the coma and until they do, there is no guarantee of her mental condition." LT looked down and smoothed his tie, "there is no telling what kind of state her mind will be in. The best we can hope for is that she remembers little of her captivity and her brain is clear of the drug, but on the other end, if she does remember or the drug has permanently damaged her, it might take years, if possible, if it's even possible, to bring her back to the way she was going in."

"LT, that is about what one of the docs from the base told me just this morning on the way to England; we were on the same flight. I want to thank you for the updates, I don't think I could focus on my work if I didn't have you keeping me abreast of Melody's condition." Jeremy looked at his watch. "I have to leave her in the next fifteen minutes if I'm to make my flight back to the base." Looking back at LT, Jeremy continued. "I had a long talk with the Colonel and, well, I have an assignment in the field that starts in the morning. However, after this last assignment, I'm taking on a different job."

LT looked hard at the young man, "You're not thinking about leaving the service, are you?"

Jeremy smiled, "No, no what I am going to do is something I've been offered before but was reluctant to take, I'm going on to a desk job." The young man took a drink of his wine and continued. "For the past eight months or so, my Colonel has been after me to be a permanent liaison in the energy sector. I am to be based in the U. S. with the rank of Major. Until now, I was happy to spend my time in the field, but now … well … let's just say I have personal reasons for wanting to be in the United States as much as possible."

As he set the empty glass on the desk, Jeremy shook LT's hand, turned and headed for the door. "I'll be out of contact for a few days, but as soon as I can, I'll call." Turning back again to face LT he said, "Take care of my girl for me." Without another word he was gone.

A movement near Melody jolted LT from his memories of the funeral and wake. The nurse periodically checked her patient's vital signs and LT's attention was drawn back to his goddaughter.

She looked so small on the gurney that had been strapped into the plane. Dr. Li had estimated that Melody had lost more than fifteen pounds since her birthday. She had always been so well proportioned and no weight loss or gain was necessary. Now, she looked almost emaciated. LT prayed again for her recovery and return to good health.

The limousine turning into the entrance to the hospital brought LT back to the present. The driver opened his door and LT instructed him to take the Bellamys to Farr House and then return for him. He didn't know how long Cousin George was going to let him stay, but whatever happened, he would be sleeping in his own bed this night.

Dr. George Harris was one of the long line of Harris doctors who was descended from Elbeth Chadwick and Dr. John Harris. Both of them had been blessed with red hair and George Harris still had a tinge of red mixed with his graying mane. At more than six feet, he and LT also showed the traits of Big Red Chadwick, the brother of Elbeth.

George was waiting for the ambulance to arrive at one of the off-loading bays near the emergency entrance. An orderly showed LT to the suite where Melody would be staying and from the commotion in the hall, LT could tell the doctors, nurse, and Melody were in the hallway just outside the door. LT left to let the staff do what had to be done and went to the second room of the suite.

The sitting room was outfitted with a couple of comfortable chairs, a long sofa, table, and chairs for eating, along with a mini-fridge and microwave. Everything a room could need for a family or loved ones to stay while a person close to them was in the hospital. LT had waited in a room much like this when his mother had surgery many years ago, but the level of elegance had been increased along with the difficulty in being assigned to one. LT had specifically asked his cousin to accommodate Melody in style and it looked like he was giving his best.

LT had sat long enough on the plane coming over and didn't want to do the same here. He wanted to know how his goddaughter was doing and what the program for her care would be now that she was home. It seemed he had done nothing but wait for news since she had gone missing, but at least now he knew where she was.

A shudder went through his generous frame when he remembered the last visit from DCI Applegate. The morning before they left London, was that only yesterday? No matter, it was the visit from the chief inspector that bothered him. Applegate told him the girl, Maude Harbison, who had taken Melody was being very cooperative. She was almost too talkative and a court appointed psychiatric exam was to be done to determine if she was able to stand trial for the kidnapping of Melody and the murder of Arthur Farr.

The Abbey had been processed. Several large dogs were found buried in the area around the kitchen garden and tests showed they had all been given the same drug as Melody. The abduction had not been a spur-of-the-moment thing either. Maude had first focused on Melody at the dinner party Alfred had given at his house the night before Melody left to return to Houston. When Maude heard about her departure, she had tried to put Melody out of her mind, but when Arthur and Alfred left to spend more than a month in the United States at Melody's estate, Farr House, Maude began to make plans in case Melody was indeed a threat.

DCI Applegate closed his notebook and looked at LT. "Take her ladyship away, get her to Houston where she can be treated. I doubt if we shall need any testimony from Lady Melody for the trial. The illegal firearms charge and shooting death of Lord Arthur will be enough. She disputes nothing but is quite willing to plead guilty to all charges. Maude Harbison shall never be a threat in the future."

Applegate cleared his throat before continuing. "I hope you and her ladyship will not think badly of us here. From my information, everyone had a very high opinion of your goddaughter and now that she has property in England, well, we do hope to have her visit us again."

LT frowned at the last remark, "DCI, thank you for that report and the sentiment. I have plans to leave with Melody tomorrow. The central focus for her is to recover from this ordeal. Any plans she may have in the future, well, that is too far ahead to be thinking. First health, then plans." Bellamy was at the door to see the chief inspector out.

"Bellamy, thank you for the assist. You and the others did a super job of it and it will be remembered. Next time you're here, perhaps a pint down at the local?" Bellamy nodded his assent as he closed the heavy oak door.

The door to Melody's room opened and LT couldn't see her for the number of medical personnel surrounding her bed. George, Dr. Li, and the English nurse left the room but others came to take their places around the comatose patient. The nurse was led away by a resident who would show her where she could get something to eat before going to a hotel. Dr. Li and George motioned LT to the sitting area.

Dr. George Augustus Harris III, MD, cousin of LT, began. "Dr. Li and Nurse Margaret have finished giving us a very thorough case briefing on Melody. She has been officially handed off to my staff. Nurse Margaret will be leaving to return to London tomorrow afternoon but Barbara, uh, Dr. Li will stay on for a few days." George could barely conceal his admiration for Dr. Li, but now it was time to get down to business.

"Dr. Li and I think we should begin the process of waking Melody in the morning. Some of the drugs she has been given to keep her in the coma will be stopped this evening, but it will take time for them to leave her system. I'd say we will get started about seven or eight. If you want to stay here tonight, that sofa makes a bed or just make sure you are here in the morning before we start. I know Melody doesn't know Dr. Li, nor any of the staff here, and may not remember me. She needs to see someone she knows when she starts waking up and it should be you. Once she is stable, we can take over, but initially, you need to be here." LT nodded his agreement.

Turning to Dr. Li, George told her about the arrangements that had been made for her in a local hotel. "It's within walking distance of the hospital and has a four-star restaurant. I would like you to be my guest." Turning to LT, "of course, you can come too."

LT knew he needed to get home. The invitation was not really one his cousin wished him to accept. George wanted to have the lovely Dr. Li to himself. "No George, I haven't slept in my own bed for weeks. I'll call my driver and be back early in the morning for Melody."

George smiled, LT had understood and was cooperating. "I'll see you in the morning." LT said his goodbyes and left.

xxxxx

The curtains were drawn over the window and the main light in the room was dimmed. Equipment that had been used to feed, breath, and address sanitary issues for Melody were slowly removed. The last of the tests had been made and Dr. Li believed it was time to awaken the girl.

LT stood at the foot of the bed and tried to stay out of the medical personnel's way. When they needed him, he would be at hand, but it could take a while. George assured him that everything was looking fine, but seeing Melody like this, he wasn't sure she would ever be the same. A commotion in the room next to Melody's drew LT's gaze and he saw Jeremy Higgins arrive.

Dr. Li frowned at the interruption. "I would like as much quiet as possible. We don't want to frighten Melody. She has been in a state of total blackness for the last 12 days and we need to ease her back." Looking at where Jeremy stood, "young man, please wait in the sitting room until we call you." Nodding to one of the nurses, "nurse, please close the door."

"Good, the time is now, 8:23. Let's begin." Dr. Li removed a syringe from the tray next to the bed and injected the pinkish liquid into the port of the IV in Melody's arm. The liquid disappeared into the flow from the bottle of saline that hung above. Minutes ticked by and nothing happened. At 8:43 Dr. Li took a second syringe and injected it into the port and at 9:00 the third and last syringe was administered. Dr. Li looked around at the gathered company, "Now we wait. It may take a few minutes or maybe hours."

Dr. Li had taken great pains to explain what the medically induced coma would mean, how it would look from Melody's side, and some of things they could expect. For many people, coming out of this would trigger nightmare or hallucinogenic type dreams. Having the lights dim, noise at a minimum, and a familiar voice at her side would or at least should, reduce the possibilities of these less than optimum effects. Melody's mind needed to heal and adding trauma to her cure was not what Dr. Li wanted to effect.

Two hours later, the first signs of voluntary movement began to appear. In another thirty odd minutes her eyes began to flutter and a slight moan could be heard coming from her throat. A nurse opened a packet of lemon glycerin swabs and applied them to Melody's lips and another type was used in each nostril. The oxygen cannula was replaced so the flow would help Melody to breathe and to oxygenate her blood. A cool cloth wiped her brow and hands. Before the third hour had passed, her eyes opened to see the shock of white hair and friendly face of LT. A slight whisper escaped her lips which was barely audible, "Pinky" was all Melody managed to say.

xxxxx

LT and Jeremy took turns sitting with Melody as she drifted in and out of sleep. Both men were amazed and concerned that she could sleep given the fact she had been "out" for so long. Dr. Li was quick to point out that Melody's body needed to readjust to consciousness and this was how she was coping. "You will find she spends more time awake and alert as the hours roll by. Take it easy with her. She may start to question you, this is good, but please don't be alarmed if she asks you the same or a similar question more than once."

Through the night and into the next day the scenario Dr. Li had mentioned seemed to play out. Melody did start to ask questions the more alert she was while awake, but she did re-question both men on more than one occasion. By the next day, with both men exhausted from their vigil, Melody finally awoke as herself.

Melody slipped the oxygen cannula from under her nose, tried sitting up, and while fumbling for the control to raise the back of the bed, pushed the nurse's call-button. The disembodied voice emanating from the speaker on the wall behind the bed woke the two men from their naps. Melody was hungry.

Dr. Li had ordered a clear liquid first meal be brought to Melody when she expressed hunger. The two men watched while first the broth and then a juice was consumed. Melody tolerated both well and a soft meal was promised for later. "You just wait until I can get some real food into you," LT said, "brisket and the fixin's will put you right!" The relief in his voice was palpable.

Questions flowed like rain and the men answered as best they could or thought was prudent. Melody was flabbergasted to learn who her captor was and expressed sympathy for the state of mind Maude must have suffered to have been so wrong about her intentions toward anyone.

The subject of Arthur soon surfaced. LT looked at Jeremy, but before the question was answered Dr. Li and Dr. George Harris came into the room. LT introduced his cousin George to Melody again and this time, she remembered who he was.

"Melody," George began, "Dr. Li tells me you are making wonderful progress. Today we will be getting you out of bed and have you sit in a chair. I know you have been sitting in bed, but it's time to make progress in your treatment. And, later, if all goes well, there is an in-patient rehabilitation facility nearer your home where we want to take you for the next few weeks while you regain your strength. Their physical-therapy program is very good for cases like yours. How does that sound to you, ready to get closer to going home?"

Melody looked around at the two doctors, LT, and Jeremy. "I really do want to go home, but being closer will make it easier on LT and Jeremy. They just haven't been getting any sleep."

Dr. Li chuckled and stepped up to the bed. "I have a therapist coming now to get you up and then, well, I must get back to my hospital. I'll be leaving this afternoon to return to London." Noticing the pained look on George's face Dr. Li continued, "Yes, George, I really do have other patients. This is a grand hospital and your offer to stay is generous, but London is my home." Taking Melody's hand, she gave it a little squeeze but without another word, turned and left. Dr. Li's work was done.

xxxxx

Melody progressed quite well. She was moved from the hospital to the rehabilitation center where she grew stronger each day. Three weeks after entering the center, she was cleared to leave. Melody was anxious to go home.

Her time at the rehabilitation hospital hadn't just been about her physical condition, but also her mental health. Trauma such as what she had suffered at the hands of Maude Harbison, needed to be addressed. Dr. Pollard and Melody spent an hour each day talking over what happened, and his assessment was the medicine she had been given had done no detectable harm to her memory. He was also able to report she seemed quite well adjusted.

The adjustment he detected in her was helped by LT and Jeremy. As Melody talked to them, they were able to fill in information about what happened to her. The most traumatic was the news that Arthur was dead. Tears flowed freely when she first was told he had died. More came as she learned how and where he was shot and by whom. By the time LT got to re-counting the funeral and wake, Melody was almost "cried-out" as her late mother would have called the end of the tears.

"I remember Smyth. He came to see Arthur at the London house a few days before my birthday. The card he had was so strange, it simply said "Smyth" with no other words. Arthur said they had been around for so long they were way beyond "Smyth and Sons" or "Smyth Brothers." They would need a huge card to list the generations that still worked at the firm. He said if you needed to be told who Smyth's was, they wouldn't want you as a client." Melody sighed. "I just wish Arthur hadn't changed his will. I told him we had no proof of the connection between him and Alfred or where it might have happened, but, I guess he went with the information he had read in my readings of the journals of Jillian's grandmother."

LT looked down at his well-polished boots. "Actually, he did have some proof. After you were taken, we were all together in the dining room in the London house looking at some photos the police had provided us with when the subject came up. He was feeling guilty for you being in England and in harm's way but I knew better and told him so. I, uh, well, I have the proof of the connection between Alfred and Arthur. It confirmed what he believed. He signed the changes to the will the next day."

Melody looked carefully at LT. "But, proof would need to be DNA! Where would you have …" Her voice trailed off. "When? In Houston? Why did you do it?"

"I did it because it is my job to look after you. You came back early from England and I wanted to know what had happened. Then there is the tale of the two men who were interested in you and the possibility there was a family tie between them." Sounding a bit sterner than he had expected. "I did what needed to be done or at least what I thought was necessary. If I had to do it over, I would do the same."

"OK, ok, ok. I give up. Can we just, please, take me home?" Melody was packed and ready to leave. Jeremy slipped out to get a wheelchair.

"Get in and I'll take you home." Jeremy ordered. "LT's car should be down stairs and all of the paperwork has been signed. Let's go!"

The short drive to her house was the first Melody had been out since the ride in the ambulance from the hospital to the clinic. As the car turned on the drive that ran past her house, the anticipation of seeing her house, the church across the road, and the familiar gate with the dragon, had Melody on the edge of her seat. The limousine pulled up in front of the house and before the driver could open her door, Bellamy was there to help her out.

"Welcome home Miss Melody. The staff is waiting in the hall." Bellamy walked behind her and LT. Jeremy came in just behind him. Mrs. Bellamy, Paul, and Glen all gave a cheery "Welcome Home" as Melody thanked each one for all they had done for her while she had been in the hospital and clinic.

"Your cards and visits were so wonderful. It can be so lonely being cooped up like that. Thank you so much." Melody looked at Mrs. Bellamy. "Do we need to do some menus or can that wait until tomorrow?"

Mrs. Bellamy smiled, "Tomorrow will be just fine." Looking at the maids, "why don't you two give Miss Melody a hand? I'm sure she wants to change out of the clothes she had to wear at the clinic."

Melody started up the stairs but turned to tell Bellamy to get LT and Jeremy a drink while she changed. "I'll be right back down. I want to see the new pool and lanai enclosure."

Twenty minutes later a more relaxed Melody joined her guests. "I am so happy to be home!" she exclaimed. "I just had to take a minute to shower in my own bathroom. Something about public facilities in the clinic just wasn't clean enough."

Bellamy handed his employer a drink and left to check on dinner. LT and Jeremy spent the next forty-five or so minutes looking over and discussing the changes made to the original pool and enclosure. The barbeque pit, bar, and outdoor kitchen were of particular interest to LT and he jumped at the invitation by Melody to have a cookout on the weekend.

"I hope that Gina will be back by then.' Melody said. "She has been gone for the last month and a half. The company she was working with sold out to a firm in California and moved the offices there. Gina was sent on an extended trip to the Far East to get revised contracts for the new owners. I can't wait to see her." Turning to LT, "How much of what happened to me have you told her?"

"As you said, she has been gone quite some time. Getting in contact with her has been difficult and, well, I didn't want to say too much. She couldn't get here and I didn't want to worry her." LT said as he sipped his drink.

Melody was happy her best friend had been spared the gory details. "I'll fill her in when she arrives."

Bellamy appeared at the door to the lanai and announced dinner.

xxxxx

LT watched his goddaughter as they sat at the dinner table. Mrs. Bellamy, as always, had made a superb meal. Jeremy, Melody, and LT talked and laughed as each course was brought to them. For the first time since the birthday dinner in London, Melody looked relaxed and like her old self. He was also happy to see how she interacted with Jeremy.

Lord Alfred either called or messaged Melody on a daily basis, but since the death of Arthur, he seemed different. He still professed his love for Melody, but it felt as if he hadn't yet come to grips with everything that happened. LT didn't question him about his feelings, but he could see that some of the conversations he engaged in with Melody had left her confused and LT didn't want his goddaughter confused about anything.

"Have you found a place to live yet?" Melody asked Jeremy. The topic had turned to Jeremy's new posting. The Marines had given him the choice of three cities; Tulsa, Oklahoma, Dallas or Houston, Texas. Jeremy had chosen Houston. He would be working out of an office in the Energy Corridor not far from the Chadwick Building.

"I have an agent looking for me. He has my list of "wants" and "needs," but it is taking him longer than I expected. Right now, I am staying with LT, but that can't go on for too much longer."

LT laughed, "I want him to stay, but it seems he wants to have his own place. But, in a way, I can understand that."

Melody put her napkin next to her plate, signaling the end of the meal. "I want to see my pool at night." Turning to Bellamy, "Please bring us some coffee and brandy at the pool."

Sitting next to the fully lit pool with the water jets playing on the water, the last few weeks seemed so far away. The longer Melody was in the safety and security of her own home, the more distant the recent events in England seemed to be. LT could see the stress melt off of her and he was happy for the sanctuary Farr House had become for her, but he also knew it was the first day home and she needed to rest.

Putting his drink down on the nearby table, LT stood. "Jeremy, let's go. I can see our girl is trying hard to stay awake." Turning to Melody, "you go on up, we can show ourselves out. I'll call you tomorrow, but not too early. You still need your rest."

Jeremy took Melody's hand and gave her a kiss on the cheek. "We still need to try out your helmet, you know the one I got you for your birthday? How about a ride tomorrow afternoon? This is my last week of transition leave and with you out of the clinic, I need to get things done!"

Melody nodded. She hadn't realized just how tired she was. Being at home, in her own house, was such a change that it had crept up on her. Now though, it was definitely time for bed.

Bellamy locked the door after the guests and waited to hear Melody's door close before he turned out the last light. He smiled to himself; it was good having things back to normal.

xxxxx

Breakfast was finished, menus had been planned with Mr. Bellamy, and Melody had taken her second cup of coffee to the study when LT called. "Melody, would you be free about eleven this morning? I still have a couple of things to finish here but there are some items we need to discuss. I can come there if it is more convenient."

Melody laughed, "LT, eleven is just fine and the sherry and cherry cake will be waiting for you."

"Can I help it if I enjoy the tradition you've started? Besides, I like Mrs. Bellamy's cherry cake." LT said as he ended the call.

An instant message from Alfred was waiting for her when she turned on her computer. He was at Aldwin House, his family's ancestral home near Farr Cottage. Since the death of Arthur, he seemed to be spending more of his time in the country and less in London. Alfred was still working with Nicky Somersby on the refurbishment of the docklands properties, but he had stopped the work on his London home and Aldwin House. Melody had the feeling that Alfred had put his life on hold while he mourned the loss of his newly found cousin Arthur.

Alfred wasn't online when Melody answered his message but she also wrote a lengthy email to accompany her brief reply. Other items on her desk also needed her attention. The mail, most of it unimportant, was opened and sorted into the wastebasket, interesting but not urgent, or in need of reply piles. By the time Bellamy wheeled in the cart with Mrs. Bellamy's cherry cake and sherry, LT was ensconced in the chair opposite Melody at the big partner's desk.

Bellamy removed the empty plates and glasses before serving each person a cup of coffee. LT thanked Melody's butler and asked him to express his thanks for the delicious cake to Mrs. Bellamy. When the two were alone again, LT began his meeting with Melody.

The overstuffed briefcase yielded several different items he discussed with his goddaughter. The last item was the communique from Smyth's in London. "They have sent the initial paperwork on your inheritance. I've retained them to be your agent in Britain, but if you are unhappy with them, you can choose someone else. They recommended an accountancy firm, which I checked out myself that will do the audit and inventory on the properties."

"No, uh, that's fine. They have been with the family for generations and should have all of the information needed. I can't get my head around the fact Arthur is gone. I mean, I know it's true, but he was so steady, solid." Turning to the photo she had of him on the desk then looking back at LT, "You know what I mean? I just thought he was a part of Farr Cottage and would always be there."

Nodding in agreement, LT continued. "There is one problem with the inheritance, the titles. According to British law, you have to be at least one-quarter British to inherit and Richard Farr is too distant for that to be true."

Melody countered, "But I am one-quarter. My grandmother Fitzhugh was English."

LT interrupted, "Melody, I met your grandmother Fitzhugh and she was not English but a Boston harpy! When your father died she came to "help" your mother through her grieving and within three days I had to put her back on the plane to Boston to get her away from your mother. There was nothing even remotely English about the woman."

Melody laughed. "LT you met Grandfather Fitzhugh's second wife, Augustine Pollard. My mother's mother was Amelia Louise deLisser. Her father was the vicar at the Church of the Martyrs in Oxford. Grandfather met her during the war and her father married them. He brought her home to Boston when the war ended. Mother was four when her mum died. Grandfather married Augustine about a year later. Mother could never put up with her and after you "escorted" her out of Houston, mother told her never to come back. She was after mom to break Father's will. At the time I didn't understand it, but I think that was the last of Augustine Fitzhugh."

"Okay then, I'll write to Smyth's and give them that information. The marriage should be registered in the church and the civil records in Oxford." LT said. "Now, the question is, do you want the titles? They are only good in England, but even if you aren't interested in them, your children may feel differently. This is not something to dismiss lightly. Think about it before you decide."

Melody sighed. "I know, but right now, I need to have time to digest all of this." She waived her hand over the mound of papers they had already gone over. "If you will give me a couple of weeks, maybe even a month, to get my mind around the enormity of it all, then, I will be ready to jump in and work at learning what is here."

LT chuckled, "Take as long as you need. There is no rush. Right now, things are pretty much running along without any need to meddle. I know you want to be made aware of all there is, but don't be in a hurry."

Melody looked at her watch. "Will you stay for lunch? I'm getting a little hungry and it's almost time. Can I tell Mrs. Bellamy to set an extra place?"

LT beamed, "I thought you'd never ask!"

xxxxx

Melody watched as LT's limo left the front of Farr House. She turned to go back to the study and work on some of the papers LT had left when a familiar car pulled up to the door. Gina Russell, Melody's best friend jumped out and bounded up the stairs.

The two young women hugged each other as both started talking. Bellamy greeted the visitor as Gina and Melody moved to the study.

"You look terrible! What happened to you?" Gina blurted out. "I go away and you get lost and the British police have to find you? Tell me all about it."

Melody laughed. "Slow down and thank you for telling me I look bad. You are looking great even if you do look as if you are in need of sleep."

Bellamy brought the two young women refreshments in the lounge where Melody started to tell Gina what had happened. After more than two hours, dozens of questions, and a lot of tears, the story was told.

Gina was horrified at the abduction, imprisonment, and rescue of her friend. The death of someone she had been introduced to, dined with, and was a close friend of Melody, touched her deeply. Gina opined. "So you didn't know who had taken you? All that time? That must have been some powerful drug!"

"They found several dogs on the property that Maude had tried this stuff on before she even took me. All but one had died of an overdose. She was trying to get the right amount of it for someone of my size to be able to knock me out but not kill me. Problem is, it is accumulative and the more she gave me, the more it built up in my system. Dr. Li, the London doctor, said Maude was one or two doses away from killing me." Melody shuddered to think of it all.

"Look, enough about me, what is happening with you? Are you really going to move away from here?" Melody was in a hurry to change the subject.

Gina brightened when the topic turned to her. "If I want to stay with the same company. The people who bought it are anxious to have me move to California and work out of their offices. The trip from which I just came home was such a success they are sweetening the salary quite a bit. But, I'm not sure I want to leave my home here."

Melody noticed a slight blush on Gina's face. "Do I detect more than just a passing interest in someone here? I know you love Houston and we are best friends, but is there, perhaps, a certain tall doctor with red hair who is on your mind?"

Melody was right. The slight blush on Gina's face turned to a red as deep as Dr. George Augustus (Auggie) Harris IV's hair. Gina had met the son of the same Dr. George Harris who treated Melody in the hospital, at the last barbeque LT had thrown the Sunday before he moved to his apartment atop the Chadwick Holdings' building. It was the young doctor who had escorted her to the ball last December and squired her to several Holiday parties.

Gina had dated before, but never the same guy for more than a month or so. For her to be seeing a man for this long, it must be serious. "Do I detect a relationship growing here?" Melody chided her friend. "What does he think about your plans to follow your job?"

Gina demurred, "Auggie still has to finish his residency. You know the web of family at the hospital. He is expected to finish all of his education and work at the institution his great-great grandfather established. Everyone just assumes this is what he will do."

A bit conspiratorially Gina continued. "Actually, he has applied for a residency at a fabulous teaching hospital in California, not far from where I would need to be located for this job. I'm hoping he gets it, but he is up against pretty stiff competition. He'll know in a couple of weeks if he's accepted into their program." Gina looked a little sad when she said, "But I have to be at the new offices before he'll find out about his future plans." She chuckled, "It kind of makes it hard to take such a serious step."

Melody knew what her friend was going through. The breakup of her parent's marriage happened within weeks of her moving into the college dorm-room she has shared with Melody that first semester at college. And, although Gina was originally from Colorado, she had made a home and found friends in Houston. It would be hard to make another move.

She tried to lift her friend's spirits. "Hey, there are planes that go from here to California all the time! You wouldn't be that far away and we already talk on the phone several times a day, at least when you're in the country. I think it will all work out." Melody saw how tired Gina looked from her long travels. "You look like you need sleep. Why don't you come for brunch on Saturday? That gives you a couple of days to decompress and re-orient your internal clock to Houston time."

Gina nodded. She had slept during part of the eighteen hour flight but realized she would need much more. "Sounds great. I'll bring the fresh croissants and you supply the mimosas!"

Melody walked her friend to the door. "Don't forget to bring your bathing suit, I want you to try out that new pool. Oh, and LT is doing a barbeque here on Sunday, maybe you should bring Auggie and I can have a chance to get to know him."

xxxxx

The low growl of Jeremy's motorcycle stopped when they reached the front door. Melody sat behind him on the machine and pulled off her new helmet. "It fits great and you're right, with this earpiece I can hear everything you said."

Jeremy had arrived about six and wanted to take Melody for a spin so she could use the birthday present he had given her. "You don't find it to snug do you? I can take it to the shop and they can adjust it for you if it is."

Melody nodded, "nope, fits just fine, but it is a bit hot. Maybe if they had something in "air-conditioned"!" She shook her long chestnut tresses out and felt the coolness of the evening through her hair. "Let's go in, I think Mrs. Bellamy might have dinner ready for us."

Bellamy had the door open and the air-conditioned foyer felt good. "Miss, Mr. LT is in the lanai waiting for your return. He arrived about ten minutes ago. I've given him a drink."

"Hmm, I didn't know he was coming tonight. I wonder what's up." Melody said as she headed for the pool area.

LT was relaxing on one of the chairs near the outdoor bar. As soon as he heard Jeremy and Melody coming he stood up. "Hi, sorry to intrude on your dinner date, but I had some news for Jeremy."

Melody gave LT a peck on the cheek. "Pinky, you could never intrude. What's up?"

LT winced at the nickname Pinky. "I have some great news. A friend of mine is going to the orient for at least a year and needs someone to live in his house. It's not that I want to see you go son, but I know you want a place of your own. This would be perfect. It's a condo in a very exclusive building. They don't allow sublets so he won't charge you rent, but he did say it would be great if you could replenish any of the liquor, food from the fridge or pantry you used, and oh, watered his flowers."

Jeremy and LT talked about the man and his home. LT gave Jeremy the name and number. "Call him tomorrow and setup an appointment. He is leaving in a couple of days and is desperate to find someone to house-sit." Looking over at Melody, "and now that I have done my duty, I shall leave you two to your dinner."

"Oh, you can stay, can't you?" Melody asked.

"No dear, I have some work to catchup with. I'm still trying to work through the backlog." LT set his empty glass on the bar and left.

Endings

Melody looked around the dining room table. For the first time since she had returned from England almost six months before, every seat was full. LT and Jeremy were there as well as Gina and her fiancé Dr. Auggie Harris. They had arrived from California to celebrate Melody's birthday and their engagement.

Melody's birthday. A year ago she looked forward to the occasion with anticipation but before the next day was over she was kidnapped and held by a deranged woman who thought Alfred Oswin was meant for her and not for Melody. Maude Harbison didn't stand trial for the abduction, at least not yet. The judge found her mentally insufficient to stand trial so she was sent to an institution for females who were criminally insane. If she ever recovered enough to stand trial, she would, but until that time, she was still locked away from society.

Alfred hadn't come for the party. He sent a gift and talked to Melody that morning, but he was still mourning the death of Arthur Farr, his cousin. While the two did IM quite often and talked at least once a week, Alfred had begun to realize he didn't have the same feelings for Melody he had shown before the abduction. Now, they were good friends and confidents. Melody was helping him to accept the death of Arthur, but it would be a long slow process.

Besides the friends who were present, a new face had joined the group. Brian Wong. LT had sent him over about six months ago to help with the transfer of Melody's inheritance into her care. Brian was in his mid-twenties and had worked for Chadwick Holdings for over three years, since he had graduated from university. His expertise was accounting and management. He made a fantastic executive assistant.

LT didn't want to wait to start moving responsibility for her estate to her birthday but wanted Melody to have a chance to ease into the oversight gradually. When the final documents on the inheritance from Arthur Farr arrived a few months later, LT was glad he'd done so.

Just after the New Year, a young man from Smyth's arrived to meet with LT and Melody. He was the grandson of the elderly partner whom LT had been in contact with since the death of Arthur. LT met him in his office with Melody in attendance.

"Martin Smyth." The impeccably dressed solicitor said as an introduction. "Grandfather does not travel anymore and has sent me in his place." The young man set a substantial folder on the desk. "These are the final documents on the estate of Lord Arthur Roland Farr, Viscount of Gibbons. The financial statements and audit papers are on this thumb drive" he said as he extracted the device from the inside pocket of the folder, "and the rest of these papers detail the full worth and inventory of the London house, Farr Cottage, and various other properties."

Martin Smyth sat down and continued. "The death duties have been paid from the estate. The bank documents have been sent from Lloyd's. They should arrive within the next week. There is, though, a listing of the accounts in the financial documents. Do you have any questions?"

LT looked at Melody. "Yes, has the decision been made about Melody inheriting the titles?"

Mr. Smyth cleared his throat. "Of course! Didn't grandfather relay that decision to you? Lady Melody Farr has inherited the title of Vicountess of Gibbons. When she is in England, visiting a Commonwealth country, or in a United Kingdom Embassy, she will be known as and receive the honors due her title. In America it will not matter, but we still recognize the peerage."

Melody was the next to speak. "If I should marry and have children, will they be able to inherit also?"

"If they are your true children, yes, the will be allowed to inherit and until that time, will be styled as "Honorable"." The young man seemed to be in a hurry to return home. "I will leave these with you. I'm staying at the Crown Plaza just down the way. If you have any questions, please call me there. I leave for London on Monday." With that, he left.

The workload on Brian increased with the documents from London. Melody was impressed with the size of the holdings. LT was also but opined that since the Farr family had more than a thousand years to accumulate the wealth, it should be substantial. He was, however, impressed with their prudence.

"This makes you something of a significant target for every fortune hunter in the world. I'm surprised you've not had young men beating a path to your door already. You need to be careful." LT said.

Melody nodded in agreement. "I think it is already happening. The British Consulate in Houston has sent several invitations already. I have declined each one, but Jeremy and I thought we might go to their celebration of St. George's Day, the patron saint of England, next month."

"That might be alright. If Jeremy is with you, he can fend off any predators," LT said with a smile.

Melody and Jeremy did attend the celebration at the Consulate and true to LT's prediction, more than one eligible young gentleman rushed to Melody's side when she was introduced to the assemblage. Jeremy, dressed in his formal Marine uniform, was a deterrent to most, but two in particular dogged Melody's every step. A word with the Consul, however, did solve the problem.

Tonight, Melody was dressed in the same green silk dress she had worn to the Consulate party. She had put the weight back on she'd lost during her kidnapping and drugging by Maude. Daily use of the pool had turned some of the curves into muscles. The results was a more beautiful shape than she had prior to the incident in England.

LT nodded to Melody from his seat near her. She cleared her throat and the room became quiet. "Shall we go to the lounge for some cake, coffee, and perhaps champagne?" With that she rose and the rest of the guests followed her.

The two maids, dressed in waiter's uniforms, had helped Bellamy serve at dinner. Paul and Glen followed the guests into the room with a serving cart containing the coffee/tea service, brandy, and glasses for champagne. Behind them Mrs. Bellamy followed her husband as he pushed a serving cart with a lovely cake with the candles already lit. The assembled guest applauded the beautiful cake and the baker, Mrs. Bellamy, who had made it.

Melody blew out her candles and cut the first piece of cake. Mrs. Bellamy cut pieces for all while Glen and Paul served the guests. As each person finished their cake and coffee the girls cleared the things and replaced them with brandies for anyone who wanted one. A nod from LT to Bellamy and the girls, Glen and Paul, began passing among the guests with trays full of glasses of champagne.

LT rose and looked at where Melody was sitting. Very few people in this room, in fact few people in total knew about the abduction by Maude Harbison just after the last time his god-daughter celebrated her birthday. So much had changed. Last year they were all gay and unaware of the danger lurking around the corner. Arthur was still alive and Alfred was on hand for the festivities. This year was different with Arthur in his grave and Alfred still unable to come to terms with the loss of his only blood relative.

Raising his glass, LT cleared his throat, and the room became quiet. "Friends, I want to give a toast to my Goddaughter, Melody. Today you have reached a milestone. I pray you live long, are healthy, find love, and enjoy the life God has given you. Blessings on you!"

The guests responded with "Here, Here!" and followed LT's invitation to drink to Melody's health. Jeremy who had been on Melody's right-hand and within reach the entire evening, left his chair and stood next to her. A brief glance passed between the young Marine Major and LT. With a wink of an eye from the older man, Jeremy removed a small velvet box from his uniform pocket.

Jeremy had helped to rescue Melody from Maude, sat with her as she lay in a coma, and been at her side through the recovery. In the intervening year they had grown very close and were never far from each other when Jeremy was not on duty or away on Marine business. Jeremy turned to Melody, sank to one knee, and declared his love to her in front of the assembled company. Blushing a deep crimson, Melody said "yes" and allowed the ring to be slipped onto her finger.

The room erupted. "Yiiii Haaaaww!" Shouted LT as Jeremy rose to his full height and pulled Melody into his embrace for a kiss. This was no peck on the cheek or brief brush of the lips but a full, "we're engaged to be married" smacker. Congratulations were shouted from around the room and Gina was the first to hug her best-friend in joy.

"I am gonna' give you the best darn wedding Texas has ever seen and the biggest they'll see for the next ten years. It's on me girl. When you momma and daddy asked me to be godfather all those years ago, they knew I would be there to stand in for 'em if they couldn't be here. Well," he said as he gave Melody a big bear-hug, "You just leave it to ol' LT and we are going to do this wedding up right!"

xxxxx

LT and his date, Lillian Vargas were the last guests to leave. Jeremy and Melody stood at the top of the front door steps and watched as the limousine carrying them headed toward the gate of Farr House.

Jeremy could feel just how tired his bride was as Melody sagged against him for support. Scooping her into his arms, he carried her across the threshold and into the foyer. Bellamy closed and locked the door behind them. Jeremy carried her up the stairs to the bedroom they would share on the wedding night.

Both Melody and Jeremy were happy now they had decided not to start the trip to New York until the next afternoon. It had been a long day and to get onto an airplane and begin their honeymoon trip would have put extra strain on both of them.

It hadn't been the biggest wedding Texas would ever see and Melody imagined it would not even be remembered by more than just the three hundred people who had come to celebrate with them, but it was just fine for her and Jeremy.

The Texas Bluebonnets were in bloom and mixed in with them, Melody had asked the florist to add white Freesia for a light fragrance. The men, except for Jeremy and his best-man, both of whom were in their full-dress Marine uniforms, had red roses in their lapels. Two months before Melody had been the Maid-of-Honor for her best friend Gina's wedding and Gina returned the favor by acting as Melody's Matron-of-Honor.

The two girls had flown to New York within days of the engagement on Melody's birthday to shop for wedding dresses.

Louisa, Melody's dressmaker, and LT went along to pay for his goddaughter's dress.

Dressed in a gown reminiscent of the hey-day of Hollywood in the 1950's, the white silk dress fit Melody beautifully. Gina and Melody had made a pact that neither would ask the other to wear ugly bridesmaid's dresses and the blue silk Gina wore was proof the agreement had held. LT took the occasion to splurge on a new Armani tuxedo in which to escort the bride down the aisle.

After the ceremony in St. John's the attendees left to enjoy the reception at Farr House. Melody and Jeremy, however, took the opportunity to visit her family's area of the cemetery and to also see Jeremy's namesakes grave.

Before leaving, LT pulled Melody aside and handed her a small envelope. "Open this later. It can even wait until tomorrow. I think it is the last of the things I still have for you of your inheritance. I don't know what it is, but it feels like a small key. You can figure it out."

The couple still had an hour before Bellamy was going to drive them to the airport when Melody remembered the envelope. Opening it, it did indeed hold a small key. By the patina, the key looked very old. A tag was attached. "A small room; chair, table, and lantern. As you sit, I'm on the right."

Melody looked at Jeremy. She had shown him some of the secrets of the study, but the little room behind the panel with the table, lamp, and chair had seemed so unimportant she hadn't thought about it. Now she wanted to take another look inside.

Looking at the room for only the second time. The smallness of it gave Melody pause. She couldn't remember the converted butler's pantry where Maude had kept her imprisoned, but she instinctively felt a wave of apprehension. Sensing this, Jeremy put his hand on Melody's shoulder. "Do you want me to go inside?" her husband said.

"No, no, I'll be ok." Melody took the key in her hand and sat in the chair. She looked to the right. There was nothing. Up and down the panel her gaze traveled but she didn't see anything. Melody was about to get up when she remembered the chair might have been moved. She looked to her left. There, about six inches from the floor was a small indentation. She slipped the key in, turned it and a door opened.

Inside the cache lay a wooden box. Melody tried to lift it from where she was sitting but couldn't. Jeremy pulled the box out and set it on the desk. It wasn't locked and the top came off easily as Melody opened it. Inside were many small velvet bags. Opening one, a gold coin slid into Melody's hand.

Jeremy gave a low whistle. "It's a 1908 $20 Saint-Gaudens Gold Double Eagle!" He opened another, and another, and another. The box was full of them! Each little bag held its own mint condition gold coin and all of them were the same. By the time the box had been emptied, Melody and Jeremy had counted fifty bags. They looked at each other. Without a word, the coins were put back into their individual sacks and back into the box. All except one of them were returned to the niche in the little room and the door closed.

Melody and Jeremy were invited to have lunch with Abraham Newhouse while they were in New York and she wanted to ask him about the coin. It would make for an interesting conversation.

xxxxx

Abraham Newhouse greeted the newlyweds at the door of the Plaza's main dining room. "Melody you are as lovely as ever. And this must be the lucky man who won your heart!"

Melody introduced Jeremy to Mr. Newhouse and everyone sat for lunch. After the waiter had taken their order, Melody reached into her purse and took the small velvet bag from it. "Mr. Newhouse," she began, "I…"

Abraham interrupted, "Abraham, my dear, Abraham."

"Hmm, yes, Abraham." She put the bag on the table near Abraham Newhouse. "Could you please look at this and tell me if you know what it is?"

Abraham took the bag and tipped the contents into his hand. Immediately he looked over his spectacles at Melody and then to Jeremy. "Well, hmm. This is a lovely item. It's a, uh," looking closer at the coin, "a 1908 Saint-Gaudens Gold Double Eagle, twenty-dollar gold piece. Very rare and it looks to be in mint condition." He put the coin back into the bag. "There are very few of these left and even less are uncirculated. From the look of it, this has never been in general use."

"The Saint-Gaudens is of particular beauty. The sculptor, Augustus Saint-Gaudens did the design for that coin. May I ask if it is for sale? I would pay well for it."

The waiter brought the wine and after serving it, left. The talk about the gold coin resumed. "Part of my inheritance was a box of 50 of these. The one in your hand is just one of them." Melody said.

Abraham stared at her. "Oh, my. That is some little stash you have. At the current market rate, that would be almost two hundred thousand dollars, give or take a bit. No, you don't want to split that up. And they are all 1908?" Melody nodded.

"Hmm, I may know where they came from. I want to check something when I get home. Now, enough about things like this. Tell me about your wedding and your honeymoon plans!" Abraham Newhouse turned the conversation to lighter fare as the lunch was being served. Before they parted after the meal, Abraham reached into his coat pocket and extracted an envelope addressed to Melody and Jeremy. "Here, a little something from the Newhouse family to you on your marriage."

Jeremy and Melody thanked the old gentleman for the gift, shook hands, and headed back to their room. It was later in the evening when the phone in the room rang. It was their lunch partner.

"Melody, this is Abraham. I was going over some old journals my grandfather left. I can tell you now the coins were bought by your great-grandfather Avery Farr when he finished his apprenticeship in New York. His father, Richard Farr had sent an order to his son along with the funds to purchase the coins. At the time, they were worth $20 each but Richard had specified they be new, uncirculated coins in the original packaging. At the time, Newhouse bank put their coins in the little blue velvet bags to be given as gifts. The order was for one-thousand dollars' worth and that is what you said you have."

Melody thanked Mr. Newhouse for the information. "Keep them safe and you will always have some instant wealth. Enjoy your travels!" Abraham hung up before Melody and Jeremy could thank the old man for his wedding gift.

Afterword

The Reverend Charles Paxton, Vicar of St. Alban's Church, stood at the ancient Baptismal Font intoning the Rite of Holy Baptism while a crowd of people were gathered round. A visibly pregnant Gina Harris was holding a baby and so was a Marine Major clad in his full dress uniform. Gina had been Melody's Matron-of-Honor and Major Fred Gomez was Jeremy's best man. Now they were godparents to Jeremy Richard Higgins-Farr and Abigail Lucinda Higgins-Farr, the three month-old twins of Melody and Jeremy. Born in London, the children could inherit the titles as well as the estates of the Farr clan. The line had been preserved and Melody's duty to the future had been done.